FOOL ME TWICE

NONA UPPAL

EBURY
PRESS

An imprint of Penguin Random House

EBURY PRESS

USA | Canada | UK | Ireland | Australia
New Zealand | India | South Africa | China | Singapore

Ebury Press is part of the Penguin Random House group of companies
whose addresses can be found at global.penguinrandomhouse.com

Published by Penguin Random House India Pvt. Ltd
4th Floor, Capital Tower 1, MG Road,
Gurugram 122 002, Haryana, India

First published in Ebury Press by Penguin Random House India 2024

ISBN 9780143462347

Typeset in Sabon LT Std by MAP Systems, Bengaluru, India
Printed at

www.penguin.co.in

To anyone who has loved and lost

'Life changes in the instant. The ordinary instant.'

—Joan Didion, *The Year of Magical Thinking*

Chapter One

'Ashish, can you cut it out, please? You're going to get us arrested.' Bani had been game for Ashish's plan in theory, which meant she, half-drunk on a pint of beer, had nodded furiously when he had explained it. Now that they were mid-execution, it seemed at least slightly criminal.

'I'm too young and pretty to go to jail.'

Ashish turned around to glare at Bani. 'I've got this,' he hissed back.

'*Bhaiya, in sabka kitna* (How much for these)?' Ashish asked the man handling the roadside bird shop, pointing to all the birds on display. 'And the ones at the back too.'

The shop, called 'Flying Dreemz'—a five-minute walk from our school, Horizon High International, in Hauz Khas—adorned the streets with the pastel hues of pink, blue and green cages that could only do so much to hide the sad faces of the birds trapped in them.

The shopkeeper was understandably suspicious. Was he being recorded for a prank on TV?

'*Sab*? Fifty *ke* fifty? *Pakka*?' he confirmed. The deal was one of those too-good-to-be-true kinds.

'*Haan, pakka*. All birds, no discount. *Kitna*?'

Ashish had no way to determine if the price the shopkeeper quoted was a steal or a loot. When his father had handed him the stack of notes, he'd been ultra-generous. 'Make sure you get her something nice,' he had said, patting Ashish on the back.

Handing the shopkeeper the money warily, Ashish wondered if this was going to be a disaster.

'*Badiya* sir,' the shopkeeper said, comically bobbing his head as he retrieved the notes from Ashish.

Having successfully completed the transaction, Ashish looked at Bani with his 'Are you game?' eyes.

'This could either be epic or an epic blunder,' she blurted out, her hands fixed on her phone camera, with Ashish positioned in the centre of the shaky frame.

'*Lekar kaise jaayenge aap inhe* (How will you take these)?' The guy asked Ashish, eyeing his i10. 'Truck-*wruck ka kuch* arrangement?'

But carrying the birds home was not what Ashish had in mind.

One by one, he unlocked the cages that weren't really locked in the first place. Having been born and bred in captivity, it took a few seconds for the birds to realize what an open cage meant. Only when one of them dared to flap its wings and fly into the blue sky did the others realize they could do it too.

'*Yeh kya kar rahe hain aap?*' the shopkeeper shrieked, finally looking up from counting his earnings. '*Saala paagal!*' he scrambled to lock the leftover cages, yelling profanities at Ashish and Bani, but it was too late. The last bird had already flown away.

Ashish hadn't gone mad, though. Far from it.

Every day for the past two years, Ashish, Bani and I had walked out of our school's main gate soon after the final school bell for a quick ice cream before heading back home. Our trusted Kwality Walls cart was usually parked right next to this bird shop, the ownership of which had been passed down to many different men over the years. Despite looking forward to my Cola bar all day, my skin burning from the sweltering heat, one look at the birds would make me lose all my appetite. I admit that it was mostly silly. But I couldn't drown it out. All those pretty birds locked away in pastel-coloured cages, waiting for someone to set them free. Instead, they were bought by rich people and carried in cars to jazz up their maximalist homes.

It was one of those things I thought no one was noticing, a two-second glitch on my face that the most attentive of eyes could miss. Here's where I got it wrong—Ashish was always looking. So, for my eighteenth birthday, when his consistent pleading for me to tell him what he could gift me failed, he rejigged his strategy. What could he *do* that would mean more than buying me a pair of shoes I would ditch for my Bata chappals or a bag to fill with stuff I would much rather carry in my hands?

After capturing the rainbow colours in the sky as the birds flew away, Bani panned the camera towards Ashish's face. 'Look here,' Bani signalled.

Ashish faced the camera. 'I don't know if this is stupid,' he said. 'Umm, it probably is. But, fuck it. It fits because I'm stupidly in love with you. Happy birthday, Sana.'

Bani turned the camera around to record herself. 'If you think it's stupid, it was all his idea,' she said, laughing. 'But I love you too, munchkin.'

The end was a lot choppier than the rest—the camera being stuffed, while still on, in Bani's bag, as they escaped in Ashish's i10 that drove like it was always in second gear. I saw the video and heard the entire story a week later, on the night of my birthday, as Ashish and Bani sat next to me and played it on Bani's laptop. Scrunching up the fabric of my loose t-shirt to wipe the fat tears trickling down my cheeks, I broke out laughing as the end scenes rolled. This kind of luck and love, I realized, might just be illegal to possess.

* * *

Present day

Months later, here I am, perched at the Hauz Khas fort, our trusted after-school hang, licking ice lollies—with Bani sitting across from Ashish and me—and reminiscing about the best birthday present I have ever received.

At five feet and (barely) an inch, Bani is the shortest of us, but her throaty voice and bold fashion sense (cowboy boots in New Delhi summer) are enough to make up for it. Her pasty white face and jet-black hair cascading down to her waist are so glorious that her mother held out hope for an Indian adaptation of Rapunzel for long enough. Her hair is still the same length, but the pop of blue streaks gives them a very *Bani* edge. She always smells like she has a woody perfume on (I don't know what wood smells like, but I imagine it's similar), except when I need a hug. Then, I always catch a whiff of Johnson's baby powder.

Ashish, on the other hand, is the antithesis of Bani. My boyfriend is stereotypically tall (six feet, three inches to be precise, without counting the height his curly hair add), dark (sun-tanned from all the football) and handsome (he doesn't believe it when I say this to him though, because for most of our school life, I never noticed him), with light brown eyes that even make disbelievers swoon. Everywhere we go, he towers over my otherwise generous five foot-six self. He is lanky except for his broad shoulders that feel like clouds embracing me when his arms wrap around my torso. And while Ashish has never used a drop of perfume in his life that hasn't been forcefully sprayed on to him (*'You think cavemen used perfume?'*), I still think I could bottle his fragrance up and make a fortune selling it for as much as Chanel or Gucci.

And if Bani and Ashish had a baby (*'Okay, ew, could you not think of a better way to say this?'* I hear

Bani scowl in my head), that would be me. I am a blend
of little bits of her and some parts of him, with an
added enthusiasm for drama, romantic comedies and a
high-achiever's complex for good measure.

What I really am, though, is a regular girl
living in Malviya Nagar, New Delhi. With a life so
perfect that I knock on wood, take the long way
home at the hint of a black cat and paste evil eyes
on everything I own. I have a best friend I love, a
boyfriend who loves me, and the convenience of the
fact that the two most important people in my life
just happen to adore each other too. I desire little
else (except to top the school, maybe even the city,
in the upcoming Board exams).

But my good luck is in a war against time.

In less than two months, as Bani and I kickstart our
college lives in New Delhi, Ashish will be jet-setting off
to the United States for an all-too-fancy design degree
in Chicago that his parents can barely afford. The bird-
gate scandal was back in November, and here we are,
sitting on a bench at Haus Khaz fort on a surprisingly
warm day in February, fighting against reaching a
finish line we never thought would arrive.

'I can't believe it's ending,' I say, sighing, but I can
imagine it's hard to take me seriously as I lick the cola
running down my hand.

I feel Ashish's arm drape over me, a weight I have
grown so accustomed to that it feels like air rustling
against my shirt. 'It literally feels like yesterday when
Bani forced me to be friends with you,' he says,

cheekily. I stick my tongue out at him as Bani jumps to my defence.

'Forced you?! I gave you your love story, you loser. You think you could've pulled someone like Sana without my help?' Bani chimes in, tossing her ice cream wrapper in the bin and wiping her sticky hands on Ashish's shirt. He doesn't react.

'I can't believe it's been two years already.' Bani looks around, vaguely nostalgic, even though she perpetually lives in the present. 'I can't believe we won't be here anymore, guys.'

Everything is changing so fast. Our farewell is old news, the gossip of my friend-turned-nemesis Tanya's not-safe-for-work blouse is just beginning to die down and Boards are right around the corner. A wave of longing for the future, while simultaneously craving for time to slow down, gushes at me like an unexpected, cold wind in July heat. I open my phone to look at our farewell photos for the hundredth time and cringe at the flashback of the too-light concealer the makeup aunty dabbed under my eyes and how the pleats of my saree fell loose and asymmetrical, despite Ma's best efforts. I flick through about twenty photos to find a picture of Ashish and me, something I can set as my phone wallpaper, but come up short. Bani has photobombed every last one of them. Finally, I settle on the one where Bani and I are standing back-to-back, making the James Bond pose, and Ashish is on the ground with his hands behind his head. Locking my phone, happy with the results, I look at these idiots in front of me, the loves of my goddamn life, and wonder how anything that college has to offer could possibly match this love, this friendship.

'I love you both. So much. Thank you for adopting me into your tiny gang,' I say, being my usual sentimental self, never without an 'I love you' at the tip of my tongue. 'I would've probably made cooler friends if it weren't for you two, but this also works.'

'Oh yeah, like Tanya and Neha?' Bani quips.

* * *

Three years ago

I remember it raining all morning and the ride to school not feeling like an ordinary one—the sky all grey, not a single person on the streets. 'Hogwarts, they're taking us to Hogwarts,' I thought. Not out loud, though, lest my muggle friends overheard.

But my dreams quickly fizzled away when the bus turned left on to the same street I had seen for the last twelve years. Still, the rain helped soften the edge on what I knew was going to be an awful day. After a range of bullying incidents the year before, the school administration, in a bid to rejig the cliques, shuffled up all sections leading up to the tenth grade. Rumour had it that teachers put in extra effort to break apart best friends and large groups. In the 'lottery', I was assigned Section E. Blasphemous, if you ask me—slotting a top-grade student with the 'discards' lot that was Section E.

Besides, I had always been a Section A kid. That was half of my entire personality, which made it hard not to take my placement personally, especially when not a single person I knew or cared to get to know had ended up in the same section as me.

A little wet around the edges, I walked up to the gate of my classroom, my school bus being the last to reach because of unanticipated traffic.

'Ma'am, may I come in?' my voice quivered as my umbrella dripped water all over the door.

'Come in. Please leave your umbrella outside,' a teacher I did not recognize replied, not bothering to face me, writing enough numbers on the board to let me know it was maths period. Great. A maths teacher was going to be my class teacher. This was disaster upon disaster.

'Can you put your bag down, please?' I asked the girl occupying half of the closest table to the door, her bag placed on the empty seat. She wore her hair in two braids down to her shoulders, held together by yellow and orange rubber bands. I was already in awe of her defiance of the black-rubber-band-only norm until I remembered this was the section for rebels. And here I was, the rule-abiding scaredy cat, thrown in with the tigers, just for fun. Would the shiny gleam of Section A wear off now? Would I be assumed a 'problem-child' too?

'Excuse me,' I muttered again, frustrated at her non-response. Mildly drenched from the rain and the only person standing in a classroom full of students scribbling in their notebooks, I wanted to blend in as soon as possible. But the girl wouldn't budge. So I did the only thing I could think of: I grabbed her bag, put it atop her side of the table, accidentally placing it on her open notebook, and took my seat. I felt her glaring at me with a 'How dare you?' that I could feel all over my body before she grabbed her bag and put it next to her on the floor.

I expected the rest of the period to pass in an awkward silence despite the both of us sitting too close for comfort, which is why I jumped a little when I heard her whisper as the teacher explained the difference between linear and quadratic equations.

'It's a new bag.'

I was unsure if it was even meant for me, this declaration, and so I didn't respond. She reiterated, now louder. 'I'm sorry. It's a new bag. I did not want to keep it on the floor.'

'Oh. Umm, that's okay.' What was her plan of action here? Hijacking a table for the rest of time so her precious Adidas bag remained pristine? 'I'm Sana,' I said, holding my hand outstretched, for the lack of anything better to say.

'Bani,' she took my hand and shook it lightly.

'Don't say sorry. It's okay. I understand,' I said, even though I was far from actually understanding.

'So, what section were you in before this? I have never seen you around,' she whispered, as if I needed another reminder of my perfect past. Suddenly, it hit me with the weight of a million bricks: how badly I craved the familiarity of my best friends, now scattered across sections.

'Section A. You?' I responded, my answer dripping with wishful thinking.

'Oh, I have always been in E,' she said, shrugging off the question. 'Do you know anyone in this section?'

'Umm, not really. I mean, I know some people, but none of my friends are here.'

'We can be friends if you want,' she replied meekly, as though every other time she had extended the invitation, no one had RSVPed yes. 'Only if you want.'

Lying through my teeth, I took a mental picture of her face in DSLR quality to remember which seat to avoid taking tomorrow. 'Yes, of course, I'd love to be friends.'

'I have another friend. I can introduce you to him, too,' Bani announced like it was some super clutch one-plus-one deal I was signing up for.

Shaking my head, feigning excitement I wasn't even close to feeling, I said, 'Of course! I would love that.'

* * *

'You hardly spend time with us, Sana,' Neha squealed from across the canteen table. 'It's like you've forgotten us already.'

The last month had been a logistical and emotional nightmare and we weren't coping well; we being Neha, Tanya, Sakshi and I, my best friends for life and beyond, the only people I would share my prized possession, always out of stock in the canteen, aloo patty, with. The administration had taken it a step too far by arranging all tenth-grade sections on different floors and I was the furthest away from the three of them. The only time we got to see each other any more was during the lunch break, often cut short by teachers bleeding class discussions into them. We already knew our lucky streak of being in the same section would come to a close in eleventh grade when all of us took different streams, but the authorities also stole the last year of togetherness we had.

'Neha, you think I am having fun being all alone? At least you have Sakshi with you. I have no one. My only friend is that weird Bani girl.'

'I heard she failed tenth grade last year. Explains why no one around knows her,' Sakshi said, munching on a samosa. 'Stay away from her, Sana, I mean, who fails tenth grade?!'

'Really? Praneet told me she had a full-blown meltdown and her parents made her stay home the rest of the year,' Tanya added. 'Sounds like a mental case, if you ask me.'

Hearing all of this, I lost my appetite. Out of all the possible Section E weirdos, why was she the one I had chosen to sit next to?

'You can sit here,' I heard her call me towards the empty seat next to her, as I walked back to the classroom after the lunch break.

Clearly, Bani wanted to be friends.

'Thanks,' I mouthed quietly, unable to find any reason that would justify not taking her up on the offer. 'You mentioned you were in Section E last year?' I asked, looking over at her.

'Yeah, why do you ask?'

The conversation with the girls had sparked my curiosity and I just needed to know what her deal was. Besides, what was going to happen? I was going to lose someone I didn't even want to be friends with?

'I don't know. I just heard . . .'

'That I failed last year? Or that I went all looney tunes and my family had to drag me home?' My un-shocked, poker face answered her instantly. 'Yeah, I'm not surprised,' Bani chuckled.

'So . . . did you?' I felt guilty for judging Bani so harshly, but there never was smoke without fire, and most rumours had a degree of truth.

'Did I what? Fail? Or go looney tunes?' Bani guffawed, inviting the sharp stare of the teacher. 'What do you think?' she asked, narrowing her eyes at me.

'I have no idea. I don't know you,' I shrugged.

'Do you know the people who told you these things?'

'Yeah. They are my friends.'

'Then you should believe them.'

Suddenly, it started feeling like I was losing control of my side of the rope in a tug of war. 'I just wanted to confirm . . .'

'My father died last year. Rupali ma'am gave me the news like she was grading me for an assignment and I'd gotten an F. Like it was a casual, everyday thing,' she said, looking down at her notebook. 'So yeah. I went a little off the rails. And if I hadn't, I would've probably failed. I didn't return to school for a year because . . . well, I couldn't.' She said it all in one go, flatly. Like she had been holding her breath, rehearsing for when someone finally asked her about the story instead of just assuming it.

Bringing the conversation full-circle, Bani finished with: 'Basically, your friends are right. I'm repeating tenth grade.'

Suddenly exposed to the reality of her supposed weirdness, I felt disgusted at my own naivety. How blissfully unaware I had been of the fact that this girl, who was so easily laughed at, was living on the other side of the same coin of life as me. Different embossing, but we were made up of the same material.

My father left my mother around when I turned five and never returned. According to what I overheard Ma telling my grandmother while she thought I was asleep, the alimony cheques came in only for a few months after the divorce was finalized. And since then, he has been absent, except for the large, brass clock on my bedroom wall, that he bought as a gift for me when I finally learned how to read time. The clock was a pathetic pick for a kid mostly into pinks and blues, but I let it stay there and ding loudly at the turn of every hour—the last mark of my father over me. A constant, hourly reminder of his absence.

A part of me could empathize with Bani. Another part had no idea how to grieve what I didn't have. All of me, though, felt awful.

'I'm sorry. I had no idea.'

'Chill. No one knows. Well, except one person, right over there,' Bani said, pointing to a boy with curly hair, sitting in the front seat, his head bobbing in sync with the teacher's hand on the chalkboard. 'I did not want to be pitied,' she said nonchalantly, like we were talking about a haircut gone wrong.

'I get it,' I said, defeated. 'I mean, I don't get it . . . but, my dad left when I was a kid. Haven't seen him in years. So I can understand, I guess.'

'Left . . . for where?'

'Oh, I mean . . . left, as in divorced my mom. I don't really see him, ever.'

'Do you miss him?' Bani asked.

'No, I don't think so,' I said, honestly. 'But if he died, I think I would. Do you miss your dad?'

I saw Bani scribbling down something indecipherable in her notebook, working through her answer as though it was a linear equation. 'All the time.'

Bani and I sat in silence under the weight of her answer. But unlike the quiet between us on the first day, this silence felt comfortable. I barely knew Bani any more today than I did last week, but I *knew* she wasn't a weirdo. Far from it.

I looked over at her, hoping she would glance back. 'I don't pity you. But I *am* sorry. For believing the rumours. I mean, not believing them, but . . . you know?'

She shook her head as though it was nothing, facing the chalkboard. 'Thank you for asking. And not just assuming I'm crazy,' she whispered. And then something happened: Bani looked sideways at me and smiled.

As all the kids bolted out of the classroom at the instant the shrieking school bell sounded, I noticed the boy Bani had pointed to walking towards our seat. His hair was curlier at the front, a few strands trickling down to his forehead that he compulsively pushed back thrice in just the few seconds I had been observing him. And *God*, was I observing him; his tall stature, perfectly sharp smile with pearly white teeth and that cut in his left eyebrow that I would later trace, asking for a backstory. In one single second, Ashish popped that little ambivalent bubble I was in, oblivious of the boys around me, and caused that fluttering feeling in my chest—the one that goes, 'Oh, you're *nice* to look at.'

How had I never seen him around before? Why were none of the girls talking about him?

'Bro, I'm starving, let's go to the canteen?' he asked Bani, ignoring me—and, thankfully, missing my glare that had been pierced to his face for the last few seconds.

'It was literally lunch break half an hour ago, Ashish.'

And suddenly, the brown-eyed boy had a name. Ashish.

Perching himself on our table, right in front of my face, Ashish sing-songed, 'I didn't eat, *naaaaa*. I had football practice. *Pleaseeeee* come?'

Bani smacked Ashish on the head and I felt a longing bubble inside my chest, like I wanted to be that familiar with him, and with her, too. 'First say hi to my new friend,' she said, pointing at me. 'This is Sana.' When she noticed me staring at Ashish already, Bani gave me a knowing smile, like she already saw how it would go, before quickly letting it fade. 'And Sana, this is my annoying childhood bestie, Ashish, who is only ever hungry at inconvenient times.'

'Nice to meet you,' I said quietly, a touch too shy for my general confident self.

Finally, he turned his glare from Bani and towards me. 'Welcome to Section E, Sana.' Before I could respond, he moved to Bani again, ending the moment. 'Can we go now, please?'

'*Accha*, fine. Quickly, but,' Bani said, rising, before quickly turning back to look at me. 'Sana, you want to come along?'

I realized I really, *really* did. Funny how I had just been at the canteen half an hour ago, shit-talking the same person who was now extending an invitation for me to tag along, right as I felt hungry. Not for food, but to find out more about these two people who had suddenly caught my attention.

So, I nodded yes. 'Yeah, if you guys don't mind,' I said, looking at Ashish specifically.

'Come, come,' he said, nonchalantly, like they had a new person accompany them daily. 'We can have chow mein samosa.'

We sat in a triangle on the ground in the park opposite the school canteen, right next to kindergartners playing on the merry-go-round, filling our ears with pitchy screams. While Bani and I weren't hungry, Ashish was famished enough for ten people. In front of us, on the grass, sat two plates of spring rolls, one chow mein samosa and two regular ones.

'Sure you don't want more food to feed the thirty elephants you have in there?' Bani said, pointing to Ashish's stomach.

Ashish stuck his tongue out at Bani, before turning around to look at me. This was the first time his eyes properly met mine. 'So, Sana, how do you know Bani?'

'We just found out we're long-lost sisters. Our fathers were brothers,' Bani quipped, looking me in the eye and winking. 'Right, Sana?'

Ashish punched Bani in the arm and the cosy familiarity between the two of them made me eager to be on the other side too. Over bits and pieces of oily goodness that Ashish finally convinced Bani and I to share with him, I learned how their mothers were childhood friends, that Bani and Ashish had known each other since they were very little and how she had always helped him with schoolwork until she had to skip the year and they landed in the same grade and section.

'Do you have any other friends in our section?' Ashish asked.

I shook my head no. 'Nope, all my friends are in other sections.'

'What do you mean? Aren't we friends?' Bani asked, her eagerness latching on straight to my vulnerability.

'Maybe she had cooler friends before,' Ashish said, interrupting. 'Section E is not as bad as they say it is, you know?'

'I don't think anyone thinks you're bad. Just rebellious.'

Ashish looked at Bani and grabbed her shoulder, proudly. 'That's just this girl. The rest of us are pretty normal.'

'HEY!' Bani yelled at him. 'He's not normal at all, Sana. Do you want me to tell her what you did to Shalini ma'am?'

'Tell me, please!' I begged.

'So you know na? Shalini ma'am? I think she taught you guys moral science too.'

'Yeah, yeah, she did.'

'So for our class, two years ago, she *literally* took a test. For moral science!' Bani said, cackling already.

'It was the stupidest thing in this world, Sana,' Ashish added. Him saying my name suddenly felt like a door held wide open for a friendship. One that, if I wanted, I could just walk through. 'She made us all come to her desk, where she had a bowl with chits with different morals written on it, like honesty, justice, whatever' he recited, trying his best to not burst out laughing. 'And we were expected to write an essay about whatever moral we picked.'

'So basically,' Bani took over, 'Ashish gets truth or honesty or something like that as his moral . . .'

'Honesty,' Ashish corrected Bani.

'Yeah, whatever. So he gets that and just . . . Sana, just guess what he wrote his essay on.'

'I come out of this looking bad,' Ashish adds as he throws his head back, clasping his eyes shut. 'But I promise it was for a higher moral purpose.'

'I can't guess. Tell me!'

'Ashish wrote, in his perfect, beautiful handwriting, three pages of being super . . . honest,' she said, emphasizing Ashish's prompt, 'about Shalini ma'am and how *her* handwriting sucks. And how he hasn't been able to read anything she has written on the board for the entire year, which is why he can't write an essay on honesty.'

'You did WHAT?!' I shrieked out loud. 'What did she do? Did you get suspended for this?'

'No, but our next class was about how not all morals are absolute. And we should exercise,' Bani said, looking at Ashish, 'what was that word she used, Ashish?'

'Discretion . . .'

'Yeah,' Bani said, double quoting the word, 'we should use "discretion" while exercising morals.'

Ashish stood up to take a bow. 'You know the funniest part? She gave me an F. For a test in a class that was literally not meant to be graded.'

'She had this whole thing where she protested the administration to include moral science scores on the report card. But the administration wouldn't budge,' Bani said, before delivering the punchline, 'because, get this, it wasn't "*moral*" of them to first say a subject was not graded and then change their minds.'

Taking a pause to laugh, Bani adds, 'I swear, for some reason, that made you even hotter to the girls,' she says, looking at Ashish.

'Not to Shalini ma'am,' Ashish chuckles.

Suddenly, from just the two of them laughing, it was now three. Our voices seemed to drown out the kids as I held my stomach, trying so hard to calm the cramping from the giggles.

Right there, just like magic, a switch flipped in my brain: I might like these two a lot.

Chapter Two

People sometimes take you by surprise, yes, but Ashish and Bani took me like a romantic comedy with a thriller-level third-act twist built in towards the end. Very generously, the two of them adopted me into their fold, showing me the ropes of which Section E kids lived up to the stereotype and had to be avoided, which ones were the nerds, friendship with whom helped during exam time, and which teachers spat the most as they taught so I knew when to let go of the front seats.

Even though Bani and Ashish had been a tiny gang before me, it never felt like I was the 'third'. There were no awkward glances, no whispers behind my back. The day I joined forces with them, it was suddenly like it had always been the three of us, together.

'Friends here, friends there, friends everywhere!' I told Ma excitedly, feeling like Hannah Montana with the best of both worlds, sitting in the passenger seat as she drove me to Neha's place where the girls had planned a long-awaited hang. Finally, after four full months of planning, we were going to be able to spend time together for longer than just a lunch break. It thrilled me, anticipating the look on their faces when I would tell them how wrong all of us had been about Bani, that she wasn't a weirdo and that Ashish was kind of cute actually, that maybe all of us could be a big gang of best friends! Mostly, I just wanted to tell them how much I missed hanging out with them, even though I was having more fun than I had expected.

Which is why, when I walked into the conversation that the three of them were already having in Neha's living room, all the energy fizzled out of me like a can of Coke left out for too long.

'Guys, we need to do something about her hanging out with Bani. It doesn't look good on all of us at all,' Tanya said, making a face. It was the very moment Neha's mother had shown me the way to where the girls were sitting.

'Are you guys talking about me?' I said, sitting down next to Tanya.

'We're just looking out for you, Sannu,' Neha said, wrapping her arms around me tight.

Sakshi nodded in confirmation. 'Yeah, come on, Sana. You couldn't find anyone better? You can be friends with Poorvi. I know her from the choir! I can introduce you two to each other.'

'I will never understand what Ashish sees in her, *yaar*. He is literally Greek God material *lekin* all he is interested in doing is spending time with Bani,' Tanya added. 'What a waste of good hair.'

Okay, so it turned out girls were dying over him. My *own* girls were!

'I didn't know he was *that* popular,' I added, nonchalantly. I wondered if even Ashish knew how much he is talked about.

'What are you saying, dude? Literally every girl has a crush on him,' Sakshi confirmed. 'Even Neha was swooning after him last year!'

Neha shrugged, 'like *how could I not?*' before adding, 'Anyway, doesn't matter. If he's into *that*, he clearly has poor taste.'

I quickly interrupted. 'They aren't dating, guys. They've just been best friends for ages.'

'Even worse,' Tanya chided. 'Why would anybody want to be *friends* with her?'

Until now, I had only been exposed to Tanya's viciousness when it was about somebody else; like when she'd gone to extreme lengths to make sure that the new girl in the seventh grade was excluded by every last clique in school, just because she sat next to her then-crush, obviously unknowingly. I'd shrugged it off, then. But suddenly it wasn't about a stranger. It was about a friend. A buzzing thought entered my brain, like a fly that wouldn't budge no matter how much you flail your arms around: what did she say about me when I wasn't around?

'Guys, can we please not? You don't know Bani and you don't know what happened. The rumours are so far from the truth,' I announced, exasperated, suddenly feeling protective over my new friend.

'Oh, so now you're her best friend or what? You know what really happened and the rest of us are just fools?' Tanya said, mockingly. 'Come on, Sannu. We know you're desperate to make new friends, *par* at least have *thorre se* standards.'

I felt my heart drop. This was something I had been looking forward to all of last week. And for what?

'Yaar, it's not that. I'm just saying she is a nice person. They both are,' I said. 'Can we stop this now, please?'

Neha looked over at me. 'Of course, Ashish is a nice person. Have you seen his face? How are you not crushing on him already?!'

'Hey! No. He's mine,' Tanya snapped, from across the room, on her way to the washroom.

Classic Tanya.

Whenever the topic of a cute boy came up, she would call dibs before anyone had a chance to see what the boy in question looked like, perpetually banning us from ever crushing on him because of girl code and all. This time, she was doing it with someone who was *my* friend.

'He's okay, I guess? I don't know. I just don't see him that way,' I said, defensively.

'Anyway, find new friends, okay, Sannu?' Neha said.

Tanya, returning from the washroom, chimed in. 'Yeah, don't become too uncool for us, haan?'

Eventually, and after enough pleading, the girls let go of the topic. And while the rest of the day was fun,

I eventually left Neha's place with a bitter taste in my mouth—literally. The dahi her mother had served with the rajma chawal had gone rancid.

Fitting, I thought, as I sat in the passenger seat when Ma came to pick me up.

* * *

'I HAVE THE BEST IDEA IN THE WORLD!' Bani exclaimed, showing up ten minutes late to our time-sensitive lunch date, scheduled at the same park adjacent to the football field we had our first trio hang-out in. Ashish took one look at Bani before violently lunging for her backpack, which he shoved on the dusty ground in front of us. 'HEY! My BAG!' Bani yelled.

'Shut up and sit,' he motioned at her, retrieving her lunch box from it.

It had been two months since the hang-out at Neha's place and my lunch breaks at school were now mostly spent eating, ranting and gallivanting with Bani and Ashish, instead of scheduling meet-ups with the girls for yet another round of '**Why Sana Should Pick Better Friends**'.

I would still occasionally pass them by in the hallway and mutter a chirpy 'Hi!' but the distance between us lurched in the background, constantly. Eventually, the 'Hi's became a smile and a nod, before finally fading into averting glances and pretending we never saw each other. Years of friendship disappeared in a flash, but I didn't have any regrets. My heart had jumped ship and where I was currently felt like a far safer place to dock.

'Bani, can I ask you something?'

She sat down close to me, using my hand as support. 'Of course!'

'What's with the bag?'

Bani smiled, gazing down at the grass and then back up at me. 'The last ever birthday gift from Dad.'

A tiny sliver of information and very quickly, what I thought was 'eccentric' about Bani from our first conversation suddenly made so much sense.

'So, what idea were you talking about?' Ashish asked.

'Oh yeah! Okay, hear me out. The next two periods are Samira ma'am's, right?' Ashish and I nodded. 'I just heard she is out for the day for that debate competition in Barakhamba, and that snoozy teacher, Rimple ma'am, is substituting for her. She never takes attendance, like, ever,' Bani spit-balled. 'You know what that means, guys . . . this is THE time for an Adventure Island adventure!' Ashish and I simultaneously rolled our eyes before returning to our food. Bani exclusively lived for the thrill of being spontaneous and breaking rules that, to her, seemed stupid. Luckily for me though, Ashish floated more on my end of the risk-taking spectrum.

Only a ten-minute metro ride from our school, the amusement park, named Adventure Island, was perhaps the most pivotal part of our school's folklore—located right at the exit gate of INA metro station. Owing to its proximity and nostalgic, childhood charm, every

year, countless students attempted to pull off a massive
bunk, usually around lunchtime and like clockwork,
some would get caught. Suspensions were the standard
response, in addition to the grounding enforced by
parents. All in all, it was a high-risk-high-reward kind
of activity.

'GUYS?!' Bani yelled, grabbing Ashish's arm and
flinging it around vigorously. 'What say?'

'I say . . . that I finally understand the rumours. You
are crazy,' Ashish remarked.

Bani smacked the top of Ashish's head, resetting
him like a broken TV. 'Shut up and PLEASE. I never
ask you two to do anything fun because you're both
such losers.'

The blatant lie of it all made Ashish laugh. 'You
have an idea like this every week.'

'I'll go if Ashish goes,' I blurted out, out of turn,
only because I already knew he would quash it. Ashish
was in the running for head boy, the election for which
was a few months away, and there was no way he was
going to risk his chances at something so important
to him for an hour of thrill. I patted my back for the
wonderful plan—for the first time, I wouldn't have to be
the usual party pooper. Especially after my exceedingly
strict but otherwise lovely mother had solidified my
reputation as the girl who would always bail on parties
because, 'I'm sorry but Ma said no.' I was never mad
about it, though. I knew my mother's protectiveness
came from a fear of losing me too. But it *had* turned me
into a little bit of a wimp, overall.

'You know what,' he said, looking straight at me, 'let's go,' he declared, instantly launching up from the ground and dusting himself off, extending his hand towards my face that was gaping at him, shocked. 'Come,' he said, pointing to his outstretched hand.

I grabbed hold of him, and butterflies rose with me, as I lifted off weightlessly from the ground. 'What are you doing? Aren't you scared of getting caught?' I whispered in his ear as Bani skipped to the back gate.

Dropping my hand, Ashish grabbed his bag from the ground and hung it over his shoulder. His response: '*Darr ke aage jeet hai*, Sana.' And then, he winked at me.

* * *

The three of us executed Bani's prison break instructions to near perfection, as Rampal *bhaiya*, our lovely but very incompetent security guard's repeated snores filled me with the confidence I desperately needed. Holding my breath, I took my turn, sandwiched between Ashish and Bani, and ran out of the back gate to find cover behind a car. Once we were generously out of his line of sight, I felt the adrenaline settle down.

'I can't believe you guys are making me do this,' I said, complaining, even though now that we were out, I was at least a little excited, too.

'Consider yourself an official Section E kid now,' Bani announced.

'What's the worst that can happen?' Ashish asked.

'We could get kidnapped! Or worse . . . expelled!' I guffawed, as Bani and Ashish stared at me, before walking away. 'Come on, guys! It's a *Harry Potter* reference,' I yelped, following up to them.

The gate of Adventure Island was gigantic and reminiscent of McDonald's branding—with a red marquee that had the name written in big, bold, yellow colours flashing right at the top. On the left-hand side of the gate stood a kiosk with a guy handling tickets and coupons.

'How will we pay?' I knew the plan had loopholes, and here was one glaring at us. As a freshly minted tenth grader, I had already spent my daily allowance on an aloo patty and a new Pilot pen.

'I've got it,' Bani said, whipping out three fresh five-hundred-rupee notes from her pocket. 'Since it was my idea, it's also my treat.' If only Bani's mother knew what Bani did with her hefty monthly allowance, double of mine and Ashish's *combined*, she would tighten up the purse strings, for sure. And save both Ashish and me from a lot of trouble.

At first glance, Adventure Island gave the illusion of a whole different world, cordoned off from civilization whilst existing so close to it. Unlike Bani and Ashish, or most of our school, I did not grow up coming here. The last time I ever saw the inside of an amusement park was when I was six years old, wailing on a Columbus ride because I felt extremely nauseous, and watching Ma almost murder the conductor, trying to make him stop the ride midway.

I couldn't recall doing anything quite as adventurous since.

How had this place, so mythical, filled with rides, roller coasters and live entertainment shows, existed in the same perimeter as our school? Every corner of it was speckled with joy—someone selling French fries, someone selling ice creams, all of them selling an idea of fun I wasn't used to having. And why had Ma not given me another shot at it? Maybe I'd just eaten something bad that day!

'Okay, which one first?' I asked Bani. The entire expanse, which seemed to stretch on endlessly, was covered in roller-coaster rides of different sizes, all painted in bright primary colours. The chain restaurants located metres away from each other only added to the visual overload.

'That one,' Bani pointed to the tallest roller coaster, or anything, I had ever seen in my entire life. Nodding, I walked behind her, with Ashish right next to me, towards 'The Ocean Dive'. Although entirely in-air, the ride was designed to feel like an underwater experience with water splashes throughout, like a 4D movie, simulating how it would feel to dive straight into an ocean. From two hundred feet above the ground, that is.

I glanced upwards to take in the height of the roller coaster, and the fact that my neck couldn't curve just enough to capture its full breadth led to my mouth drying up. The sun in my eyes stung tears right into them.

Was I . . . afraid of roller coasters? I couldn't be! How can you fear something you've never experienced?

'You okay?' I felt Ashish's breath on my shoulder. Suddenly, my flesh was goose-pimpled by his proximity.

I nodded. 'Just a little scared.'

Ashish grabbed my hand, touching me for the second time today, and squeezed it three times. 'I'll sit with you, okay? You'll be fine, I promise.'

As we hopped on to the ride, Bani willingly took the seat next to a stranger, leaving me to fiddle with the belt as Ashish watched, amused.

'How many times are you going to check it?'

'As many times as I can before they start the ride.'

'Check mine too?' Ashish asked cheekily and I made a face.

He looked at me, sincerely this time. 'Chill, silly,' he said, with a twinkle in his eyes.

'Trying.'

The ride gave us little time to prepare. Before I could say a prayer, the front columns were already ascending. The rumble of the tracks and the click-click-click of their friction against the wheels was jarring, my ears flinching with every rising decibel.

If it looked steep from the ground up, the view from the top was sobering. I realized that I might not know if I'm afraid of roller coasters, but I damn well have a fear of heights. Instantly, I shut my eyes and my nose scrunched up involuntarily in the process, as though I was trying to make my face disappear inside my skull.

Right as I prepared myself for the mighty fall, I felt a gush of wind hit me in the face, and it only took it going away for me to realize it wasn't the wind. It was Ashish, who had scooted in to kiss my cheek gently, before moving away so fast, almost pretending it didn't happen. As our coach plummeted to the ground, I felt my heart soaring in rebellion; the warm feeling of Ashish's lips on my cheek plastered like a tattoo.

Little did I know then, I was falling in more ways than one.

Chapter Three

Present day

'Where did you go?' Ashish knocks on my head, bringing me back to today: T-minus three months to intercontinental long-distance.

'I was just thinking about that day at Adventure Island,' I announce, flicking my ice cream wrapper in the dustbin beside us.

Bani looks up at the sky as though a film reel from that day is playing on the horizon. 'Fuck, that was a great day. And to think you were being such a bitch about not going!'

Something pokes me in my stomach; Ashish's hand wrapped around my waist, edging up and down, asking for attention. 'That's how we started, Sana,' he whispered, soft enough so only I could hear it, before lightly kissing the corner of my cheek the same way he had done that day, years ago.

He does not have to remind me how it started. I know our story like the back of my hand. And also because my ego suffered a bruise before it started, too.

* * *

Two years ago

After that day at Adventure Island, I was mildly heartbroken when Ashish pretended nothing had happened, despite the fact that I made several not-so-subtle nods that I had a crush on him. Eventually, I retreated too, and the remaining months of tenth grade passed with both of us pretending we were friends. He no longer seemed interested in anything more and I did not want to run after attention when he had put it directly on my lap. Well, before snatching it away too.

'He's not doing anything because he's scared about not getting head boy,' Bani said as she joined me in the canteen for lunch. Ashish had been away for the last week for all our lunches, busy campaigning for the elections. While Ashish, if elected, would only formally be the head boy two months later, when we went on to the eleventh grade, the elections were conducted a few months prior to give the new batch of Student Council members a chance to test the waters in the presence of their senior mentors.

I looked up from my food. 'Huh?' I asked.

'About the fact that he likes you,' she announced. Bani knew? 'He's not doing anything because he thinks it'll lower his chances of getting the position. You know? How teachers don't pick the boys or girls who are dating because they'll be too distracted to work?' she added, pretending to gag.

I looked down at my food, fiddling with the canteen biryani, suddenly losing my appetite. 'How do you know about this? Did Ashish say something?'

'He didn't have to.'

I blush, caught a little by surprise at how transparent my feelings have been, until the red feels like a ball slammed into my face. He had taken the punt to skip school to go to Adventure Island, but this—*us*—wasn't worth the risk?

'He's doing the right thing,' I said, defeated.

'You're both so stupid. It's just head boy, not the prime minister,' Bani replied, frustrated, choosing to focus on her spinach and corn sandwich, instead.

On the day of his faux-election (because the final votes were always subservient to what the teachers had pre-decided, just in case the student body went really berserk), I stood with Bani in the audience as our seniors counted the votes in such a dramatic fashion, it *did* feel like Lok Sabha tallies. Tanya, by a thumping majority, was announced head girl first. And then came the time for the head boy announcements.

While Tanya's win had been obvious—she was smart *and* pretty, what could be better?—Ashish's was a close call. He was the crowd favourite and very well liked overall, but not nearly as academically gifted as one needed to be to bag the position. Which is also why he had been so nervous in the weeks leading up to the election.

Still, his massive good-guy, popular appeal had successfully skewed the votes in his favour. When Ashish's name was finally announced as the head boy, after a few minutes of debilitating contestation, the smile I saw on his face made it all worth it. I had never, ever seen his eyes glimmer like that.

As the audience dispersed and the anointed king and queen returned to their subjects, Ashish made his way to Bani and me.

'Congratulations, I'm so proud of you!' I said, playing with his hair, the way I knew he hated.

But this time, Ashish didn't protest or get annoyed. Instead, he said: 'Be my girlfriend.'

Right next to me, I could hear Bani squeal in excitement.

'What?'

'I like you, Sana. So much. Will you be my girlfriend, please?'

All the feelings of rejection I had stifled came rushing back. He had picked this thing over how he felt about me, and now that he had won one, he wanted both.

'Why? They could still take head boy away from you if they find out we're dating, you know?' I said, dryly, a little late to taking offence at how he had not wanted me enough.

'I don't care if they take it away, Sana. I just needed to know I could win. That's all,' he said, affirmatively.

'And what if you had lost? What then?'

'It wouldn't have changed what I'm asking right now,' Ashish said, smiling.

'Haan, but then I would've been the consolation prize, na?' I could tell I had stumped Ashish because he did not have a smooth answer at the tip of his tongue.

'Okay, you two are not ruining this,' Bani said, intervening. By which I mean, she used her hands to part us, stood in-between, and smacked both of us on our shoulders. 'There is no way you can be just friends after this, and we all know that. Sana,' she said, looking over at me, 'he's a little bit of a loser and his priorities are sometimes all over the place, like in this case, and you can be as mad at him as you like. But I also know that he really likes you.'

A few weeks later, I learned that Ashish had set his mind on a design school in the US, specifically Chicago. His research had told him that besides good grades, which he didn't yet have, and a general talent for design, he also needed splendid extracurriculars and glowing recommendations to secure a scholarship that would get him out of the country. And so, whether it was the most absurd inter-school competitions or wanting to be head boy, he needed every notch on his belt possible.

'And you,' she said, pointing her finger at Ashish, 'you are the stupidest person I have ever met. Who puts being head boy over a girl like this?' she said, pointing at me with both her arms exaggeratedly. 'If you do this again, I will be the first one to ask her to break up with you, but because I know you,' she said, and then looked at me tenderly, 'and because I know you, you two have never been just friends. I saw this coming from the first day.'

'Please, you did not,' Ashish snorts.

'Ashish, I caught you literally smelling her *hair*,' she yelled, making his cheeks flush and eyes dart to the ground. 'And you,' she said, pointing at me, 'don't shut up about him even though we spend the entire day with him. And I know he's not *that* interesting. So yes, I saw it coming from a kilometre away. Can you please cut the crap and get together already?'

Before I could blink or process what Bani had just said, Ashish knelt down on one knee. 'Sana, for the second time, will you please be my girlfriend?'

In one quick, crazy way, Ashish managed to prove to me what really mattered to him, above it all.

'Oh my GOD, get up! The principal is right over there,' I shrieked.

'Not until you say yes.'

'Yes, you idiot,' I said, as he finally let up and gained height. Looking in his eyes, I repeated, 'Yes, I will.'

In our group dynamics, there had always been Bani and Ashish and Bani and Sana; suddenly, from that day on, Ashish and I were a subgroup too. In the middle of the day, amid breaks between classes, we stole moments, escaped from the crowded hallways, and found cosy nooks and alleys to touch, hug, kiss and love in.

'You're too pretty for me,' Ashish said after we kissed for the first time behind his school bus, five minutes before the bus yard started filling up with people. Both of us had left class for a pee break. Bani would bring our bags to us when the bell rang.

As I looked down at my feet, too shy to still look him in the eyes, he kissed me again. 'If we get caught and they take head boy away from you, you will hate me forever,' I said, casually disguising a fear as a joke.

'I'll still have the best prize in this world possible,' Ashish said, grabbing my hand. 'I really like you, Sana.'

'I really like you too, Ashish.'

'No, I mean, *really* like you.'

'Hmm, I really, *really* like you too.'

He scratched his head and turned away. 'I really, really, really like you.'

And because he had asked me to be his girlfriend, I decided to take the lead on this one. 'I love you, Ashish.'

In front of me, I watched Ashish take it in—that I was right there with him, on the same page. 'I love you, Sana. I am so glad you're mine,' he whispered like a kid does to their favourite toy, scared someone will find them talking to it. As we kissed, our hands never left each other's, until he squeezed mine thrice before letting it go—something he would come to do over and over again.

* * *

Present day

It's him squeezing my hand again that brings me back to this moment, right now.

'You know, none of this would've happened without you, Bani,' I say, reaching out for her hand that she smacks out of her way. 'Hey!' I squeal. 'That hurt.'

'Please don't give me credit for this okay?' she says, scowling in Ashish's direction. 'Have you looked at his face? There's not that much to be thankful for.'

Ashish launches up in Bani's direction and yanks her rubber band out of her hair, pulling apart her ponytail and running away with it. When Bani's little legs struggle to catch up with him, I just sit there thinking how much I'll miss this.

The next phase of life, college, feels like tenth grade all over again. But back then, the fear of moving on from my girlfriends led me to finding the best friends in the world. That kind of luck does not strike twice. The unfamiliarity aside, I can't fathom the idea of Bani and I not sitting next to each other, Ashish not even being in the same time zone as us.

'We need to set some ground rules, guys,' I say, standing up, commanding attention and making the two stop their goose chase. 'Ashish, return her rubber band, stat.' A few days ago, I realized that fearing the change and the distance would not help. What would help was a plan. And so, I came up with a few ground rules for our friendship as it enters a new phase and compiled them all on my Notes app. It was now time to vote on the clauses. 'Yes, ma'am,' Ashish complies instantly, motioning it over to Bani, who grabs it and makes a *kuh-CHHHH* sound that she only makes amongst the three of us to imply just how whipped he is.

'Okay, guys, here we go,' I say, after giving them a brief primer on what's to come. 'Feel free to discuss, debate, modify,' I announce, clearing my throat as I read from my phone's Notes app.

Ashish and Bani glare at me like I have lost my mind.

'Okay. **Rule number 1: A weekly call on a predetermined date and time is non-negotiable.** Anything else needs to be scheduled against it. Missing the weekly call results in penalties, to be determined by the impacted parties.'

'Impacted parties,' Ashish repeats, holding in a chuckle.

'You're really going full Sana on us,' Bani says, before my stare shuts her up. 'Okay, okay, sorry yaar, go on.'

'**Rule number 2: The group chat should not remain dormant for more than a day.** Regular updates about daily life, new friends, college drama, etcetera, must be sent in the form of photos, voice notes and texts that catch the remaining members up adequately.'

Ashish nods. 'Fair enough.'

'**Rule number 3,**' I recite from my heart. I have just added this one to the list this morning. 'This one's for you, specifically, Ashish. **Should you fall in love with someone new, you must instantly call Bani.**'

Then, I look over at Bani. '**Rule number 4**, this one's for you, Bani. **Should Ashish call you to say he's falling in love with someone new, you must make the case for why I am the best girlfriend in this universe and why he's a piece of shit for even looking in a different direction.**'

Bani nods, always taking my silliness seriously. 'I would fly to Chicago and slap him across the face if he even dares.'

While Bani and I have our moment, Ashish rises up from his bench and kneels down in front of me, just like he had done so many years ago. 'You really think I can fall in love with anyone else after you?'

'Who knows? You might find that you like white girls with blue eyes.'

'Actually, I've come to realize brown girls with black eyes are kind of what get me going,' he says, before planting a kiss on my lips.

I fight back the distraction and push him away. We have a lot to discuss.

'**Rule number 5**,' I say, resuming. '**All fights have to be resolved within twenty-four hours of the first sign of occurrence. Should that time elapse, the fight is automatically resolved, and all involved participants have to move on.**'

'I interject,' Ashish laughs, throwing his head between his knees. 'Sana, you can't make sure we don't fight,' he says, looking up at me, his elbows resting on his knees.

'He's right,' Bani nodded in Ashish's direction. 'Fights are how we become closer. Don't you remember? Our massive allergy debacle?!'

The allergy debacle had been something about me making fun of Bani's gluten allergies (which were fake, as we would find out a year later) and Ashish agreeing with me, and Bani breaking down and crying. Eventually, she mentioned that she had been feeling, for a while, that ever since Ashish and I started dating, we sometimes forgot she existed. Instantly, Ashish and I had done whatever we could to fix that feeling.

There was no way I was going to make Bani feel like an outsider when she was the whole reason why I was on the inside.

Still, while this was a good example, that was not the point. 'Guys, I'm not saying we won't fight. All I'm saying is that the fights must have a finish line,' I add. 'I don't ever want there to be days, weeks that I go without speaking to you two just because we had a stupid argument,' I say, before I can't say anything more.

The thought of this impending separation has made me emotional every time it has come up; reading out these rules makes it that much more real.

'Okay, I propose an amendment,' Bani says, raising her hand.

I giggle, 'You may proceed,' wiping my tears.

'Instead of setting a time limit for resolving the fight, why don't we make it a rule that we'll never resort to silent treatment? That at any point, if there is any difference, we'll talk, yell even . . . but we will never ice each other.'

Ashish nods. 'I like that. What do you say, Sana?'

'Amendment accepted,' I say, laughing, as I edit the rule on my Notes app. 'The amended rule number 5 goes, **All fights must be resolved without resorting to silent treatment. If at any point the parties disagree, they will converse about it instead of avoiding each other.**'

Bani passionately nods her head. 'Exactly!'

'I really love you guys. I don't know how I'm going to find this in Chicago,' Ashish says. 'No one's going to compare to you two.'

'Of course they won't. We're literally the loves of your life,' Bani chirps in.

'She's the love of my life,' Ashish says, pointing to me, 'you're just my ugly best friend who won't stop third-wheeling.' Before I can stop it, there is another goose chase; Bani running behind Ashish to attack him, Ashish with his long legs evading her smacks till the two of them are sprinting in circles around me.

'HEY! I have ten more rules left to go over.'

* * *

The only rule I couldn't make to resolve all the challenges distance was going to throw our way was how Ashish and I would make up for not being able to touch each other for months at a stretch.

'Fuck, Sana, you feel so good,' Ashish groans, his gaze piercing my body as he tucks loose strands of my hair behind my ear so his view of my face is clear. As we lie shirtless with Ashish on top of me, I try not to explode under the heat of his touch. Every time he holds me, it feels like I'm naked in a snowstorm; like I'm walking barefoot on burning coals. It's embarrassing, the effect he has on me, even after two years of being tethered.

Right now, as Ashish and I lie in my bedroom, my mind flashes to the first time he was here, alone, back in the eleventh grade. We'd been dating for a few months at that point and were slowly realizing that the quick kisses we snuck in at school were not enough. Our teenage hormones were raging and we needed more. One day, I offered up a solution—he could come over to my place after school. Ma, being a high-flying journalist for NDTV for ten years now, had erratic work hours and was usually never home before eight on most days, giving us a good four to five hours, as long as we kept track of time.

* * *

Two years ago

'Can I . . .?' Ashish asked me as he sat on the bed next to me, our mouths dry from kissing each other senseless. I had no idea how, until that moment, I had existed in a world where I wasn't kissed for an hour at a stretch. We were still in our school uniform and his hands were already grazing my thighs, so far up my skirt that I felt it stupid that he thought to ask.

As I nodded yes, Ashish undid the first button of my shirt—his lips resting in the nook between my shoulder and neck. My shirt didn't come off, not entirely, but his hands went all the way inside, gripping and exploring me. It wasn't until he pulled my shirt over my head that the dim buzz of the doorbell to my front door knocked me back to reality.

'Shit, shit, shit,' I screamed. 'Oh my god! Get dressed! Now!'

'Are we sure that's her?' Ashish asked.

'Who else will it be, Ashish?' I yelled, scrambling to find a way to make him disappear before my mother opened the door with her key. 'Go hide in the washroom!'

'Sana, we'll just say I came over for a bit. She's not going to kill you.'

'Yeah, and then I'll come live with you and your parents when she kicks me out, cool?' I replied, signalling him to sit quietly. 'Washroom. Now!'

The fact that my mother was cool with me having a boyfriend was a big, bold aberration to her general strictness. I had curfews, was regularly grounded and rarely ever attended a school party that she had the slightest reservation would be serving alcohol. Luckily, when it came to Ashish, she'd been the stereotypical 'cool mom,' asking me to invite him home for lunch the day I told her about our relationship. For years, Ma had worn the hats of two parents and done a fine job at it. Because of that, we weren't *friends* like Bani and her mom were, but I knew everything my mother did was for my happiness at the end of the day.

Still, I knew that expecting her to be cool with *this* was pushing it.

'You're home! Early!' I said, faking cheerfulness as I unlatched the door to my mother—like I wasn't planning a heist in the background. 'Light day at work?'

Handing over her lunch bag to me, she replied, 'What took you so long?'

'I was in the washroom.'

'Why are you still in your uniform?

'Oh, that,' I said, suddenly falling short on excuses. 'Napped right after coming home. Just woke up a few minutes ago.'

She eyed me suspiciously before asking: 'Had lunch?'
I nodded yes. 'It was delicious!'

Something in her face arose, suspicious. She glanced over to the kitchen sink. 'Why are there two plates?'

'Huh? What do you mean?' I said, my brain fixed on Ashish sitting cross-legged in my washroom, before I saw what she was talking about. There were two sets of cutlery in the sink. 'Oh, I got myself seconds. You know how much I love rajma.'

Lucky me, my inquisitive mother probably decided she was too tired for this interrogation. 'Okay, well, I'm going to take a bath. Can you make me chai, please?'

Nodding enthusiastically, I watched as my mother disappeared into her bedroom. When she locked the door behind her, I knew I had to execute this in two minutes, tops.

Shoving the door open to my washroom, I yelped, 'QUICK! You need to leave.'

'Hey! You can't come in without knocking,' Ashish quipped. 'I could've been peeing in here!'

'Ashish, now is not the time for jokes. You have to get out of here,' I said, grabbing his arms and pulling him towards the main door—only the fear of my mother's wrath would give me the Herculean strength to drag a giant like him out.

'Sana, I'm not joking. It is important to set some ground rules for our relationship, such as not walking into the washroom without knocking,' he smiled, twisting his arms across his chest.

'I will kill you,' I said, punching his belly, before pushing him out the door, unlatching it as quietly as possible. Obediently, Ashish stepped out of my house and into the hallway, and right as I was about to shut the door on him, he grabbed my shoulders and kissed me for a beat too long.

'I love you so much,' he mouthed, bolting towards the staircase before I could say anything. From the other side of the door, I heard my mother's door opening.

'Who is at the gate?' she asked, looking at me facing an empty doorway.

'Oh, no one. I thought I heard the bell ring,' I said, shutting the door. Ever since that day in the eleventh grade, we were extra cautious about keeping a watch on time. So when it came to having sex for the first time, on the day of our last Board exam, we knew we couldn't risk Ma interrupting something this important.

* * *

A *few months ago*

When we made it to my house after a quick lunch with our extended school group, the impatience fluttering between the both of us was palpable. We'd been waiting for this moment for years and it was finally here. Both of us finally felt ready. As I ripped open a condom packet, Ashish ripped off my clothes, feverishly trying to touch me all over like it was the first time, all over again. We had bought a few extra packets of condoms, just in case, which came in handy because we kept trying to put it on upside down. Finally, a few sex-ed YouTube videos later, we nailed it down so it wouldn't slide off and Ashish took his position on top of me.

'Is this good?' he asked, moving inside me slowly.

It hurt like a bitch already, but I knew that wasn't the answer anyone is looking for when they ask that question. 'Ah, not great, but keep going,' I said, between forced breaths, before Ashish collapsed on my face, laughing.

'You're such an idiot, Sana,' he said, kissing my forehead. 'You know we don't have to do this right now? I'll get some lube the next time, and it'll be easier.'

No. This was non-negotiable. We had already started now and our first time was not going to end up becoming a dud. This was not the story I wanted to recite in never have I ever or other such drinking games. 'No, it doesn't hurt that much,' I said, lying.

'You sure?' Ashish asked, moving my hair off my forehead. I nodded yes and Ashish took that as a sign to move further inside me, instantly causing me to yell.

'You said it did not hurt!' he said, quickly detaching, his eyes dripping with concern. 'Are you okay?'

'I did not mean to go full throttle, asshole,' I said, grabbing a pillow and shoving it in Ashish's face, laughing as he moved off from being on top of me.

'Okay, enough, we're not doing this today,' he concluded, rolling over to his side with an I-told-you-so look.

'Wow, way to make me sound like a horny idiot.'

'Aren't you?' he said as his hands slipped between my legs.

Even though our first time having sex was a disaster, we still managed to make the most of it in other ways.

* * *

Present day

But this was a few months ago. Now, I'm more prepped and primed. Now, we have the right tools. Now, Ashish's movements are softer and deeper, his touch melting over me like I'm hot iron. He knows all the tricks to ease me up, I know all the tricks to make him last, and together, we make a really great team.

As Ashish climbs on top of me, adjusting his grip on the pillow, he asks me, like he always does, 'This okay?'

'More than okay,' I say, digging my nails deep into Ashish's back, my permission for him to go all the way.

Between wet, slobbering kisses, tossing and turning, getting off the bed and pushing me against the wall, grabbing me everywhere as though I would slip out from under him, Ashish spends the next two hours exploring my body like he hasn't walked down this road a hundred times before. He holds me, my waist, my legs, like he's afraid someone will snatch me away from his touch. He moves inside me like he's worried there's a part of him he has found in me that he won't be whole without. As usual, we try our best to keep these feelings in, until it's too much and Ashish collapses on top of me—our chests heavy, reeling from the last one hour we've just had.

'Are you listening to me?' Ashish asks as our breathing steadies.

'Hmm?'

'My Apple Watch is literally worried about my health,' Ashish says, pulling up from over me.

'Why? It wasn't that good!'

'Oh? It wasn't? Do you need me to go again?'

I shake my head no. 'I need some time to recover, Ashish,' I say, panting.

'You can say thank you any time.'

'Please,' I say, scoffing, 'I more than returned the favour.'

'I can't believe I won't get to do this to you in a month,' Ashish says, turning over to face me, running his fingers over my stomach in the way that makes me shiver.

As soon as he says it, I roll out of bed. Just the thought of him moving has reminded me to pee after sex. 'Can we not talk about that?' I ask, standing up.

Ever since the date has gotten too close for comfort, I have been riding the avoidance train daily. Besides, we've had long, long conversations about it already. The logistical stuff, how we'll manage the time-zone problem. I have my lists ready and our calendars aligned for date night video calls. Everything is planned out.

Now it's just time to make the most of what remains.

Ashish grabs my hand and pulls me back down on the bed. 'That's not how this works, Sana,' he says, kissing me.

'Gotta pee, gotta pee, gotta pee,' I say, slithering out of his touch. 'I'm not getting a UTI in the days we have left to do this over and over again.'

'Over and over again?' Ashish looks down at his crotch and dramatically exhales, 'Rest in peace, my man.'

'Shut up,' I throw a pillow in his face. 'I'll be right back.'

Chapter Four

There were fifty items on my list of things the three of us absolutely needed to do before Ashish left for college. The original draft had run up to about 120, but I had to be realistic and pare it down. Some of the highlights were: see the Qutub Minar for the first time without a teacher forcing us to stay in a queue, experience one night of clubbing, smoke a single (only one, I promise) drag of a cigarette to know what I would be missing for the rest of my life, take a road trip to Chandigarh.

But, to my dismay and to Ashish's surprise, moving continents required a lot more prep than any of us had anticipated.

For the most part, our hang-outs ended up being the three of us at his place, in his bedroom, talking about the same old things as Ashish tried to meet more of his packing goals. Today wasn't going to be any different. Except that it was going to be the last time.

But before I have time to fixate on that, Bani blowing up my WhatsApp jerks me out of a thought spiral.

Bani: I'm downstairs!!!!!! Where r u

Sana: WAIT. Coming. Mom's annoying me

Bani: Should I screenshot and send this to her?

Sana: Only if you want me to tell your mom what you were really doing when we went for 'a run' yesterday

After two whole years of biting my ears about being single, Bani had recently hopped on the dating app trend and was filling up her post-grad days with as many first-dates as possible. Yesterday's specimen was an all-tattooed up boy, much older than us, who picked up Bani in his Mini Cooper. 'Sana, he wears leather jackets. In *summers*. He's, like, my soulmate,' she'd told me when they'd matched on hinge. As usual, to her mother, I was her cover-up story.

Bani: In case mom asks, we ran 3 km

Sana: Oh I'm sure you got a lot of 'exercise' in

'About time, bitch,' Bani says, flinging the door open to the passenger seat. I move into Bani's scorching hot car and turn the AC on full blast.

'One time you reach early and you won't let me hear the end of it.'

'Whatever,' she replies. 'It's finally time,' Bani says, clutching the steering wheel.

It has been a long time coming but I'm not even close to ready for this. 'Please don't, unless you want me to start crying.'

Bani nods, putting the car in first gear. We zoom out of the parking lot and I realize this will be the last time that we will be driving to Ashish's place together for a while. I push that thought aside. I need to be on my A-game today.

'Namaste, aunty,' I say, greeting Ashish's mother as we walk into his house in a cute colony in Hauz Khas, a convenient ten minutes away from both Bani's and my place. It's nothing like where I live, considering it's one, a bungalow, and two, largely white and brown while mine is copper and brassy; but something about it has always felt like home. His comfy couch we watched Shinchan on, his kitchen the three of us made and burned countless Maggi's in, his bedroom we sneaked many make out sessions in as Bani guarded the door ... his home is a time capsule of countless moments of our friendship.

'Sana, Bani,' Rana aunty says, pulling us into a hug that instantly makes me emotional. Wasn't it just yesterday that Ashish dropped his bag next to my chair in the classroom and stared me in the eyes, before announcing proudly that he had told his parents about us? How his mother had hugged him and asked to meet me instantly, how she'd made my favourite, rajma chawal, when I'd visited? How warmly his parents had opened up their home to me and never made me feel any less than Bani, who had been around forever?

Where did the years go?

What reason will I have to visit when Ashish is gone?

'Suresh, look who's here!' Rana aunty says as his dad looks up from the newspaper.

He looks unimpressed in his usual, deadpan manner. 'Let me guess, you're here to help him finish packing, haan?'

A month ago, Ashish's parents had offered to pay for movers and packers to help ease the process of shifting continents for him. Suresh uncle had emphasized that it was far more complicated than Ashish was thinking it to be and that neither him, nor his mom had the energy to help him out.

'Are you guys crazy?' Ashish had exclaimed. 'Who hires movers and packers for college?'

Let's just say: he regretted passing on that deal more than I regret some of my bold, but ultimately unsuccessful, Janpath shopping bargains.

'Sana, I am not packed at all. I should've just said yes for the movers and packers,' he said on the phone last night, grovelling for my help.

'That boy is never going to grow up,' Suresh uncle mutters to himself. 'God knows how he's going to live in Chicago all alone.'

'*Tum chup raho* (Keep quiet, you)! If he has any problem, you will be the first one to take a flight to help him,' Rana aunty says lovingly, showing us the way to Ashish's room as though we haven't visited a billion times before.

Bani and I open the door not to his bedroom, but a royal mess. 'I'm so fucked,' Ashish announces, collapsing on his bed, holding his head in his hands.

'Who asked you to be so cocky when your parents were offering to help you?!' Bani says, already on the job, folding Ashish's fresh laundry into the suitcase.

I fling my phone out. 'Okay, let's get to work. How many suitcases can you take?'

Ashish points to the three big ones and two carry-ons parked in front of his bed.

'Hmm,' I say, taking a moment to look over the organization chart on my phone, 'here's how we're going to do it,' I say, as I walk the two of them through the system. 'All the chunky, breakable items will go in the big suitcases; the weightless ones will go in the carry-on as well as the things Ashish would absolutely need as soon as he lands, in case his check-in baggage gets lost. As for the items, we will go category by category; approaching the packing the way one would approach a day. What is the first thing you do when you wake up? Brush your teeth! Yes. And in goes the toothbrush.'

While they both looked at me like I'm crazy, to no one's surprise, my method worked.

'I love you so much, you're literally my life saviour,' he says, pulling me into a hug when we're halfway through.

'Oh hello, love birds,' Bani says throwing Ashish's toiletry bag a little south of Ashish's crotch, but close enough to startle us upright. 'You're not here to do *aashiqui*, Sana,' she says, looking at me. 'And get off your ass, Ashish. We won't be there to save your butt in Chicago.'

It takes seven hours, three cans of Red Bull and the light shifting from blazing afternoon to orange sunset, but finally, all of Ashish's life is packed into five bags. His bedroom, once a panoply of Pink Floyd posters, random motivational quotes chipping from the corners and framed photos of the three of us reimagined by him on Adobe Illustrator, is now a bare four by four, stripped of all its Ashish-ness.

'I've never loved you guys more,' Ashish says, crashing into his bed.

'Okay, I have to head home now or mom will kill me.' I know Bani is leaving so I can get some time alone with Ashish. 'So. This is it,' Bani mutters quietly, her hands in her jeans pockets. I can see her struggling to not cry. The same Bani who didn't shed a tear when she skinned her knees raw on a rocky pavement as she ran behind Ashish after he called her too ugly to even be Buttercup in the *Powerpuff Girls*.

'Come here,' Ashish says, pulling her into a hug. This is not a regular sight. These two are never affectionate.

Why is this happening? Why is it all changing?

'I'm not even going to miss you that much,' Bani says, her voice obviously strained, pulling away from Ashish as he wipes her tears.

Ashish shrugs. 'I am, Bani. I'm going to miss you like crazy,' he says, so sincerely.

When Bani leaves and it's just the two of us, though, I feel the energy shift, a little. This often happens, usually in a good way, but right now, something feels off; in the way he thuds his washroom door while coming out of it, or how he hasn't said a word to me in a few minutes.

'All okay?' I ask him.

Ashish is zipping his backpack, the same one he has been loyal to for years. 'I still don't understand why you won't come to the airport to see me off.'

We've discussed this before. 'Ashish, your entire family will be there,' I reply. 'I won't even be able to kiss you when you leave. I want to say bye on my terms.'

'Come on, Sana. They know we're dating. You're over at my place most days.'

'That's different . . .'

'Haan, *toh*, *matlab* whatever is good for you, we'll do that?'

'Ashish . . .'

He sits next to me on his bed, stretching out his legs and resting his head on my shoulder. 'Sorry, I didn't mean that.' He holds out the palm of his hand towards me in truce.

'I'm scared,' he whispers as though he is afraid someone else will hear it.

'Talk to me,' I say, looking at him, holding his face in my hand. 'What is scaring you?'

'Ask me what's not.'

'Tell me?'

'I'm scared I'll fall apart there. I have never, ever, for a single day in my life, functioned by myself. There has always been mom and dad and then Bani and eventually, you,' he says, looking at the floor, his head still on my shoulder. 'And suddenly, I'll wake up in a place where every new person I see is a stranger.'

'That's true, but have you thought of how fun it's going to be?' I say, cheery and enthusiastic, even though this is the last thing I want to be. Instead, I want to say the stupid stuff. Like: if you're scared, don't go. Stay back. We'll study in Delhi together. It doesn't have to be this hard.

Ashish stands up, frustrated. 'This is the problem. You always come back to this, how fun it's going to be for me there. Can I, for once, be scared for a second without you pointing out that I'll be having such a great time without you?'

'Who said you can't be scared?' I ask.

'Sana, all we ever talk about is how scared *you* are of my move. Have you ever thought of what I'll do without you? How I'll function in a completely new country, on a completely new time zone, with a culture shock?'

'Because you never talk about it, Ashish,' I reason. 'You're making it sound like I only care about myself just because I *talk* about my feelings.'

Ashish mock-laughs. 'I don't talk about it? Every time I try, you tell me not to! You say it's too tough and you don't want to talk about it. Except when you want to discuss how you'll cope, then it's all fair game.'

My mind instantly goes to the last day we spent at my home. Ashish goes on. 'Have we ever talked about how I'll figure my shit out? How I'll cook? How I'll make friends? How I'll manage everything by myself?' he asks, staring into my eyes until he answers for me. 'No, we haven't.'

'We haven't talked about these things because when have you *ever* wanted to talk about your feelings, Ashish? What am I supposed to do? Guess?'

Ashish furrows his brow. 'Again with the you-
don't-talk-about-your-feelings, Sana. When we were
on the roller coaster, when you were scared out of
your mind for 10,000 reasons, all of which were
written on your face, how do you think I knew that?
I saw you, I saw your face, and I held you,' Ashish
says, bitterly. 'That is all I'm asking. For you to hear
the things I'm not saying, for you to just think, for
once, that you are not the only one who is going to
go through this. That maybe I'm going to go through
a worse version of what you'll go through, all alone
in a foreign country with no Bani to come cheer me
up when it gets especially tough.' Ashish chokes as he
approaches the end of his argument.

'Then why go?' I ask, deflated.

'What?'

'Why are you going if you're so scared?'

'Are you serious? Are you hearing yourself
right now?'

'I'm just saying, if you're this scared, then I don't
understand why you're even doing this. I thought you
were all game about it.'

Isn't this what he had done before too? Chosen the
fight to become head boy over me? Now, he's picking
a school a thousand miles away, when there are
countless good options in India. How do I stop feeling
like I'm only ever going to be his second biggest dream
at any point?

Ashish looks deflated. 'Can you please just leave?'

Really? We're ending it like this?

'Got it,' I say, slamming the door shut on my way out, forgetting to account for the fact that Ashish's parents are sitting right there in the living room, sipping on some chai.

By the reduced volume of the TV, despite 'Breaking News' flashing across the screen, I know his parents heard everything.

So much for wanting to say goodbye on my own terms.

* * *

'Back home so early?' Ma asks as I unlock the door, while she's sitting on the dining table, watching TV and eating dinner.

When I do not respond, she raises her voice. 'Hey! I'm talking to you.'

'Yeah?'

'All okay?'

I hold a thumb up and say 'Awesome' before heading to my room and slamming the door shut, a little too hard. It surprises me when she doesn't follow me in.

Flinging my bag on my study table, I remove my chappals and dive straight into bed. With the AC on blast, I bury myself inside the blanket Ashish and I were under just a few days ago. He hasn't even left yet and it already feels like a lonely hell.

Wide awake and tossing and turning in my mind, I keep opening and closing Ashish's chat—desperate to see a 'Typing' sign under his name, desperate for him to just text me something so I know it's not over. When he doesn't come through, I send Bani a text.

Ashish and I are about to set the record for literally the quickest two people who have broken up while in long distance . . . aka the day before it starts, I text her.

But she doesn't reply, either . . . right when I need her the most. Frustrated, I put my phone back on my nightstand—not before checking Ashish's chat window thirty more times.

Four hours later, I wake up to my phone screeching with an alarm. It's 3 a.m. Confused and disoriented, I grab my phone to snooze it and find one new notification from Bani.

Rule Number 5: All fights must be resolved without resorting to silent treatment. If at any point the parties disagree, they will converse about it instead of avoiding each other.

As my alarm fades into the quiet, I wonder what to do. Should I call? Should I text and say sorry? I re-read Bani's text five more times, until it finally sinks in: this is not how it will end for us. Rushing to my mother's bedroom, I push her door open far too loudly, considering how late in the night it is. Luckily, she is awake.

'Wait, why are you up?' I ask, suddenly delirious.

Ma looks up from her phone. 'Why are you awake?'

'I asked first.'

'I'm the mom.'

I walk over to her bed and sit down in front of her, on the edge. 'I need you to take me to the airport, Ma.'

'I thought you'd decided not to go?'

'I know, but we had a huge, and I mean huge, fight and I just . . . I walked out of his home without saying goodbye,' I say, tugging at my cuticles. 'Ma, I can't stand the idea of him being in that flight for hours, thinking that I didn't care enough to make it right.'

'So that's why you were being moody?' she says, raising her eyebrows.

'I was not!'

'Worse than when you were thirteen,' she quips, before checking the time on her phone. 'What time is his flight?'

'I'm . . . not sure.' I reply. 'I didn't ask.'

'You didn't *ask* what time your boyfriend is flying out of the country?'

Suddenly, a fog lifts.

'I think I have his tickets in my chat somewhere,' I reply, holding up the PDF file to her face. 'This is his flight.'

'Okay, so he's flying out at seven thirty, he's likely going to reach the airport by three thirty,' she says, staring into my phone. 'It's almost three, Sana. I don't know if we can make it.'

'Ma, we have to try.'

That is all the ammunition she needs. In record time, we make our way downstairs and to the parking lot, which she backs out of like the pro driver she is, while I fix the Google Maps location to Terminal 2.

The sound of my mother yelling into my ear jolts me. 'SANA! No international flight leaves from Terminal 2,' she says, scolding, and I quickly fix the location to Terminal 3.

'How am I supposed to know?! I've never flown international!'

The maps on the screen estimate the time of arrival as 3.30 a.m., right on the nose. In the end, my relationship of two years is going to come down to seconds.

'You know you can speed a little, there is literally no one on the road,' I say, quietly, looking at my mother.

'There is no one on the road that you can see, until some drunk idiot crashes into you and you lose control of the car. I know you love Ashish and you're doing a romantic thing right now, Sana, but please don't be stupid,' she says, changing the gear to fourth. 'Why don't you just give him a call? Ask him to wait a minute at the gate? He has plenty of time,' she says.

'No, I don't want to do that. I either get there and surprise him or he leaves without meeting me.'

If he leaves, I'll know it was supposed to be over.

Ma scoffs and ever so slightly accelerates, and, with just one minute to spare, we turn left towards T3. As we make it to the drop-off, she looks over at me and yells animatedly, unlocking the car doors. 'What are you waiting for?! Go. I'll catch up with you.'

I run like Geet does in *Jab We Met* when she sees her train leaving the platform without her. I have one goal in mind: spot Ashish. 'There!' My mind goes. On the far-edge, right in front of Gate Number 4, I see his parents, standing and waving.

'Did he leave? Is he gone?' I say, running over to join them, panting with my palms on my knees.

'Sana! We thought you weren't going to come,' Rana aunty hugs me. 'He was just next in line,' she says.

'So he's gone,' I say thinly into the air, wondering what this means for us.

If I could just see him again, I would tell him that I was sorry, that I messed up, that I—

Wait. What was that? I turn around, responding to the two finger taps on my shoulder and open my eyes to Ashish's face beaming at me. I break down, involuntarily, into rapturous tears. Before I can even digest the fact that he's here, he pulls me into a hug. I wish I could Fevikwik us in this moment until eternity.

'I thought you were gone,' I sigh, crying into his ears. 'I did this entire romantic airport thing and I thought you were gone and now they don't even let people inside airports without a ticket and I can't afford a ticket.'

'You've watched *Jaane Tu Ya Jaane Na* one too many times to know I couldn't possibly be gone without seeing you, Sana.'

My teary eyes light up with joy. 'You're here' I say grabbing his face. I know his parents are watching us, but I don't care.

'I saw you running like an idiot when I was showing the security guard my passport. Had to snatch it out of his hand to get here,' Ashish says, fixing the loose strands of my hair that are clinging to my tears.

'I thought we were over,' I whisper through my tears, struggling to conjure up any proper last words that would matter.

Ashish takes his handkerchief out of his back pocket and wipes my cheeks clean. 'No matter where I go, Sana, this thing will not change. We are never going to be over.'

'I'm so sorry, Ashish. I'm sorry for being a selfish piece of shit, I love you so much, I'm so sorry.'

'Shh,' Ashish says, clasping me tighter to his chest. 'I love you, Sana. So much. You don't even know how much.'

'I promise, you've got this, okay? You're going to kill it, if there's anyone who can do this, it's you,' I say. 'I'm a little slow, I know, so please just tell me when you're scared. I'll hold you, I'll fix things.'

'I know, Sana, don't you think I know that?' he says grabbing my face. 'It was just a stupid fight, I said things I don't even mean.'

A minute passes before it dawns on me—the realization that he has to leave, that we're here to say goodbye.

'How do I do this?' I ask, pleading him to show me the way. 'How do I let you go?'

'We do it the way we have always done it.'

I unclasp myself from him and take a step away.

Forcing a smile, I say, 'Text me when you land?'

'Of course I will.'

When he walks back to the security gate, I see him holding his hands up, picking at his earlobes, mimicking an apology to the entry guard. As Ashish waves me and his family a last goodbye before disappearing into the grey of the airport, Ma finally catches up to me, heaving the same way I was, minutes ago.

'Did he leave already?'

'Yeah.'

'Did you get to say goodbye?'

'Yes,' I say, half-smiling. 'Yes I did.'

Chapter Five

Luckily, Ashish flying out of the country has perfectly aligned with Bani and my college life kicking into gear. While I'm off to pursue a bachelor's degree in English at Sri Venkateswara College, always more fascinated by the South campus than the North, Bani is reluctantly pursuing fashion at NIFT Delhi—something Ashish and I convinced her to apply for, after years of laying witness to her eccentric style and excessive platform boots collection. And even though I miss Ashish constantly, I am at least a little grateful for the distraction. Besides, just like in school, our group chat, foolishly called 'Flying Dreemz' since my birthday, is constantly buzzing with notifications. In some ways, it feels like nothing has changed.

Bani: u guys can thank me whenever for saving your ass

Sana: you read out MY own rule to me, the ones you were mocking me for making up

Ashish: bani what do you do with all these compliments you keep asking for?

While I've been busy chatting with Bani and Ashish, I have also been added to a group named 'Venky English First Year,' where every last member seems to be tripping on at least a little bit of coke. There are over 400 messages already and it's been ten minutes! People are planning fresher's outfits, their second semester electives, what placements they want to sit for . . . and college hasn't even begun yet. Before I can compel myself to become a part of the conversation, feeling the FOMO trickling in, another text pops up on my screen.

Aanchal: yo, Aanchal here. I'm messaging everyone I added to the group to welcome them personally (and to make sure you don't register it as spam and leave). I'm going to be the class representative for our batch (which is why I'm having to do all this fun work of texting people on a Sunday and annoying them). Hope it wasn't too annoying! Feel free to text me for anything (I mean anything at all)! See you soon!

I smile as I read the text to myself. I already like this girl's energy. Could this be our meet cute? Does it count as a meet cute if it happens online?

Sana: Hey, hello! Sana here:) That's totally fine. I read the group's name and realized it probably wasn't spam. Although, I opened WhatsApp to 400 new messages and went like??????

Aanchal: lol - there are another 100 already just in the few seconds it took me to type this out

Sana: Who are these people and what drugs are they on? (asking for a friend in case the govt's reading this)

Aanchal: let me find out for you bestie, even though i'll just say i did NOT anticipate drug-peddling as a part of my class-representative responsibilities

Sana: oops did i take the 'feel free to text me for anything' a lil too far

It feels so strange, this conversation with a completely new person. With her, I can be whoever I want to be. Parts of me I love, I can amplify. Those that I hate, I can conveniently ditch.

Chucking my phone aside, I get back to the last few minutes of prep before my first day of college tomorrow. I ensure that my canvas tote bag, which says 'Drama Llama' with an exaggerated drawing of a cartoon llama, is filled with the necessities: a planner, a five-subject notebook, a pouch that will replace my extremely childish pencil box, and some hygiene stuff, lip balm, extra pads, etcetera. The outfit I'll be wearing—a kurta-top from Fabindia with my favourite blue jeans that never disappoint—is already hanging outside my cupboard, properly ironed, just the way I like it. If 'ready' had a face, I would be the poster child.

Which is why the fact that I forgot to set an alarm for the next morning is really the punchline of the century.

I wake up to a thumping on my bedroom door.

'You're getting late,' Ma cries as I jump out of bed. It is eight already and I need to be at college by nine.

Running to the washroom, I clean myself up, the shower a lot less intense than the version I usually like to take during summers, and everything else is ready to go. Smudging *kajal* on my waterline and my mom's stolen perfume under my neck, I shove my phone and its charger in my bag and sprint out my bedroom. This time, as a college kid, officially.

'Breakfast!' Ma yells as I rush to leave. Her voice startles me as I walk back, grab a toast from the plate and compensate with a big fat smile.

'Delicious' I say, chowing down a bite and completely ignoring the plate of scrambled eggs.

Only in the auto to the Malviya Nagar metro station do I get a second to catch my breath. What if I hate everyone in my section? What if Aanchal is actually a really well-spoken . . . bitch? What if I become the class loner? This is the flip side of a good deal, I realize. The level of security that came in my friendship with Bani and Ashish also brought with it a great proclivity for comfort. I have completely forgotten what it is like to be put on the spot and dance like a monkey for a bunch of strangers, just for the off chance that they feel entertained.

Still, I feign confidence as I step off the auto and pad towards the stairs of the metro station, despite the fact that the *autowallah* conned me out of twenty rupees and I, once again, refused to stand up for myself. But it's okay, there will be another tomorrow and so many chances for me to get this thing right.

Standing at the ticket counter, awaiting my turn to recharge my metro card, I hear a familiar voice calling out my name. 'Sana?'

I know that voice too well to still be smiling.

I turn around and face my childhood, now stretched out at the top and bottom: Tanya.

It has been months since I last saw her. After everything that happened, my brain developed an anti-Tanya filter, blurring her out in the hallways and from pictures that pop up on my Instagram. Seeing her in front of me now, too close to ignore, feels like whiplash.

'Oh, Tanya! Hi,' I say, far too awkwardly.

'Dude, I can't believe I'm running into you at, like, a *metro station*,' she quips, like we've run into each other at an abandoned island. *It's just a metro station and we live two minutes away?* I want to say, but I bite my tongue.

'Uh, yeah. So, heading to college?' I ask, trying to act, very hard, like I care.

'Yeah, B. Com. at Venky. What about you?'

Oh my god. What sort of a catastrophic hell is this?

My friendship break-up with Tanya was a lot more dramatic than my fall out with Neha and Sakshi. Those two were more like the dominoes that fell once I flicked Tanya off. Let me put it this way: if I *were* to bump into Tanya on an abandoned island with Neha and Sakshi also there, and there was no option but to eat each other, Tanya would be the one I would light a flame under. And if that's gory, it's because if *I* didn't do that, Tanya would take the first chance at burning me at the stakes. After all, I disobeyed her dibs on Ashish.

When Ashish and I got together, we decided to keep our relationship as low-key as possible to avoid the glare of teachers and high-school gossip.

But despite our best efforts, we were too known in our circles to be completely incognito. Ashish had massive 'he's going to make it big' energy and I was the grade topper by a mile, even with my shitty grasp of mathematics. All of this I had already accounted for, and to some extent, made my peace with. What I had, although, conveniently forgotten, was the 'dibs' Tanya had called on Ashish during that stupid lunch at Neha's place.

This memory had only come back to me as the gossip made its way towards me as well. One version of the story went that Ashish had asked Tanya out, and because she said no, he had settled for her 'seconds'. The more vicious of the rumours was that Ashish was actually dating Bani and using me to cover-up just how weird it would look if it came out that the two of them were dating, how bad it would be for a head boy's reputation. I was so sure that both these rumours were Tanya's creations because they had that essence of bitchiness that only she was capable of infusing in stories. And also, because, well, I heard it from the horse's mouth.

* * *

One year ago

'First *toh* he desperately grovels, *ki* please date me na, Tanya,' I heard her recite to a bunch of girls I couldn't recognize. 'It'll be so cute if the head boy and the head girl are dating, he said.'

'And then?' One of the girls asked.

'Then what, now he's dating Sana, because I was very clear I did not want to mix work with love,' Tanya exclaimed. 'Poor girl, she doesn't even know he's cheating on her with that weirdo Bani, yaar.'

'How are you sure?' the other girl inquired.

Before Tanya could respond, though, and spew out more nonsense, I made my presence loud and clear. 'Hi Tanya,' I said, interrupting.

'Oh, hey, hi San,' she said, her voice fidgety, her stance suddenly shaken up. 'Ho-how long have you been here?'

I huffed, 'Long enough,' before disappearing into the crowd. Whatever had been alive of our friendship ended that day, officially. Even for her loudmouth, Tanya was too embarrassed to look me in the eyes again.

* * *

Present day

Except now that the year has flown by, she seems to have forgotten it all—or maybe she thinks *I* have. Standing in front of a grown-up version of the girl I once called my best friend, dressed in her cool beige cargo pants and Yankees T-shirt, I can't help but wonder: how the hell am I going to avoid running into her for the next three years?

'I said, what about you?' Tanya repeats.

Confused and lost in thought, I ask, 'What about me what?'

'What college are you off to, yaar?' she asks, like I am forcing her into this conversation.

'Oh, um . . . Venky also.'

'Super! We should catch up,' Tanya mumbles.

'Oh, absolutely,' I say waving her off, adding an 'or not' as soon as she is out of sight. The first thing I do the second she is gone is whip out my phone to text Ashish and Bani.

Sana: YOU WON'T GUESS WHO IS GOING TO THE SAME COLLEGE AS ME

'Madam?!' The guy manning the counter at the metro station yells over the microphone.

I'm a public nuisance already, I realize, as five people are standing behind me, annoyed, for holding up the cue.

'Oh, sorry *bhaiya*. 250 recharge please,' I ask politely, before exiting the line—muttering a whisper of a 'sorry, sorry' to the people I held up.

Bani: WHO

Bani: you can't just say that and disappear

Bani: helllllllooo?

Sana: fucking TANYA

Bani: LOL are you excited to light the spark of your childhood friendship

Sana: I would much rather light myself on fire

Ashish: is it possible Tanya has a crush on Sana instead of me and this is just her being a super massive stalker

* * *

On the metro, I sneak in a solid five minutes of shut-eye, despite Ashish's instructions never to sleep on public transport, before it is time to brace the massive college building that will become my everyday life.

My first thought when I walk into the main gate: this feels nothing like school. Second? I'm going to, inevitably, put on a lot of weight. A thousand eateries line the road opposite my college and avoiding all of them will be a practice in extreme self-control.

But I'll leave that problem for when I have friends to share meals with. Oh my god, I'll have to make new friends.

Okay, Sana. One thing at a time.

Per the instructions on our WhatsApp group, I find myself facing an empty lecture hall at the very end of the hallway on the first floor, stopping many strangers on the way to make sure I am heading in the right direction. When I walk in to see I'm the first one to arrive, I breathe a sigh of relief which quickly turns into surprised gasp, clutching my chest and all, as a tall figure springs out from under the table at the back corner.

'I thought you were a ghost.'

'Nope, just Aanchal,' the figure says, sauntering towards me. I meet her hand in a firm, steady shake, as Aanchal sets her butt down on a table close to the podium, right where I'm standing.

She looks at me, her eyes narrowed, as though she is trying hard to place me. 'Sana, right?'

'You've got it,' I say, striding towards her and stealing the remaining side of the table.

'I'm so glad I know one person, at least! You know you were literally the only one who replied to my personal text?' Aanchal adds.

'You're kidding?'

'I'm really not. Everyone was so busy talking on the group. I was so hurt,' she says, exaggerating. 'So, are you excited? Because I'm, like, super intimidated at the idea of meeting *soooo* many new people all at once.'

If she is intimidated, no part of her actually lets that on. In fact, Aanchal oozes effortless confidence. She is significantly taller than me, five-ten from what I can gather, and her hair is brown and golden down to her shoulders. Dressed in athleisure, Aanchal is the fittest person I have ever seen in real life. She has a deep but feminine voice, and she smells like she just finished baking banana bread, which is not what you'd expect from someone wearing Nike gear top to bottom. If we become good friends, the first thing I want to know is who does her eyebrows, because she has the most perfect, slim-thick pair that gives her face a beautiful, almond shape.

'Something tells me you're an athlete,' I retort, finding the silence between us just a tad uncomfortable.

'National level badminton,' Aanchal replies, her chest puffing up proudly.

'Are you Prakash Padukone's child by any chance?'

Aanchal throws her head back laughing. 'Still waiting on that DNA result.'

As the lecture hall fills up with more and more students, Aanchal and I are still together, even making our first introductions to the same people. Eventually, we land ourselves in an everything-conversation (one where you jump topics by the second) with two girls sitting in front of us, Preksha and Samira, who are noticeably already friends, having bonded over how they have fourteen years of Bharatanatyam under their belt, each. Both of them look like the same person too—just a tad shorter than me with perfectly tanned skin and light brown hair right out of a Pantene commercial. Amongst the four of us, there are some oh-my-god-it's-such-a-small-world connections. I know the guy Preksha used to date through a mutual friend and, luckily, we both hate his guts, and Samira and Aanchal share a few friends in common too. Our love for literature, Woolf and Austen unites us, and the fear of studying them at a higher level of proficiency is a universal sentiment. Not to mention our mutual sense of disdain for people asking us what we're planning on doing with our lives with a literature degree.

Overall, though, we have little in common, other than the fact that we're all picking up on the 'vibe' of the moment. Which is really all that matters.

'Okay, guys, on the count of three, we'll all say our favourite Austen, okay?' Preksha says, breaking the flow of our conversation. 'One, two, three . . .'

The three of us collectively chime 'Emma!' in varying decibels as the rest of the lecture hall turns around to glare at us. It's that thing, that instant chemistry, right place, right time, friends' edition. We already have plans, detailed down to the next few months, about things we'll do, cafés we'll visit, trips we'll take (they don't know how strict Ma is yet, but I'm hoping she'll let up, now that I'm in college).

We'll be a gang, I recite in my head, and Aanchal and I will be closer and that'll be okay because Preksha and Samira will be best friends too.

'Guys, there is this bakery right next to college that we *need* to go to! Literally everyone is Instagramming it,' Samira announces.

I look over at her, excited. 'Oh my god, is it Bloom's?'

Bloom's, a coffee shop tucked in a lane right behind our college, which has books lined up everywhere as decoration, is number one on my list of Must-Dos for the three years at college.

Samira yells 'Yes!' and the two of us jump up and down, holding each other's hands like we've just discovered America again.

The four of us are deep into Instagram stalking a guy who has just showed up as a mutual friend for all of us when a starkly mature voice echoing through the speakers captures our attention. A tall, bespectacled, middle-aged woman, who has the look of a professor, introduces herself sans a first name—Professor Sarin—before instantly rushing to her lecture decorum requirements.

'There are some non-negotiables in my class, kids,' Professor Sarin starts. 'First, absolutely no cell phones allowed,' she asserts, and I feel her eyes specifically on me, even though every second person in the hall has their phones in their hands. 'Second, one minute late is too late. *On time* is late. Early is on time. These are the golden rules of a well-disciplined, successful life. And third, don't try to lie to me. I have two teenage boys. I will just . . . know,' she says, rolling her eyes.

'This feels so different from school,' Aanchal whispers in my ears. I nod in agreement. The teachers at school felt like second mothers. They had seen me out of my awkward growth spurt that hit early and I had seen their hair turn grey. Professor Sarin couldn't have been further from that idyllic vision of a teacher.

'Okay, class, now the second years are going to steal the show. We're going to do some ice-breaker sessions. It'll be fun,' Professor Sarin adds, in the least fun way possible, before handing the mic to an olive-skin boy in a blue linen shirt and beige khaki pants.

As he walks to the podium, I notice his hair misbehave in the way you'd want your hair to misbehave—silky straight and falling jagged, here and there, but still looking extremely put together. By everyone's eyes glued to him, I can already tell he is used to the attention. The sly smile on his face tells me he might even like it.

'Hello *fuchchas*,' he announces, grabbing a different mic from behind the podium after his initial attempts with the earlier one produces a high frequency noise loud enough to break glass. 'Now that I have officially made all of you lose your hearing, how are you all doing?' he asks, like he is emceeing a super lit party and not an orientation of fresh school graduates with bags under their eyes.

There's a depth to his voice that almost feels put on and, on the mic, it sounds like he has a flattering baritone. Although half of his frame is hidden behind the podium, I can tell that his legs are disproportionately longer than his torso and his head stands atop a very tall neck. He is about as tall as Aanchal, I think, so not *too* tall, but he seems to stretch on forever somehow.

Responding to his question, the lecture hall erupts into a 'woooohooooo' and I join in silently, wondering what they did with the coke-heads on the WhatsApp chat.

'A little more energy or I will make you all come up to the podium and introduce yourselves one by one,' he quips, and a huge roar erupts out of the lecture hall.

'Awesomeeee,' he says. 'That's more like it. But I'm still going to make you all come up here and do just that,' he says and the crowd lets out a groan. 'But first, hello, I'm Pranav, a second-year lit student who did this thing last year and is making sure the legacy and embarrassment live on.'

A few more protest-y sounds from the lecture hall and Pranav puts on his no-nonsense face. 'Option *nahi hai bhai*,' he says, chirpily, seeming to enjoy this thoroughly. 'You want to get to know each other or not? Okay, *chalo*, I'll make it a little more fun. We'll do two truths and a lie, cool? Everyone knows how it goes na?'

A few people shake their heads 'no' in the audience and as Pranav begins explaining the game, in the background, I notice Professor Sarin leaving, making this a lot easier for all of us intimidated by the thought of making a good first impression in front of our peers as well as our professor. Two very different skill sets.

'Cool? Everyone on board? Let's start from here,' he says pointing to the left-hand corner. I count up the number of people who will go before me, elated that I have more than enough time to prep my truths and lie, recite them in my head, adjust the cadence and infuse casual humour and shock value. I desperately want to make a good impression.

When my turn arrives and I walk up to the podium, I can feel Pranav scan me, top to bottom. His glare instantly makes me nervous. I grab the mic from his hand and our fingers touch. He still doesn't stop staring. But I tune him out; it's not him I have to impress.

'Umm, okay, here we go. Hi, guys! I'm Sana, from Horizon High. And for my truths and lie . . . okay, I think *Notting Hill* is the best romantic comedy ever made. I am extremely Type A and have a list on my Notes app for everything imaginable. *Aaaaand*, um, I once chased after my boyfriend at the airport to fix a fight we'd gotten into.'

The audience roars and I feel Pranav's eyes fixed on me, as though they have an in-built lie-detector that can scan me for my dishonesty.

I can see on his face that he comes up short, as he poses the question to the audience. 'Okay then, that's an interesting one. Any guesses?' Pranav asks the crowd, nonchalantly.

The lecture hall is in consensus: I am obviously lying about the boyfriend bit.

'*Pakka? Lock kardiya jaaye?*' Pranav asks, smirking at the audience, and then directly at me. 'So, Sana? Are they right? Did we catch you in the lie?'

'I actually *don't* think that Notting Hill is the best romantic comedy of all time,' I reveal and everyone erupts into hysterical laughter. My grin is ear-to-ear-wide; I have successfully bamboozled them all!

'Wow, just when I thought we were going to be friends, you go ahead and lie about the most accepted truths of our time,' Pranav mutters, giving me the stink-eye. 'Just out of curiosity, what *is* the best romantic comedy ever made, according to you?'

I put my arms on my waist, feeling more confident than ever to declare: '*Jab We Met*, duh,' I say in a very Geet-like twang when she says, '*Ohoo*, possessive!'

This part of my personality, I know, doesn't mesh well with the fact that I'm sitting with a bunch of kids right now who would scoff at Hindi cinema as being worthy of analysis. But I will stay true to my roots, while still honouring the canon. The two *can* coexist.

But Pranav does not take me seriously. 'How does it feel having such poor taste in movies, Sana?' he asks.

'I don't know, Pranav, I think you'd be able to answer that better?' I bite back and the lecture hall shoots into an *ooooooooooh*. Like, look at this fresher taking on a senior. I can't help but feel a little proud of myself.

Pranav looks down at the ground laughing, before glancing back up at me. 'Nice, I like the confidence.'

'Thanks, I worked very hard on it,' I add as a cheeky self-deprecating humour to tune out the snobbish side of me that's come out in the last few minutes.

Pranav bites his lip and looks at me with a smile twisted towards his right cheek. Before he can add anything, though, I back away, clearing space for Aanchal who has been standing in the aisle for a few seconds. I hand her the mic and pat her with a quick 'Best of luck' on her back before heading to my seat.

'Okay, hi, I'm Aanchal. I'll make this super quick. I have played badminton at the national level. I have a metal rod inside my leg because of a childhood injury. This guy right here is my brother,' Aanchal says pointing to Pranav, and the lecture hall goes ballistic as Pranav laughs heartily in the corner—an obvious giveaway.

'Any guesses?' Pranav asks the crowd, chuckling. But the answer is plastered on both of their faces, literally. How have I not noticed that they look like the male and female version of the same exact person?

Pranav steals the mic from Aanchal. 'You're definitely not cool enough to have a metal rod inside your leg,' he retorts, before Aanchal punches him in the arm and the lecture hall erupts into thunderous claps.

'Why did you not tell me he was your brother?!' I squeal in Aanchal's direction when she returns. 'I would've been nicer to him!'

Aanchal giggles. 'Please, I don't think I've ever had more fun in my life than watching someone put Pranav in his place.' I blush at the compliment. 'But as a side note, I would stay away from him. He can't control his player tendencies, honestly. I've lost track of the number of friends I have lost because he broke their hearts,' Aanchal adds as warning.

'Did you miss the part where me having a boyfriend who I chased down to the airport was the truth?'

Aanchal scoffs. 'Trust me, you don't know my brother.

Chapter Six

'Guys, check WhatsApp. We've been assigned buddies! Mine just texted,' Preksha announces in the two seconds she takes away from gaping at her phone.

Every first year is paired with a second-year buddy—a forced companionship for the rest of the college year. The buddy is supposed to sub-in for a lack of actual friends, provide the first years mentorship and guidance, and *definitely* not hook up with them and complicate their academic affairs, etcetera. The programme had been successful in the past and very organically come to replace its less-lauded alternative: the senior–junior ragging practice.

I pull my phone out of my bag and see that my screen is lit up with a message from an unknown number, as predicted. Tapping on the photo, I fling the phone in Aanchal's face. 'Wait, isn't that your brother?'

'Damn, best of luck San,' Aanchal says, laughing. 'Pranav can't be a "buddy" to another woman if he tried.'

Pranav: Hey buddy! This is your buddy, Pranav (we met at orientation, you made that ludicrous statement about how jab we met > notting hill and I tried *extremely* hard not to take offence) let me know whenever you want to catch up? would love to show you around college and (help) make things easier for you :)

Sana: hello! first of all, if you're going to be my buddy, we will have to agree to disagree over this jab we met versus notting hill debate. And second, I am free for the next 2 hours if you want to catch up right now?

Pranav: hahaha. okay. shall hash this out in person. give me 2 mins to confirm about right now?

I shut my screen off and stifle a bubbling smile; just in case Aanchal catches me. This—having a guy friend—feels good. All my life, I haven't had a lot of 'boy' friends at all, especially not if I don't count Ashish's friends who also became mine, by extension. And while I'll never admit this to Aanchal, I'm realizing that maybe I am excited to have Pranav as my buddy. Maybe college is the time to branch out?

Pranav: *cleared up my schedule for you. meet me in front of canteen in 5.*

'Okay friends, turns out I'm meeting my buddy right this second,' I tell the girls, dusting off samosa crumbs from my lap. 'Miss me? Don't eat another plate of chilli potato without me, please!'

'Tell Pranav I asked him to behave,' Aanchal retorts.

'I will absolutely not.'

'Don't say I didn't warn you that he's a man-whore.'

'LANGUAGE!' I say, narrowing my eyes at her, having just spotted Professor Sarin grabbing lunch in the canteen five minutes ago.

When I walk out, I find Pranav already sitting on the bench right outside the canteen, reading a book thick enough to give someone carpal tunnel.

'Hey,' I wave at him, as he stands up from the bench and starts walking towards me. I can tell a hug is inevitable and so, I spread my arms only to find that it was his hand he was stretching out to meet mine.

Flushed by embarrassment, I say, 'Wow. The most classic comedy sequence in the world and still I never imagined it happening to me.'

Pranav responds by casually pulling me into a hug. 'Wasn't sure if you were a hug person.'

'I have this theory that anyone who isn't a hug person just hasn't been hugged enough,' I shrug.

'Wow, savage,' Pranav chuckles like I've just said something either really funny or remarkably stupid and I notice that his head tilts forward when he's laughing; as if the joy in his body is spinning him off centre.

'Thanks for showing up, like, instantly. I can't imagine how busy you second-years are,' I say, pointing towards his novel.' He flips it to the title-side and I realize it's *Crime and Punishment*.

Pranav shakes his head. 'Never busy for my buddy,' he says, smirking. 'Besides, this isn't for class.'

'Oh, just a light read then?'

'You need something to take the edge off all those readings,' he quips. 'Do you want to go out and chat? We could also walk around campus. You pick.'

Jitters run through my body in anticipation of a shockingly cold iced latte. I realize this physiological reaction might point to a severe caffeine dependence, but I don't care. I squeal, 'Oh my god can we *please* go to Bloom's?!'

I can see I have once again disappointed Pranav—and his tastes. 'All you first years with your stupid little lists, yaar.' Still, already leading the way, he says, 'Just don't be disappointed when you find out it's overhyped as hell.'

'It can't be. It's all over everyone's Instagram!'

'Oh, of course, if it's on *Instagram*.'

As we walk to the front gate, I fear the awkward silence catching up with us. Luckily, the stretch from college to Bloom's is a little topsy-turvy, with a few left and right turns here and there, which leaves plenty of instructions for Pranav to announce to fill in the gaps. By the time we turn right on to the street where Bloom's is meant to be, my chappals are already a different colour from this morning and Pranav has eaten my ear off about the Instagram algorithm and its echo-chamber effects.

When we're almost there, Pranav points to the building, less than fifty metres away, where Bloom's is located. But suddenly, I'm distracted, looking at my phone that's beeping in my hand.

Ashish: i'm going to sleep guys, been a looooong day. hope you're having fun

Bani: HELP I'm overdressed!!! for FASHION school guys!!

Ashish: I explicitly told you to throw away those cowboy boots

Bani: I can't throw away my firstborn, Ashish

'Hello?!' Pranav flails his hand in front of my eyes, zapping me out of my screen.

'Sorry, sorry. Just had to get back to a text,' I say, shoving my phone in my jeans pocket.

'Let me guess, that's the boyfriend?'

Years in and the mention of Ashish in conversation still makes me feel giddy. 'Yep,' I say, casually, like I'm not blushing, and throw my phone in my tote bag.

'How long have you two been together?'

'Umm, two years. Ish. Maybe a little more, if you count the crush stage.'

Pranav shakes his head, looking down at the ground. 'I don't get it,' he finally says, looking back up at me.

'You don't get . . . what?'

'How do you date someone for that long without getting sick of them?' Pranav asks.

'By sharing a best friend in common who would kill us if we broke up,' I say right as we arrive at Bloom's—its name erected on a wooden flank with neon-lettering, quite an unexpected turn to the indie-core aesthetic I had been imagining. Inside, it's a teenage girl's Pinterest board gone all wrong; a mishmash of decor-genres. Bold and glittery on one end, quiet and calm pastel on the other.

'That's not the vibe I was expecting,' I say, looking at Pranav.

'Yeah, well, that's what you get for getting your recommendations off Instagram.'

Still, there is something warm and cosy in all the muddled mess that tells me I will be spending many afternoons here, tucked in with a book and an iced coffee.

Pranav pulls out a chair for me and I readily take it, waiting for him to take the seat in front of me. Instead, he sits down right next to me. The two chairs are close enough that our arms brush against each other and require an uncomfortable twenty-degree tilt for me to look him in the eye.

'Aren't you supposed to sit there?' I say, pointing to the seats in front of us.

'Why?'

'I don't know, it's just . . . the right way to sit?'

'I only sit across from a girl for the wrong reasons, Sana,' he replies casually, flicking through the spiral bound menu in front of him. 'Besides, I like the view.'

'You don't like this cafe's interiors but this,' I say, pointing to the window, 'view you like?' Facing us is a bunch of shrubbery with a few nice flowers growing out. Behind it, the main road flows with the usual Delhi traffic.

'I didn't judge you for liking *Jab We Met* more than *Notting Hill*.'

My mouth is agape. 'You absolutely did judge me! In front of my peers!' I tilt my head to look at him. 'Isn't this a little inconvenient? You know, to hold a conversation?'

'Don't worry. I can guarantee you a high-quality conversation,' he says, winking.

Over the next half hour, Pranav sprinkles his one whole year of college wisdom on to me and I do my best to soak it up. From which professors to not piss off to which cult-y societies to avoid (debating, entrepreneurship clubs), hanging out with him feels like a crash course in how to college. I'm surprised he knows so much about so much, especially for someone who looks like he wouldn't sit for more than one lecture in a day.

'Sarin *toh* you cannot mess with,' Pranav says, referring to Professor Sarin, who is taking two courses for me this semester. 'With her, you have to . . .' He pauses to look at his phone. 'One sec.'

Aanchal: REMINDER. She has a boyfriend. STAY AWAY.

Because we're sitting millimetres apart, from the corner of my eye, I can read Pranav's screen.

Pranav: get a life.

Aanchal: Seriously!! Promise me you won't fuck around Pranav please I really like her or I'll text her the same thing

Pranav: I'm putting the phone down now

Turning his phone over, Pranav places it on the table in front of us, right as mine goes off.

Aanchal: if he starts talking about his dead dog, RUN. it's a MOVE.

Internally, I thank Aanchal for throwing me a fun bait. 'So, are you going to tell me about your dead dog?' I blurt out. It doesn't come out quite as humorous as I expect.

I see his entire face change as he asks, 'Aanchal?'

Nodding, I apologize. 'I'm sorry, that came out . . . wrong.'

'No, that's okay,' Pranav replies, forcing a laugh, although I can tell I have rattled him a little. 'Did she say I use it as a move?' My silence is his answer. 'She can be a real bitch sometimes.'

'What is this move? Why do you need a dead dog for it?' I ask, following it up with the question I have been sitting on all this while. 'And are you the serial dater she paints you out to be?'

'Oh my god,' he says half-laughing, looking over at me. 'Is that what she is telling you?'

'Let's just say she has told me to be wary of you. Just in case, you know, you pull a move.'

Pranav is halfway through a sip of his coffee, as he turns his entire body to look at me. 'You have a boyfriend, why would I pull a move on you?'

'So if I didn't, you wouldn't hesitate?'

'No,' he shrugs lightly, 'then you're fair game.'

'Calling women fair game is not the move you think it is.' I add: 'You didn't answer my question, though.'

'Am I a serial dater? I don't know,' he says, playing with his hair. 'I like getting to know people. And yeah, I haven't really had a long-term thing yet, for reasons Aanchal does not know,' he responds. 'Besides, I'm just twenty, not everyone is practically married like you. She just likes to exaggerate because I dated a couple of her friends.'

'A couple?'

'Like, five.'

'You've dated FIVE of her friends? And broke up with them?'

'I mean, I'm not with any of them right now . . .'

'Wow, no wonder she warned me.'

Pranav smirks. 'Why? You would've given me a shot otherwise?'

'I feel like we keep having to circle back to the boyfriend thing. Do you have short-term memory problems or something?'

'Nope, just very high hopes.' The air between us is suddenly electrified, which he dims, instantly. 'Anyway, you have nothing to worry about. I'm not going to pull my dead-dog move on you.'

'Oh come on, just because I'm not single doesn't mean I don't like a good, sentimental story,' I scoff, attempting to convince him.

He raises an eyebrow at me. 'You can't blame me if you fall in love.'

'Oh, I'll try very, very hard not to.'

Pranav seems to mull over it, before a conclusive smile washes his face with certainty. 'Nah, I have decided we can't risk it,' he affirms. 'Anyway, it's more of a third date kind of thing.'

'But I'm never going to go on a third, or a first, date with you.'

'Your loss, then.'

* * *

The singular advice Pranav gave me re: Professor Sarin was 'Don't make your assignments sound like they didn't take you the equivalent of climbing Mount Everest to complete. She hates an obvious lack of effort.' Which was largely ambiguous to work with, at the moment, but now that my first assignment for her is due tomorrow, it's especially frustrating. I'm reading one essay on my phone, while highlighting another on my laptop, when my phone buzzes with a 'Baby Shark' tune set to Bani's phone number. She had set it up, custom, a few years ago after realizing that even while having a mobile phone on me all the time, I was just as unreachable as when we were still using our landlines to communicate.

> **Bani**: Ashish please tell your girlfriend i'm not speaking to her
> **Sana**: What??? Why??????
> **Ashish**: Bani is not speaking to you, Sana (Why +1)
> **Bani**: i don't speak to people who are ruthless ignorers
> **Sana**: i'm in the LIBRARY and your call almost got me kicked OUT Bani we really need to change this ridiculous ringtone
> **Bani**: You can change it when I'm dead

I shut WhatsApp off my laptop. I really need to get some focused study time in if I want to meet my ridiculous GPA expectations. Right as I close the window, I feel my phone buzz again. I'm going to kill Bani, I mutter under my breath.

> **Pranav**: Hey bud - Aanchal told me ya'll have an assignment tomorrow. first ever, i'm assuming? need some help?

Pranav, as a buddy, is honestly my beacon in the night. Last week, he added me to a Google Drive folder with neatly categorized sub-folders for readings, essays, PDF files of books, his past assignments and more, broken down by semester, all because I was having a mini meltdown about how this degree was nothing like what I had expected it to be.

'English in school was so easy. What the hell is this?' I said, frustrated, shoving my face into a twenty-five page reading, 'Virginia Woolf and The Art of Madness' that Sarin had instructed us to complete overnight. 'This reading will drive *me* mad.'

Pranav shook my head like he would a dog's. 'This is real life. Suck it up. Besides, that reading's actually quite fun.'

'Yeah, if you're a masochist.'

How discouraging and un-buddy-like of Pranav, I had thought at that moment, only to find later, an email pop-up notification adding me to this goldmine of a Drive—including a summary sheet on the same reading I had been complaining about before.

Sana: i'm freaked out and will happily take all the help you can offer

Pranav: wanna study together? Aanchal's with me too

Sana: YES! you are a LIFESAVER

As soon as I hear rustling in the library, I know it's the two of them, probably arguing about something as they walk in.

'That's NOT what I meant,' Aanchal says, resting her bag down next to me. 'Sana, can you please tell him I did *not* say that his dead dog thing was a move?' she says, narrowing her eyes at me.

'I *saw* your text in her phone,' he exclaims, smiling at me.

'You peeped into my phone?!' I ask, flabbergasted.

'You were sitting, like, a centimetre away from me.'

'SAN BABY, I'm so glad to see you finally,' Aanchal whisper-screams, enveloping me into a hug. I return it double-fold because we haven't seen each other in a few days owing to her off-season, inter-college badminton matches.

Aanchal takes the seat next to me, leaving Pranav opposite us. 'Please tell me you've not made new, cooler friends.'

'Yes, they're in fact right here,' I say, pointing to the two empty seats next to me. 'Say hi, guys.'

'Wow, you think you're so funny, no?' Aanchal tugs at my waist.

'Okay, what's this assignment on?' Pranav asks, plunging straight into buddy mode.

'It's actually not that tough. Prof asked us to pick any one modern reinterpretation of Austen's novels and write an essay on why we think it respects or rejects the classic. Quite interesting.'

Aanchal yelps. 'Wait, *that's* what we have to do? This means I can't just copy-paste from any of Pranav's assignments from last year, urghhh.'

'Shh,' the librarian whispers from the front desk.

'I wasn't going to let you do that anyway,' Pranav retorts, flipping his book open. His copy of *Crime and Punishment* has since been replaced by *A Suitable Boy*. 'You're here to learn.'

'*Oho*, thanks teacher,' Aanchal mumbles. 'Like you would've ever passed tenth grade maths without cheating.'

The library session lasts four, long marathon hours. Eventually, Pranav and Aanchal switch seats because I need his eyes on my assignment and Aanchal needs to sit next to someone who doesn't hyperventilate out of a fear of failing every few minutes. As he pores over my prose, smirking in the parts where I have added my skittish humour and furrowing his brow where I am making a long-winded but eventually full-circle argument, I feel the giddy curiosity for finding out what he thinks. When he flips to the final page, I am desperate for feedback—good, if possible—considering that the deadline is up in half an hour.

'I don't have any notes.'

'It's that bad?'

'You know it's excellent, Sana.' He says with so much certainty, that any speck of doubt I have evaporates. 'Good job.'

Pressing send on my assignment, I feel all the lost sleep hitting me at once. Like a zombie, I go back home, and starfish on my bed. I still need to do the readings for tomorrow and eat dinner, but the thought of shutting my eyes just for a few minutes is so tempting, I give in. They only open next morning to my phone ringing with Ashish's name. It's seven.

'Good morning,' I whisper, a little delirious, already expecting the world's worst post-nap hangover ever.

It's likely dinner time in Chicago, based on what my buffering brain is able to calculate. Still, Ashish responds, 'Good morning, baby. Just getting up?'

'What do you mean just? It's like seven in the morning,' I say, crabby. 'What's up?'

'I'll show you,' Ashish replies. 'Check your WhatsApp.'

I open my phone and the bright light almost blinds me, until the blur starts to fade away into a crisp photo on my chat window.

'ASHISH!' I yell. 'Are you really sending me unsolicited dick pics? Is that how bad it has gotten?'

'You have no idea how bad it has gotten,' he replies, a raspy edge to his voice.

And because I still have a few minutes before I have to get ready for college, I say, 'Give me an idea.'

Chapter Seven

'Are you being serious?' I ask.

'Yes,' Aanchal replies. 'She has already graded everything. She's on her way with the papers right now.'

Samira's mouth is wide open, having overheard our conversation. 'How did she read fifty assignments overnight?'

'Apparently she doesn't like any backlog,' Preksha adds.

'Dude, I've heard she's super strict in marking,' one of our classmates mutters from behind, as Professor Sarin enters the class with a fat bundle of sheets clasped in her hands, confirming Aanchal's hunch.

'I've heard she gives negative marking for takes that piss her off,' Samira retorts.

Aanchal snaps at all of us. 'Guys, you've got to chill,' she says, assertively. 'And you too. This is not boards, Sana,' she says, pinching me in the arm, as I'm absolutely losing my shit.

Even if the word 'chill' existed in my vocabulary, I wouldn't know how to spell it. This is my thing, being a good student. The fact that teachers love me, that I'm good at assignments and exams, all of this is core personality material. And now that it's college and the stakes are higher, I care a lot about how this assignment has turned out, what Professor Sarin thinks of my analysis on *Bride and Prejudice*, an underrated Bollywood interpretation of *Pride and Prejudice* starring Aishwarya Rai and Martin Hendersen. I have so carefully deconstructed the anti-colonial sentiment in the movie that even I was surprised with myself, reading it over and over like watching my own Instagram stories.

She will love it. She has to, right?

'You know it's excellent, Sana.' Pranav's voice echoes in my head, tempering the tension. Thanks to him, I'm not worried *if* I'll get a good grade, only about just how good it will be.

So when Professor Sarin hands me back my assignment, a fifteen out of twenty-five marked in red with the comment 'more analysis required', it feels like my heart just experienced a fifty feet drop into my stomach.

I glance at Aanchal's answer sheet to determine if this was some class-wide screw up, only to discover she has scored a twenty. That too, written in green! As have Preksha and Samira. Meanwhile, I'm the black sheep with the crimson mark of shame.

It doesn't matter how many times Aanchal pokes my stomach or how funny the GIFs she sends me are, the dejection I feel doubles my body weight as she pulls me towards the canteen.

'Come, we deserve some spring rolls,' Aanchal says, linking her arm with mine, as I carry my sunken head sullenly through the hallway, and then down the stairs.

'You deserve it. I practically failed.'

'Don't be dramatic, San. Half of the class didn't make it past fifteen.'

'You're really trying to make me feel better by telling me I'm average?'

This is Aanchal's first time seeing the ultra-competitive, grade-obsessed version of me that Bani and Ashish eventually learned to tune out. It's not a great side of me, but she exists, right there with the other, more redeemable parts.

And right now, she is grumpy.

We walk into the canteen, the atmosphere a touch too loud for my taste as usual, and I finally lift my head to prevent bumping into people carrying their overflowing dal makhanis when I find Pranav sitting on the far end with his friends. Our eyes meet and it's a two second thing, but he bids his friends goodbye in an instant and walks towards us.

'You look like you've had a great day,' he quips, messing with my hair.

I fling his hand away. 'I'm not in the mood, Pranav.'

'She's sulking about Sarin's grading,' Aanchal adds, like it's a disclaimer to have any conversation with me for the next few hours.

'It's not sulking if it's legitimately bad, Aanchal,' I say, curtly. Aanchal spent half the hours and a quarter of my effort on her assignment and still managed to bag those five extra points. And green marking!

Pranav grabs both of my shoulders and tries to shake the sadness out of me. '*Arre* Sana yaar, you can't be so sad over Sarin's grades. She failed half our class last year.'

'I would've preferred failing over this.'

Aanchal raises her hands, admitting defeat. 'You deal with her. I'm going to get us some spring rolls,' she says, quickly scurrying away.

'Why is she being such a bitch?'

Pranav laughs lightly, before adding, 'Probably because she now has two people like this to deal with,' he says, pointing towards himself. 'It's like I'm looking in the mirror.'

I ignore him. 'You don't have to do anything. I'm just in a mood. It'll be okay.'

Pranav tightens his squeeze on my shoulder. 'Sana, I don't know if this helps, but trust me, you can go a lot lower with Sarin.'

'You're right, it doesn't help.'

'Look at me?' he says. 'I read that assignment. It was brilliant. If Sarin has given you such a bad score, I feel like she's done it because she thinks you can do even better.'

'Don't reverse-psychology this. Let a shit thing be shit,' I reply, despondent.

Pranav doesn't seem to get frustrated the way Aanchal did. But he does seem discomforted. 'Okay, forget this. I have the perfect thing to cheer you up.'

'I really, truly doubt it.'

He pulls his phone out, distracted by trying to find whatever he is trying to find, until he lands on it. 'See this,' he says, flashing his phone in front of my face.

The entire screen space is taken up by a poster that is so *Jab We Met*-coded, I could spot it from afar, with Geet and Aditya sitting with their backs to each other in a sugarcane field, looking so desperately in love. Under the photo, it reads: 'OPEN AIR CINEMA! Today's viewing—on popular demand—*Jab We Met*! Entry closes at 5 P.M. Tickets @ link in bio. Rights of admission reserved.'

Grabbing Pranav's phone, I'm suddenly so happy I could do a somersault. 'WHERE has this thing been all along and why have you been hiding it from me?'

Pranav acts like he didn't just take a full three minutes to find this post on his Instagram. 'Reported this account, like, 10,000 times so you don't find it,' he jokes. 'But you know, desperate times.'

His sarcasm doesn't register. From gravelly rock-bottom, I am suddenly floating on cloud nine. 'I've never seen *Jab We Met* on a big screen, Pranav. You have no idea how serious this is.'

'If you're going to be this insufferable about it,' Pranav says smiling, looking at me as I jump up and down, 'I'm not going to take you two.'

'Take us where?' Aanchal asks, joining us, her hand greasy from the spring rolls. She pops one in her mouth, just as Pranav shoves his phone in her face like he did with me.

'Really cute, guys, but I'm going to have to skip. I have badminton practice at five, you know? Like I do every day?'

My face curves back into a frown. It's like making a drive all the way to a McDonald's for soft-serve and finding they're out of the chocolate dipping sauce.

That is, until, Pranav looks at me and asks: 'Hmm. You still wanna go?'

Bobbing my head like a little kid, I reply, 'Yes, please,' before looking at Aanchal to ask: 'Okay if we go without you?'

'Babe, even if I could, I wouldn't come,' she winks at me and flutters away, leaving the two of us alone. 'Pranav. Hands. To. Yourself,' Aanchal yells from afar. Pranav waves her off with his middle finger.

'So? Shall we?' he asks, beaming in my direction, right as my phone starts ringing. 'The show is in Vasant Kunj, so it'll probably take us half an hour to get there.'

'Just a sec,' I say.

It's Ashish. He's probably calling because of the fifteen separate texts I sent him about how I think I should drop out, how I chose the wrong degree, etcetera. He's checking in, like he always does, even though he knows me enough to know these things aren't a cause for alarm.

'Helllllooo,' I say, excitedly.

'You sound . . . happy.'

'You caught me at a good moment, I just finished crying,' I say, walking a little away from Pranav. 'I'm going for an open air cinema screening of *Jab We Met*. Isn't that so cool?'

'Ooo, sounds fun. With Aanchal?'

'Oh, no, with Pranav. He came up with the plan to cheer me up.'

'Who is Pranav?'

'I've told you, like, ten times. Aanchal's brother? Did our orientation two-truths-and-a-lie activity?' When Ashish doesn't respond, I add: 'He's my buddy?'

'You've mentioned him, but I don't recall you saying he was a friend.'

'We're not *friends* friends.'

'Why does he want to cheer you up so bad then?'

Plucking my phone between my ear and shoulder, I pace around as I wonder how best to proceed, as a loose pebble pricks the corner of my foot. 'Ouch,' I squirm.

'What happened?'

'Nothing, what were you saying?'

'Just that I didn't know you guys were so close.'

'What's this about?' I ask, turning my phone from one ear to another.

'He's a second-year, isn't he? Doesn't he have friends of his own?'

'You're being really weird, Ashish. Shouldn't you be excited I'm making friends?'

'Right,' he replies. 'Anyway, I have to head for dinner. I'll call soon.'

Before I can respond, he has already hung up the call. I stand there, staring at my phone, wondering what just happened.

'Is everything okay?' Pranav asks, walking up close to me.

'Uh . . . yeah, yeah, everything's fine . . .'

'The call seemed,' he says, pausing to find the right word, 'tense. Ashish?'

'Oh, yeah, he's just having a tough time at college. Homesick,' I say, casually. 'Should we head?'

'Yes ma'am,' he flings his arms forward. 'After you.'

In the auto ride, Pranav focuses on navigating us to the precise location as I cross my arms in front of my chest and rest my head on the side. By the time I open my eyes, I feel us taking a right, until the autowallah eventually presses the brakes in front of a dingy-looking gate with a half-broken hoarding, titled 'Sunset Avenue.'

'This . . . can't be right,' I say, looking at Pranav and then back at the building, confused.

'Then how come it is?' he replies, leading the way, holding the door open to reveal a large hallway, at the end of which I see a flicker of sunlight and grass. 'Look, there.'

'The light at the end of a tunnel, literally,' I say, smiling. This would be perfect, except for the sinking feeling in my stomach right now for how things ended on the call with Ashish.

Pranav holds the door open, the creak of the hinges distracting me from wondering if Ashish and I will make it through the distance, so I can walk in. 'Feel free to thank me anytime.'

'Feel free to admit defeat anytime,' I say, skipping towards the grassed avenue.

As we walk in, I realize the fatal flaw in this plan. 'Don't you need, like, no natural light for a projector to work?'

It seems the organizers allocated more budget to their marketing department than to the logistics. The 'venue' is nothing different from a colony park with a flimsy tent on its perimeters—which, hello? Open air?—some tables at the back corner with snacks, and a medium-sized projector screen on the opposite end. The set-up mimics any other wedding in my colony.

'Unless these guys have acquired some super cutting-edge technology,' he says, unimpressed. 'A mediocre set-up for a mediocre movie.'

'HEY!' I yell in his direction. 'I thought this was supposed to cheer me up!'

'It is.'

'Then you can't be mean about *Jab We Met*.'

Pranav looks down at the ground and raises his hands, admitting defeat. 'Okay, okay. No trash talking the movie until after we've watched it. Cool?'

'How about not trash talking the movie at all?'

'Very cute, but that's not how this works. I'm going to get myself some popcorn, you want something?'

I shake my head no, but Pranav returns with a large tub of popcorn and coke anyway. Which is just as well, because before the movie starts, the tub is halfway empty.

'You said you didn't want any,' Pranav says, side-eyeing me.

'You didn't say they were going to be *this* buttery,' I respond. 'Okay, okay, pay attention now,' I say as the beginning credits roll. 'I don't want you to miss a single detail.'

'I am quickly regretting this,' Pranav adds, bringing his knees close to his chest, letting me hold the popcorn for the both of us.

'You're doing this to make me happy, no?'

Pranav nods sincerely.

'It would make me very, very happy if you paid attention and gave the movie a fair shot. And remembered enough details to score well on the quiz.'

'There's a quiz?' Something melts in Pranav's eyes. 'I guess then I need you to shut up and let me watch.'

* * *

I have *Jab We Met* memorized down to the last dialogue—which makes it convenient to skip looking at the screen every few minutes to glance at Pranav to check if he's laughing adequately or smiling at all the cute moments. To my surprise, he almost always is.

'This guy is going to lose it if she does not stop talking,' Pranav says, halfway through Geet's dramatic monologue as she sits across from Aditya for the first time, who is decidedly poker-faced, staring out the window.

'This movie is too damn predictable, Sana. Of course she's going to end up with Aditya and not whoever this Anshuman guy is.'

'That's because love is predictable, Pranav. One of the two people will always be madly in love and know it, the other will be madly in love and not know it. After that point, it's just a race to find out how they get together before it's too late.'

Pranav turns to look at me. 'Accha? Is that how it went for you too?'

'What do you mean?'

'You know, with your boyfriend?'

'I don't know. We did have some of that classic will-they-won't-they drama, but we were so young back then.'

'Hmm,' Pranav says quietly, before turning his attention back to the screen.

Looking at him, I get that feeling one does when they're right at the precipice of making it to the peak of a climb. There is an entire layer to Pranav I don't understand; the things he doesn't say, when I can clearly see there's something on his mind, the things he says that are often the opposite of what he means. But still, I know, just like I know the summit will arrive, that one day I'll know these parts of him, too.

The bright sunshine has faded into the evening afterglow when I notice Pranav's face glistening with the reflection of the light from the screen. He has a strikingly good smile, I realize. For three hours, we sit there, mostly quiet, letting the sound of the film echo all around us. Holding my knees to my chin, I feel myself looking in from the outside—in a park with a new friend, watching my favourite movie, unlocking a core college memory. Even before the day ends, I'm nostalgic for it.

When I see Pranav wiping a tear off his eye at '*Kyu dekhu mai ganne ke khet?*', a sense of victory washes over me. The movie concludes to its obvious happy ending and the credits roll, right after Geet and Aditya's romantic exchange in the same *ganne ke khet*.

I know people hate the romance genre in general, for its predictability, but that's precisely why I love it. Isn't there enough uncertainty in life to seek it in cinema too? For me, there's something magical about that sequence, the promise of a happily ever after, that will never not soothe the deepest of my wounds.

What is there to fear when a happy ending is right around the corner?

As the screen fades to black, my face perched on my knees tilts up sixty degrees to catch Pranav's eyes. 'So. What do you think?'

He glares at the white projector screen before turning to face me, too. 'You really want to know?'

'You have to be fair.'

'Sana . . . I'm just a boy. Standing in front of a girl . . . admitting,' Pranav says, before taking a long, annoying pause, 'that I was wrong.'

I levitate! He likes it! Some people turn back to judge me for the nuisance but I don't care. He really likes it! 'You're not being serious! You're lying,' I say, poking him in the stomach as he stands up next to me. 'Tell me truthfully na.'

Pranav shakes his head. '*Nahi nahi*, I'm being serious. You were right,' he says through gritted teeth. The constipated look on his face tells me he's having a tough time admitting it. 'It's better than *Notting Hill*, but not by a whole lot.'

'You don't sound convincing at all, just by the way,' I say, crossing my arms.

'I don't want to. It pains me to admit this.'

'I really appreciate your commitment to the truth,' I say as I bend down to pick up my tote bag still left on the ground.

Pranav does not even try to hide how his eyes travel from my face to legs. 'I really appreciate your butt,' he says, a cheeky look on his face.

'That,' I say, 'is a compliment I'm willing to take.'

'So you're okay with flirting if it makes you feel good?'

In my pocket, I feel my phone buzzing.

Ashish: *sorry Sana, I was in a bleh mood. I love you so much, even though you can't tell when a guy is obviously flirting with you*

Sana: *that's because the only guy I have eyes for is you*

'I did have one problem with the movie though,' Pranav says, stealing my attention away from my phone and back to him.

'I knew there would be a catch,' I reply, plastering on my infamous puppy face that hasn't ever failed to work on Ashish.

'Arre, why are you getting sad?'

'Tell me.' I'm about as ready to take criticism of my favourite movie as a parent is to hear about their child's performance at a parent–teacher meeting.

'I just think it wasn't fair to make Anshuman the villain,' he says. 'Dude had no idea Geet was dropping everything and coming to him, you know? You can't do that, you can't blame him for his very justified reaction.'

I feel my phone buzzing in my hand again.

Ashish: *don't lie, I'm sure you like the attention*

Hitting send on a few random emojis, I return to the conversation with Pranav, half-distracted. 'I don't think he's necessarily portrayed as the villain, is he?' I say, putting my phone in my bag's front pocket.

'You're right, he is not. But he is shown to be the cause of why Geet is so sad and gives up everything to become a teacher in Shimla and doesn't speak to her family for months. Like . . . that's on Geet, not him,' Pranav adds, looking at me now. 'Plus he comes back to her, doesn't he?'

Shrugging, I say, 'Too late though.'

'So what, Sana? Sometimes it takes people some time to realize what they really feel. Doesn't mean he loved her any less, you know?'

'You're really trying to write an alternate ending for *Jab We Met* where she ends up with *Anshuman*?'

'No. All I'm saying is that if Aditya was never in the picture, maybe she could've had a happy life with Anshuman, too. That's all.'

'Maybe,' I concur, finding myself smiling a little too wide, despite Pranav's absurd sympathy for a character I barely even notice throughout the film.

'Thank you, for this.'

'For admitting defeat?'

'No, for . . . for getting me here. I really do feel better. Even though being sad over marks is a little bit ridiculous, I know.'

'It's not ridiculous if it matters to you,' he says, simply.

When Pranav dusts himself off after getting up from beside me, I feel a flutter in my chest: *Am* I enjoying the attention?

Chapter Eight

'You'll be so busy with college, Sana, you won't even realize how time will fly,' Ma had told me in one of our many conversations where I had expressed my deep, bratty dismay that Ashish had decided to stick with the US route for his design school dreams.

'Should I apply too?' I asked, genuinely curious.

'I thought you really wanted to go to DU.'

'I do, but . . . I don't know, Ma. I just don't want to be so far away from him.'

'You want to apply to the US because he's applying to the US?'

'No, I mean, I'm sure there are great English degrees there, too.'

'That's not the point Sana,' Ma said, mildly frustrated. 'I know how much you love Ashish and as much as it annoys me to admit, he's a good guy. But Sana, you're seventeen.' Every year, the age changed, but the sentiment persisted. 'You have your whole life ahead of you and I want you to build it independent of him. Hasn't he taken the decision to move away independently of you?' she asked. 'Because, while this thing you have with him may or may not last, which I really hope it does, the thing you have with yourself, your personality, your career, you will always have that. Besides,' she said, winking at me, 'you'll have so much fun in college, you won't even have time to miss Ashish.'

Me? Not miss Ashish? As if!

But oh how mothers know best.

While I really thought that all the time I spent away from him would be a drag, the months have seemed to fly. The internals first, the Sarin-grading fiasco next, interspersed with a lot of fun, drunk lunch adventures with the girls and sometimes, Pranav. While dance and badminton have kept Samira, Preksha and Aanchal busy, I've been spending my evenings with the creative writing society, a relatively chill, low-engagement group, all things considered, for evening reading and writing sessions over coffee.

I could swear it was only yesterday that we were getting our orientation, though, and it's already time for our end semester exams. Right now, the one thing blaring fast and loud on my mind is my GPA.

Aanchal: *how's prep. I'm dying*

Sana: *i'm already dead. or i will be when i get my results*

Pranav: *you're both REALLY dramatic for first years.*

Aanchal: *you wouldn't know mr topper*

Sana: *wait pranav is a topper??*

Aanchal: *he topped DU last year, highest first year score*

Sana: *i didn't even know that was a thing . . .*

Remember Pranav and layers? This is one I absolutely did not expect to unravel. Although looking back, collating the evidence, it makes sense. The Google Drive, the massive attention to detail, the book that's always in his hand, how he had every key to acing Professor Sarin's class. But Pranav? Topper?

Pranav: *can you not reveal my secrets i need to maintain my street cred in front of the girls*

Sana: *cute of you to think you have any street cred in my mind*

Pranav: *cute of you to think you're the 'girls' i'm referring to*

Sana: *the only other girl on this group is your SISTER*

I shut my phone off. This time, I cannot afford any distractions. I'm aware I'm being extra careful about getting every reading down pat, even as Pranav has reassured me countless times that the exams are always easy, and Aanchal and I have revised together two times already. I'm just-in-case-ing my way through this prep; on the off chance the independent invigilator decides to mess with my grades like Sarin did.

So imagine my surprise (and relief), when, considering the hours I spent buried into my books and readings, the exams are a literal copy-paste of the question paper from two years ago.

'I told you, but you wouldn't listen to me,' Aanchal yells in my ears as Preksha and Samira gleefully join us outside the examination hall. 'WE'RE FREEEEEE! Oh my god, we're finally free!'

Something jostles with my hair. Just by the touch, I know it's Pranav. 'How was it, nerd?'

'You're one to talk, Mr Topper,' I say. 'It was okay, I think.'

'Okay?! It was a cakewalk,' Aanchal yelps animatedly. 'What are your post-exam plans, big brother?'

'I still have two papers left,' he says, lightly smacking Aanchal in the shoulder before walking off. 'See you soon, Sana,' he looks at me, smiling. We won't see each other for all of winter break because I'll be booked and busy with Ashish.

'Dudeeeeee, how the hell is first sem over already?' I hear Preksha say as Pranav walks away.

Samira nods along. 'I swear, it, like, flew by in a second.'

'It flew by because you're both barely ever in class,' I add and Preksha sticks out her tongue out at me. 'I feel like a zombie.'

'No one asked you to prepare like you're going to war,' Aanchal jibes. 'We have to do something fun, ya, guys!' She is practically screaming in my ears.

Samira interrupts, on behalf of her and Preksha. I already know where this is going. 'Guys, so sorry, but we can't really do anything right now. Dance meeting.'

Aanchal looks at me and asks: 'Let's at least go to Bloom's? I don't want to be the loser who goes home straight after exams end.'

A cup of coffee does sound enticing. In fact, I could do with ten cups, coffee on an IV, if it were allowed. I nod excitedly and Aanchal and I interlink our arms, waving a goodbye to Preksha and Samira. Both of us secretly like it better when it's just us, anyway.

On our walk to the front gate, I can feel the tiredness in my eye sockets. 'Aanch, I can't believe we have to do this five more times,' I say, sinking my head down.

'At least it's over now!'

A wide smile flashes on my face. 'Yeah, it's like that Usher song . . . I feel like a zombie gone back to life, back-back to life.' I'm delirious enough to now be doing the robot-dance as my classmates walk around me.

As we arrive at the front gate, Aanchal suddenly stops walking. 'Let's just wait here for a second.'

'Umm . . . what exactly are we waiting for?'

'An auto, of course.'

'Bloom's is a minute away.'

'Can't walk, yaar, my legs hurt like a bitch.'

'Okay, then, there are like ten autos over there.'

'I'm waiting for the right one,' Aanchal says affirmatively.

I'm over my irritation and have already resigned to this ludicrous demand, when Aanchal finally shrieks. 'That one!'

'Aanch, there is someone inside,' I say, mildly annoyed. 'Are you okay? Did you hit your head?'

'No, look, it's getting empty,' she says, pointing at it.

She's right: the auto comes to a halt right in front of us, and out emerges a boy in blue jeans and dirty Nikes, once white but now busted up with mud.

Finally, I think, and walk towards the auto, before my eyes catch the guy exiting it.

'What the fuck?'

It happens over the course of a microsecond, but in my mind, it's playing out in slow motion. You know, those moments in life that catch you so unexpectedly that your brain slows them down so you can digest what's happening? Yep. That.

Everything in the background blurs, like a crisp portrait shot, and the object of my focus is the love of my life. Standing in front of me. In New Delhi. Ashish.

'What the hell is going on?' I say, feverish, because this can't possibly be real.

For the fear that this is a dream, that the second my chest meets his, he will disappear into particles, I don't move any closer to him. When he saunters towards me, lowers his gaze, and takes me in his arms, I'm afraid something will flutter and my eyes will pop open, that the softness of his skin and the hardness of his bones will melt from under me. That I'll wake up in my room all alone.

But when he wraps his arms around me, I feel them digging into my skin. When I open my eyes, he's still here. 'Hi baby,' Ashish slowly whispers into my ears.

I unlatch from him and grab his shoulders. 'You weren't supposed to come for another two weeks. How the hell are you here?!'

'It was always the plan to come today, I just didn't tell you,' he says, laughing, noticing my mouth hung wide open. 'I knew you'd be too busy with your exam to even care that my phone has been switched off for hours.'

'This is why you were being weird?!' I say, gaping at Aanchal—finally realizing we're in public, that she is right there with us, awkwardly smiling as we act like two lovers lost at sea, finally united. And that Aanchal, this wonderful, new person in my life, cutely conspired with my boyfriend to make this tired day my happiest.

'This is also why Preksha and Samira are busy with their "dance meeting", Aanchal says, double quoting the meeting, looking awfully proud. 'By the way, hi. I'm so happy to finally meet you in person,' she says, pulling her hand out to meet Ashish's, before he initiates the hug.

'How do I return this wonderful favour?' I ask Aanchal, as the sky around me is littered with confetti and there's glitter everywhere. I feel like a kid who has smacked open a piñata to find endless amounts of her favourite chocolate in there.

'Just find me someone to date by the time we're headed for our trip,' she says, pinching my arm. 'Okay, you lovebirds, I'm going to leave you both to it. Have fun.'

As she disappears into the crowd of autos, I look back at Ashish and grab his face. 'You're really here, I can't believe this!'

'I missed you so much, Sana,' Ashish says, squeezing my hand three times. 'I love your stupid face.'

As we walk to the South Campus metro station, I am still lost in the haze of the surprise.

'How was the exam?'

'*Too* easy,' I say. 'I don't know why I was so worried.'

'I'm not surprised at all,' he replies as we're walking up the stairs. 'What trip, by the way?'

'What?'

'Aanchal mentioned some trip?'

'Oh, did I not tell you? Aanchal's family owns this cottage hotel in Nainital and we're going sometime in March. Apparently they're booked out all year round, but Aanchal managed to find this little window when a few rooms were free to accommodate us.'

'Wow, that sounds like a lot of fun. Are all the girls going?'

'Yeah,' I nod. 'And Pranav.'

I can feel Ashish's body tensing up as I say his name, the grip of his hand on mine loosening.

'What's wrong?' I ask, as his face has completely shifted moods.

'Just don't understand who this Pranav guy is and why you're constantly hanging out with him.'

'Ashish, I've told you before. He's Aanchal's . . .'

'Yeah yeah, he's Aanchal's *chipku* brother who has nothing better to do than hang out with his sister's friends.'

'Why are you suddenly so pissed off?'

'I'm not pissed off.'

'You clearly *sound* pissed off,' I say, disappointed that this sweet surprise is taking a sour turn.

'I don't know, Sana. Maybe I'm a little annoyed that this dude, who you have described to me as a super massive player, is constantly around, spending time with you, doing things to cheer you up. Wouldn't you feel the same if the positions were switched?'

I want to grab him and shake this mood out of him. Is he hearing himself? Ashish? Jealous over some other guy? Just the idea itself is comical!

'Ashish. I love you. I'm so, so happy you're here. I don't want to waste time talking about Pranav, please? He's a friend, like Aanchal. Can we let this go?'

Ashish looks down at the ground and then into my eyes. There we go, I think. Those eyes, I know. 'I don't know what's wrong with me. Ever since I heard his name, my stupid brain has just fixated on it. Obviously, I know you're not into him.'

'Why don't we go to my place and I'll show you exactly who I'm into?' I whisper in Ashish's ears as we board the general compartment of the metro. I can see the goosebumps rise all over his hands, his hair standing up.

'Oh, who is that?'

'Hmm . . . he's really tall, has these brown eyes to die for, and,' I investigate, touching his arms, 'has gotten really muscular in the last few months. I prefer him clean-shaven but he's currently rocking a rowdy, grunge look and I don't know, I think it's really working.'

'Eh, doesn't sound good enough for you.'

'Oh, he's too much,' I say, sneaking in a grab.

* * *

We speed into my room, my house empty for at least six full hours, and Ashish undresses me; every last piece of layering protecting me from the Delhi winter shrugged off, just so I can feel him on my skin and finally accept that he's really here; that this isn't a dream. I unbuckle his belt, my eyes stuck on his as my hands move to places they're so familiar with, it feels like a choreographed dance. As he takes off his shirt, I shiver at the sight of the newness in his body. Only six months out, but he looks more like a man than he ever has before. It's like being touched by a new person.

Ashish closes the distance between us, kissing that part of my neck that always renders me useless and leaves me moaning senselessly. I hold him everywhere, scrambling to get more of him under my relatively tiny hands, while he travels to my back to unhook my bra that has stayed on far too long already.

'You're not going to be able to take it off,' I say, cockily, because I know how much he loves a challenge.

He looks at me. 'Oh yeah?' In a second, it's on the floor.

Under his touch, I'm warm, soothed, hot. And under my touch, he is not the 'good' boy he is known to be. He is adventurous, thirsty, famished. His hands trail down from my stomach southward and the jitters in my body follow their direction. As his fingers spread me apart and he bends down to sneak a taste, I quickly realize I can't take this foreplay. Not when he's been gone for six months.

'Get the condoms,' I squeal, out of breath before it even begins. This is not waiting.

I feel him rise to my voice, until the flash of regret leaves his face pale white. 'Fuck, fuck, FUCK!' he yells, animatedly. 'I had to stop and buy them but then the stupid fight and I . . . we don't have condoms.'

I pull my blanket to my chest, acting as coy as I can. 'It's okay, we've waited months, we can wait a little longer, no?'

Ashish grabs me by the shoulders, as though I've just said something blasphemous. 'Sana, I cannot physically wait longer,' he emphasizes, placing my hand where it connotes his urgency. I feel him throbbing and so I nod. I'm used to Ashish wanting me, yes, but I'm not used to him needing me, like I'm a thirst that needs to be quenched.

He pulls back, while my hand stays. 'I'm going to go and get some condoms and you're going to wait right here, just the way I'm leaving you.'

'It's freezing cold, Ashish, I'm not waiting here naked.'

I feel Ashish kneel down close to me, his mouth pressed on mine.

'What's the point if I'm just going to take it all off again?' he whispers, leaving those words on my tongue and planting a kiss right on top of my lips. 'Stay there, don't move.'

Chapter Nine

'Have you been . . . practising?'

Ashish gets up to laugh, reaching for a bottle of water resting on my nightstand. 'Thanks, I guess?'

'Wait, no, I'm serious,' I say, a concerned look on my face, as I sit upright with him. 'Are you cheating on me because . . . how . . . the . . . hell,' I confess through shallow breaths, 'are you suddenly that good?'

'Are you saying I wasn't good before?'

'No, you're just *too* good now,' I say with my hand on my chest.

He beams like he has come second in an ultra-competitive race. 'Just been swimming a lot.'

'Oh, that's where all this muscle comes from,' I say, grabbing his bicep as he blushes.

Ruffling his hair in the mirror, perpetually dissatisfied with the way it curls, Ashish looks at me through the reflection. 'Should we call Bani now?'

'Any longer and she might actually murder us.'

'Do you think she's jealous she can't have sex with us, considering we do everything else together?'

'Please don't say that sentence ever again.'

Because his surprise for me was so satisfying, Ashish wants to execute Version 2.0 for Bani, and so I call her pretending we had a massive fight and there's nothing left to do but cry in her lap. Bani, hands-on best friend that she is, rushes to my place in record time, her backpack jiggling with the sound of Corona bottles rattling against each other, probably stolen from her mom's stash.

I delegate Ashish to open the door to Bani to really key in the surprise. Seeing Ashish's face, Bani drops her bag to the floor.

'Oh my god, you *asshole*,' she yells, pulling Ashish into a hug. 'You scared the crap out of me.'

I want to cry, not at the sentimentality of the moment, but because I'll have to clean this wet, glassy mess up. 'Great, thanks guys,' I say, bending down to pick up the pieces while the two hug it out. Minutes later, we're all on our knees: Ashish wrenching out the remaining liquid from my mother's favourite mat, Bani wiping away the excess, me removing the glass shards.

'Well, at least you didn't need the beer,' Bani says.

'I still would've preferred drinking it to,' I say, pointing to the floor, 'doing this.'

Ashish looks up and glares at Bani's face, as though spotting something stuck in her teeth. 'Damn, six months later and you're still just as ugly.'

'Sana, you're sure you've gotten all the large chunks of the glass, na?' Bani asks.

'I hope so,' I mutter.

'Hmm, would be such a shame if one of us were to step on a piece and bleed to DEATH,' she yells in Ashish's face.

Ashish, as usual, lunges at her with his wet hands, but their dynamic is too much for me to handle on a normal day. With this mess in front of us, my tolerance point is at a zero.

'Both of you shut up and clean. You can run like dogs once I say we're done here,' I command, knowing that when it's the I'm-not-messing-around voice, they'll take me seriously.

It takes half an hour for things to look like they did before Bani came over and we're officially in the clear, enough that I can call Ma and tell her that Ashish and Bani are visiting.

'No, they've both had lunch, Ma,' I say irritated. She's after my life that I allowed this 'surprise' to happen without letting her arrange food first.

'Why couldn't you just tell me they're coming over? I would've made something.'

'Ma that's kind of how surprises work, na. Ashish didn't tell me he was just going to land in India.'

The version of the story Ma is being told is that Bani came over and brought Ashish along. It's a cute and comfortable story, one that doesn't invite questions like, 'Oh, hmm, did he come alone?'

I cut the call and look at the two of them sprawled out on my bed like it's theirs.

'Okay guys, Ma's forcing me to order food for you two, so lunch is on me.'

'Yay! I'm anyway out of all my pocket money,' Bani sighs. 'Why is aunty still so formal after all of these years?' she asks, working through the blue Lay's I've opened for her.

'Good question, I think you should ask her,' Ashish quips.

Bani throws a pillow in his face. 'And I think you should ask her permission before you bang her daughter.'

'It was actually right where you are sitting,' Ashish says, shyly, and Bani lunges up in disgust.

I fake gag as I place a Zomato order for the three of us. It's the kind of friendship where I don't need to ask because after years of trial and error, I know exactly what they like. Bani goes for a chicken dominator from Domino's and Ashish is extremely loyal to his double cheese margherita. For both, if it's not a cheese burst, it is a no-go.

'Sana, can you actually make mine a pan pizza?'

'But you always have cheese burst?'

'I've just had so much pan there now that I can't stand the idea of having cheese dripping all over me.'

'But I placed the order already,' I say, dejected.

Ashish grabs my face and kisses my cheek. 'That's okay baby,' he says, holding me. And I realize that a lot of things about us will probably change. But this, this feeling when we are holding each other, this will stay.

'What are you wearing for Kabir's party?' Bani asks flinging open my wardrobe to reveal how ridiculously disorganized it is. It's my version of Monica's hidden closet in *Friends*—it doesn't gel with my personality, but it exists.

'Shut it na yaar,' I tell Bani, irritated. She has just scratched a sore spot. 'You know Ma's not going to let me go.'

'Come ON, Sana, you're not in school any more,' Bani says, making a face. A convincing argument when you're a teenager, yes. But to a parent, it's like saying 'I'm forty-one!' when they are seventy-five.

The party in contention is Kabir's annual New Year's Eve soirée. For the last five years, it has always been *the* thing to look forward to. And now, with everyone in different colleges, countries even, it's all anyone's been talking about on our extended WhatsApp group. Kabir and I aren't necessarily friends, but he's close enough to Ashish for Bani and I to always receive an invite. Not like I've ever had the good fortune of actually RSVPing yes.

'This one will be perfect,' Bani says, holding up a very Gatsby-esque dress I picked up from Sarojini Nagar during my latest hunt with Bani.

'It would be perfect for someone who's actually going to get to go,' I say, frustrated.

While Bani loudly groans, 'Urghhhhhh,' Ashish looks at me. 'Try asking her once? It'll be so much fun to kiss you at midnight.'

And because it's too tempting an offer to refuse, on the day of the party, New Year's Eve morning, I take the plunge and try again.

* * *

'Ma, everybody is going. It's almost a reunion,' I protest. She has already said no twice. Just today.

'Sana, you graduated nine months ago. That's barely a reunion.'

'But Ma, Ashish and Bani are also going.'

'Haan, so if they jump off a cliff, would you follow suit?'

By now, you would expect that the world parent committee would come up with more creative clapbacks. But no, it's the same tardy response being regurgitated, having lost its comedic or moralistic value.

'Ma, it's just a party. Everyone parties on New Year's. Why is it such a big deal?'

'If it's not such a big deal, why do you want to go so bad?'

'What sort of a response is that?'

This is the most frustrating exchange ever, not just because I'm built to lose, but because it always follows the same template, down to the ending.

To make it all worse, she concludes it with: 'Sana, as long as you're living under my roof, it's unfair, I know, but I call the shots. You aren't going. You can spend New Year's Day with Ashish and Bani. I don't want to get into this again,' she says, returning to her newspaper.

This time, I yell, 'Fine!' and storm back to my room, slamming the door shut. I sit at my desk and grab my head in frustration, exhaling a scream into the void. Why do I even try?

'What's wrong? Why are you crying?' Ashish asks as he picks up the phone to the sounds of my sniffles and sobs.

'I just don't get it yaar. It's like she doesn't want me to have fun, Ashish, just because all she does is work, eat, sleep.'

'Sana, *baba*, that's of course not the case,' Ashish says, in his usual, calm temperament. 'Every parent is strict about one thing or the other.'

'No one's as strict as her. Anyway,' I mutter, totally overcome by the FOMO of it all.

'Don't be so sad na.'

'You'll be gone in ten days . . .'

'We have the rest of our lives to celebrate every last one of our New Year's Eves together, you know that, right?'

'Yeah?' I ask. 'Well, can the rest of our life begin, like, right now?'

'If it did, we won't have any fun, juicy stories to tell the kids.'

'I swear, when I have kids, I will let them do whatever they want.'

Ashish laughs over the other side. 'How many do you want?'

'Three, but I want to adopt one.'

'What if the adopted one thinks we love them less?'

'Will you love them less?'

'No, of course not.'

'Then they won't feel like that.'

Ashish chuckles, simply accepting what I say. This is so easy. Everything about us is already figured out.

'Accha, I have to go get ready now.'

My smile fades into a frown again. 'Will you at least call me at midnight to wish me a happy new year?' I ask, grumpily.

'Have I ever missed a single year?' he asks.

He hasn't. Not even in the tenth grade, when he called through his dad's office landline because his mother was hoarding the house phone. When he hangs up, I feel the weight of the silence. And the FOMO of the fact that my best friends will be bringing in the new year without me and having fun at yet another party I'm not allowed to go to.

Pranav: *hey buddy wassup*

Sana: *hi buddy. Not much wby*

Pranav: *no fun NYE plans?*

Sana: *no yaar I like to stay in! don't like NYE parties*

Pranav: *oh wow you're so cool and different haan?*

Sana: *that's NOT what i said but ok. what are you up to?*

Pranav: *i'm reading actually*

Pranav sends me a photo of him lying on his bed and on his blanket, with little hearts all over it, holding a book titled *A Short History of Tractors in Ukrainian*.

Pranav: *it's about an eighty-four-year-old man marrying a much younger woman who lets him fondle her boobs*

Sana: *that's . . . a good pick i guess?*
Pranav: *good pick? bro is out here living my dream life Sana*
Sana: *have some shame*

When I have successfully scrolled through the depths of Instagram, when no more of Twitter would load to reveal new content, and when YouTube is as dead as the night around me because everyone is partying in cooler places, I put my phone back on my nightstand and try to lull myself to sleep. Luckily, my dreams cooperate. Almost instantly, I am off to a coastal wonderland, where there is wind in my hair, sand in my crevices, salty air in my mouth and not a care on my mind. This is where Ma's rules don't exist, where my bikini can be as tight and revealing as I want it to be, where Ashish can touch me in broad daylight because there is no one around for miles and miles. As the sunlight fades, we drown the night chills in the hot jacuzzi and underwater, I can feel Ashish undoing the strings of my swimsuit, boldly cupping me in his hands.

Until suddenly, there is a rude interruption. I can't tell what it is. For a second, it sounds like a knock on our door, but it quickly begins feeling like someone is jostling our entire jacuzzi.

I want to throw hands, shoo them away. 'Can't you see? I'm on vacation!' But the coast keeps fading, the water retreating further and further, until Ashish, too, disappears pixel by pixel. A switch flips and suddenly I'm awake—the coastal wonderland all but gone as I open my eyes to my mother sitting at the edge of my bed in my dimly lit room.

'Ma, what are you doing? You scared me,' I say, rising up in my bed, clutching my chest.

'Sana, can you wake up?'

'I'm awake, I'm awake.' The room is dark but her face shines pasty white. 'Ma, you look like you've seen a ghost. What's wrong?'

She's holding me now.

'Ashish and Bani were in a car accident,' she says without skipping a beat.

I instantly rise up in my bed and my eyes dart to the time. It's 4 a.m.. He was supposed to call! 'Where are they? Are they okay?'

Big fat teardrops escape my mother's eyes and suddenly, my limbic system is in overdrive. Why is she crying? Accidents happen.

'Bani is in the hospital recovering,' she says wiping her nose and I feel my body relax, until she adds, 'Ashish . . .'

As she says his name, her face contorts into a sadness I've never seen before.

Still, I ask, restless: 'What? Where is Ashish?'

No one ever prepares you for when your mother breaks down.

'Where's Ashish, Ma? Which hospital is he in?' I say, getting up from my bed and putting on my chappals. I feel myself losing balance, my body and my brain in disarray. 'He had to call me! Why hasn't he called?' I'm scrambling to find my phone. It's on the nightstand, I could swear I put it on the nightstand, but why can't I see it there then?

'Baby, listen to me,' Ma says, holding my arm, her grip firm and sturdy.

But I can't listen to her. I need to hold out for his ringtone to blare through my phone. He has to call. He'll be calling anytime.

'Sana . . .'

'Please don't say it.'

'I'm so sorry, Sana,' my mom says, looking down, her shoulders trembling with the tears. She can no longer look at me. 'Ashish didn't make it.'

What a horrid joke to crack! What an evil, bizarre thing to do! I have to call Ashish. My mother has lost her mind. He needs to talk to her, tell her he's okay!

'Where the hell is my phone?' I yell. Why can't I find it? Why won't it ring?

'Sana, baby, I'm here,' Ma says, clutching my hand, breaking my pacing.

'Here for what? What exactly are you here for?' I say, shrieking, my back breaking out with sweat. 'Nothing has happened!'

Suddenly, my phone goes off. *There*, I think, as relief floods my system. The clock on my wall is probably missing numbers or something. See, there's Ashish—he's calling. I walk to the sound of my phone on my nightstand, but before I can swipe right on the call, I see Bani's photo filling up the screen. My ears are suddenly alert. It's not the regular ringtone. It's Baby shark do-do-do-do-do.

I cut the call. I need to wait for Ashish to call. I can't keep my phone busy.

Bani calls again.

Baby shark do-do-do-do-do.

'Stop it! Make it STOP,' I yell in my mother's face. 'MAKE IT STOP!'

'Sana, baby, just listen to me,' she says, grabbing hold of my body, trying to steady me. Only when she does that, do I realize I have been trembling. 'Pick up the call, baby,' Ma whispers in my ear. 'Please.'

I look at her. 'I don't want to, Ma.'

'You have to,' she says, her forehead pressed against my arm. I'm sitting in her lap like I'm five again.

'Hello?' I swipe to receive the call. It's the third time Bani has called.

'Sana,' Bani says, her voice breaking, the single syllable in my name expanding into three, the cracks in her voice punctuating them. 'Ashish,' she says. This time, the name is a quiver; said in an instant to let it out. She doesn't say much else.

My phone falls to the ground. Or to my lap, or somewhere.

'Ma,' I yelp, like a wounded puppy. Like this is a cut on my hand she can nurse back to health with some Dettol and cotton. 'Ma, please,' I beg. 'Please.'

'Baby, I'm so sorry,' she says, her forehead still pressed into me. 'I'm so, so sorry.'

Chapter Ten

It's 7 a.m. Ashish has been dead for seven hours already, but in my world, it's just been three. How could he be dead for so many hours and I didn't know about it? It's obvious there's been a glitch. I shut my eyes. If I focus hard enough, maybe I can pull myself to the other side where things make sense. But I keep opening them back up to the same scene. Me on the floor, my mother, next to me, holding my hand.

'Ding!' goes the bell and my mother leaves my hand to check the door.

'It was the milk,' she says.

'Why would we need milk?' I want to ask. 'He's dead!'

But I just nod. Like it's totally okay for things to proceed as they normally do; like I need a glass of milk when I have this huge dagger wedged straight into my chest. Like it's all right for the *kudhewallah* to come collect the garbage, for the newspaper boy to fling today's paper in the balcony. Like I care which countries are warring. Like anything matters when *my* world, as I've known it, has come to an end.

Ma offers me facts. Here's what has settled in: Bani's mom called Ma. Yes, he's dead. Dead, like, dead-dead. Yes, they tried reviving him. No, he's definitely dead. Yes, like laying in a mortuary kind of dead. No, they can't just try again, this is not *Grey's Anatomy*. It was a drunk driver. Ashish's car was parked still when the guy crashed into him, cannonballing directly into his seat. There was never a pulse and so, they declared the time of death 'undetermined', but based on estimates, it was most likely midnight, New Year's Day.

Right as everyone on Indian Standard Time was screaming 'Happy New Year'—as kisses were being exchanged, condoms were being broken, shots and drinks were being downed, celebrations were underway to bring forth the shiny, bright opportunity a new year holds—my world was ceasing to exist. And I was asleep through it all. Suddenly, I understand how people snooze through earthquakes.

Ma tells me that the cremation is today.

Cremation. I repeat the word in my mind. It's like one of those—mutual funds, LIC, savings—'big words for adults'. What am I doing here then, reciting it over and over in my head?

'He was supposed to call,' I say, curled up in a foetal position on my floor. I haven't moved in hours. I don't plan to. If someone were to move me, which is the only way I would go, they would find bed sores.

'What was that, baby?'

I sniffle, staring into the nothingness of my bedroom wall, finding it superior to watching the sun rise outside my window. The sun means it's a new day. It means that his death is already 'last' night. It means it's the start of a full day without him. A sunrise Ashish will never, ever see.

'He was supposed to . . . he was supposed to call. At midnight,' I say, slightly pausing, for no dramatic effect whatsoever, but mostly because it tastes acrid, the anticipation of the words on my tongue: 'Instead, he died. At midnight.'

Now that I've said it, I expect the lights to flicker on and the cast of a stupid prank reality TV show to come out, yelling 'You've got punked!' or something in my face, probably squirting slime all over me. Right as I would be about to shriek, Ashish would walk out from behind the scenes, my home, a set, without me knowing. My mother would be in on it, obviously.

'Of course I'm not dead, you idiot,' he would whisper into my ear. 'How can I die?'

'Exactly! That's what I've been saying all along!'

I realize I say it out loud when my mother asks, 'What, baby?'

'Nothing. Nothing.'

Minutes pass before another word is exchanged, until Ma says, 'We have to go see the body.'

From Ashish, my boyfriend, love of my life, friend, son, boy, to . . . body. Body, I repeat in my head. We have to go see the body. The body that is dead. The body that once was alive enough to be called . . . Ashish.

I thought it would take a hurricane to move me, but it just takes that—the realization that this is the last time I will ever get to see him. I get up and brush my teeth, even though it doesn't matter—he's not going to be able to tell my breath stinks because I'm never going to get to kiss him again.

Am I never going to kiss him again? That can't be right. Just because he's dead, that can't mean I won't be able to kiss him again, right?

Wait. He's dead?

'Ready to go?' Ma asks.

I put on a white kurta with jeans under it because I'm too young to own a full-white ensemble. What would I need it for, other than Holi? I look in the mirror, my eyes puffed to the size of golf balls, and dab some moisturizer on my face. It's so stupid. He's dead and I'm moisturizing.

Here's everything I yell in the car, but Ma does not listen.

Or maybe I don't say it, I can't be sure: Don't take me there. Please, I don't want to go. Please don't press the bell, please, no, I can't do this. Please don't open the door. Please, please, please don't be on the floor.

Oh, but there you are, my love. On the floor. Wearing white. Wrapped in white. Cotton balls up your nose. Flowers around your neck. Flowers around a photo of you. Your hands crossed and placed one atop the other at your waist. Your mother's hand on yours. Your head propped up on a tiny pillow.

'You look so gorgeous' is my first thought as I walk in the door. My second thought: Why aren't they waking you up? Why won't they shake you out of this stupid state? Surely someone as young as you would respond to a good jolt or two? Have any of them tried? Should I?

But I realize then, what I think others too have realized before me. You look so gorgeous, yes, but you look gorgeous for a dead person. Because you most certainly are. Dead. I've never seen a dead person before, and yet, I know you are. There's that thing on your face, a gaping nothingness, an endless vacuum that tells me you have all but left, floating now in a dimension I can't access. You have left behind for us, this mould of you, this casing that once held you because you care, because you want us to say goodbye.

It hadn't sunk in before this. I don't know if it'll ever sink in. But I swallow it, at this moment. You really are gone.

And so, right there, in front of his parents, in front of most of his family, in front of guests I don't recognize—parts of him that will forever remain unknown—I fall to my knees, my eyes glued to his face. His face that won't look back at me. His mouth that won't talk. I'm talking to him. But he's not even here any more.

'Ashish,' I yelp, quietly, so no one hears me, until something convinces me that if I scream louder, make a big enough scene, he will come back.

'Wake up, please,' I say, my throat filling up with phlegm. I think maybe if I rock him, shake him out of this, his eyes will open.

'Ashish,' I say, feeling myself being pulled closer to him, like gravity. 'Can you hear me?' I whisper in his ears. Maybe if I kiss him, soft, wet from my tears, he'll get embarrassed. He will come back, just to say, 'Not in front of my parents, Sana.'

I can bring him back if I try, I tell myself. And if he doesn't want to come back, if he is so determined to be in this new world, then I can hold him and dissolve into him. If he tells me he wants to stay there, I'll pack my bags and go too.

'Ashish,' I say, once again, assertive, demanding. 'Why aren't you listening to me?'

I hold his hand and squeeze it three times. He doesn't squeeze mine back.

'Please come back,' I say one more time, louder, less wary. 'Why can't you just come back?'

I have things to say, arguments to make in favour of this world. But my time is cut short as I feel my mother's hands on my back, pulling me away. And so, I retreat, not before glancing at Rana aunty, sitting a few feet away from me. In her eyes, I see everything that I think she sees in mine. She nods at me and reaches for my hand and I hold it, squeezing a few times to tell her I'm here, until she has other hands to hold. Here's what

I think we both say to each other: Hello. How are you? Broken? Do you think it'll get better? Hmm. Do you think we'll get through the day? No? Ever?

In the corner, I watch Suresh uncle staring at the ceiling, as though not seeing the truth will help him avoid it somehow. I wish it were that easy. I saunter to him, thinking twice before lightly tapping his shoulder. When I do, he finally looks down, first at me, then at Ashish. He holds my hand, still placed on his shoulder, and with the other hand he palms his mouth shut, holding back his tears at the sight of his lifeless son lying there on the floor.

As long as he is holding my hand, I promise myself I won't cry.

* * *

My mother and I leave a while later, leaving the family to grieve as more of Ashish's relatives start pouring in. Truthfully, though, we leave because I can't stand to see Ashish like that any longer. I would've rather not seen him dead at all and just remember him alive, forever. Now, every image of him is followed by this concluding picture.

'Do you want to go see Bani?' Ma asks as we walk back to her car, where we will wait until it's time for the cremation, and I think, what a stupid question to ask. Why would I want to meet someone right now?

And then it hits me. Oh, Bani.

'Is she not going to be at the cremation?'

Ma looks over at me and pauses before she says, 'She hasn't been discharged yet.'

'Maybe tomorrow,' I say, bringing my knees close to my chest as I make myself small in the front seat, feeling mad at Bani for being hurt. How can she not be there? How can Ashish just . . . leave without her getting to say goodbye?

Before I have a chance to protest, my eyes force themselves shut the moment I rest my head on the car window. The body wants what the body wants, I guess—even as I try to deny it everything it needs. Water, trips to the washroom, sleep. When I open my eyes, shaken awake by my mother gently caressing my hair, I don't know how many hours I've slept, but I do know it's time to head to the crematorium in Lodi Garden. As I walk inside, the hours of sleep I have already lost hit me all at once. My head feels woozy and the path in front of me seems like it's disintegrating into three, four lanes. A dream-like fog is blanketing my vision. I know it's real, I know this is happening. It's happened. Why is my brain still tricking me into thinking it hasn't?

From across the gate of the crematorium, I see Ashish's mother's silhouette in front of the pyre, the four-by-four square box assigned to his body to rest in, for his family to cry in, as he is burned. Burned. Put to fire. Cremated. Extinguished. Gone, forever.

What are you doing here? I ask Ashish, as a foggy, semi-opaque outline of him crystallizes in front of my eyes. *Don't you know you're not supposed to be here?*

He says: *I'm not here, baby.*
But that's you, right there, I reply.
Yes, but that's not me.
Who is that then? I ask.
Just something I left behind, he says, before disappearing into the back of my mind. Any blind faith I had in your revival is being eviscerated in front of my eyes as Suresh uncle lights you on fire. He's trembling.

Instantly, a memory comes knocking back—how Ashish had told me that when it was his time to go, I should cremate him electrically. I'd scoffed then, but I'm never going to get to make that decision for him now, am I?

As the fire spreads to all of him, I feel my knees weaken.
Why is he doing that to you?
That's not me, Sana.
But I can see you! That's you!
Sana, baby, I'm right here.
Promise it doesn't hurt?
I promise.
It's not that hot, no?
I can't feel a thing.
You melt in front of me and suddenly, you're all around. In the air, in my hair, in my eyes, coming out as tears. I stretch my arms to try and hold you, these little bits and bobs of black floating all around me. That one could be your brain. That one, your left leg that you broke in the tenth grade. Which one is your sweet, sweet smile? And what about your strong hands? I raise

my hands in the air, trying to grab what's left of you. But you keep slipping out of my grip.

One by one, the crowd thins. They have their days to start, breakfasts to have, colleges or work to attend. This is only a pause button for their lives.

'Let's go, Sana,' Ma says, sitting right next to me. She seems to want to hurry me out of everything, while I can't help but wish for this moment to stretch on forever. To only ever live a life with you, even if it means living in the very minute of your death and never after it.

'No, we have to stay.'

'What do you mean, baba?'

'He's still there, Ma,' I say. I can't even see the shape of you through the flames, but I know you haven't fully left. Until you do, I won't either. 'I have to stay. I'm not leaving till it's over. Not till he is gone'

'Baby, it's going to take a long time. Maybe even the whole day for it to finish. And you need to eat something.'

I shake my head. 'I'll leave when it's over.' My mother does not protest, she does not respond.

Both of us watch as Ashish's mother bids everyone namaste, as one by one, all the people leave. Until it's just his parents, grandparents, me and my mom. Suddenly, Rana aunty's eyes meet mine and I can tell, in an instant, that she is going to come to me now. Ma and I squeeze in to make space for her.

We sit in silence, until she decides to take a pin to it and pop it.

'He'd talk of marrying you all the time.'

My throat itches with build-up—a cocktail of phlegm, bile, tears. The declaration surprises me. What else did he tell her that he didn't tell me?

'I would tell him he was too young to talk about things like these . . .' Her lips quiver in preparation of the end of that sentence and I wish there was some TV remote to shut her off. *Please, just don't say it*, I think. *What good is going to come of it?*

'How do I tell him he's too young to die?'

I break down, once again, wailing, yelping cries leaving my system, my hand clutching my chest, afraid of my heart pumping out of my system and escaping, considering how hard it is beating. The love of my life, now gone, for all my life. What do I do now? Run away? Disappear? Go back in time and plead with him not to go to that party without me?

My cheeks are wet, my mouth is snotty and I search for a handkerchief I have never carried, because I have never needed to. Because Ashish always carried one for me.

'Just in case,' he had said when I had asked him why. 'There are napkins everywhere.'

'Still. Just in case.'

Chapter Eleven

'I could never leave you,' he would promise me all the time.

In all categories of questions, in all scenarios.

'What if you find someone hotter in college?'

'What if I do something really bad, like murder someone? Or really badly injure them?'

'What if I want to become a star of a reality TV show?'

The answer was always the same, 'I could never leave you.'

It's night three today and I'm tossing and turning in bed, wondering what if I'd asked more times? Would that have made him stay? I go to sleep hoping to wake up with an answer, hoping to wake up to a world that I don't feel I'm viewing through a looking glass. And yet, I keep rising to the same reality, over and over again. Every morning it's *Groundhog Day*.

Here's the real kicker, though: it's him I want to call, to text and say, 'You won't believe this!' I want him to pick up the phone, say 'Yes baby?' and I want to hear him go 'I know, love, I know,' as I tell him just how crazy it is that he is not here any more. I want to trash talk the 'friends' that have taken to Instagram stories to grieve him, choosing the same, tired Wiz Khalifa song as the background music. I want to dish about the guy who dared to use a picture from the party after which he passed away.

'Isn't it ridiculous? They're all name-dropping you like it's your birthday and they just have to make an Instagram story about it.'

And then he would say: 'It's okay baba, it's all innocent.' He'd say this next thing seriously and disguise it as a joke: 'You should put up a story too.'

'How can you even joke about stuff like that?'

'Your friends are all worried, Sana.'

I look to my phone piling with the notifications I keep ignoring.

Should I just come out with it? Make a grand announcement on my Instagram stories? Put it up as my WhatsApp status? Or if not the world, at least tell Aanchal, tell Pranav, make it real? So that they stop with the questions, the interrogating. Where are you? How are you? Are you okay?

How can I be okay?! How can you even ask that?

Aanchal: *how dare you not wish me a happy new year!!!! Okay anyway I'll do it happy new year san I'm so glad you're in my life, we'll have the best year together <3*

Aanchal: *ok where the hell are you?*

Aanchal: *SANA*

Aanchal: *please text me back. I'm worried.*

Pranav: *partied too hard on NYE or something? Where are you lost*

Pranav: *where are you?*

Pranav: *hey. tried calling you. I know you probably can't respond if something really bad happened, but if everything's okay, can you just tell me?*

I'm here. Don't you see me? I have been here all along, on the other side of this wall, banging, yelling, screaming, for someone to let me out, the real Sana out. Not this caricature of me, sitting catatonic on her bed in yesterday's clothing.

Preksha: *BABE why not texting on group, are you ok*

Samira: *Sana tell me the name of that book you were raving about in sarin's class na*

Samira: *where are you????????*

Samira: *i found it nvm*

I could tell them. But I could also live in this world that they are living in; where I just disappeared for no reason, where nothing happened, where Ashish didn't die. In their world, my story just stops getting written, without any tragic ending. If that possibility exists in Aanchal, Preksha, Samira's world, it means it's at least half true. Somewhere, if not in my life, Ashish is still alive.

So this is what I'll do. This is where I'll stay. This is where you'll find me, until it's absolutely impossible to not walk over to the other side any more.

* * *

Two more weeks pass in this haze. Mornings blend into evenings that turn into cold nights and I rarely ever leave my bed. I just sit here, watching the hours tick by on that ugly clock my father gifted me. I have no way of knowing what day or date it is, even though I can see my phone screen delivering me this information on a single tap. Words, letters, numbers, they don't make sense. What does my phone mean it's 15 January? It's supposed to be the first of January, the day he died, the day hell froze over. But time does not seem to want to stop with me. It wants to keep moving on, making space for new things, more things, while I'm still trying, arms outstretched, to hold on to the ones it has already taken away.

'Knock knock,' Ma announces, walking in with a tray in her hand.

'Why knock if you're going to come in, anyway?'

'No points for guessing what's for lunch,' she says, lowering the tray to my bed. She uncovers the lids of the dish to reveal a steaming bowl of rajma and jeera rice. Instantly, the room smells like garam masala and my stomach grumbles in the anticipation of its taste. In classic Ma fashion, it looks as elaborate as ever, spread out with countless tiny contraptions—yogurt, pickle, laccha onion, extra salt.

I can't remember a single day in my life, in its 'Before' era when my mother let me eat a meal in my room, forget the bed. Now, this is all I do.

'I'm not hungry,' I say, grunting. 'I'll eat later.'

The 'later' keeps getting added to the basic things I once used to do without thinking. Brushing, bathing, eating. But for eating, the 'later' is already due. I rejected yesterday's dinner and today's breakfast.

I watch as she grabs the serving spoon to pour me a serving. She hands me the plate, the amounts perfectly portioned to my preferences. I fiddle with the spoon before shoving a mouthful of it in, noticing her glare on me that would not go away until she sees me eat.

'Tastes okay?'

'It's great.'

And then a memory, like a pinprick on my naked body.

'You know, Ma' I say, looking at her, as she is lying down in front of me, across the breadth of my bed. 'Ashish hates rajma,' I reveal finally.

He'd told me this nearly a year into eating it for lunch at my place whenever he came along with Bani.

'You're joking,' she says, her mouth open. For a second, it feels like he is in the room with us. 'I made him rajma every single time he came over. He licked the plates clean!' And snap. Him being referred to in past tense zaps me right out.

I look down at my plate of food, thinking of all the times she made the same dish for him, and the times she didn't know she was making it for him—when he sneakily came over and we served ourselves lunch like we were married. How the faint leftovers made Ma wonder if I had a beast appetite.

'He just hated it in general. Nothing about the way you prepared it.'

'Why did he request it all the time then?'

'I'm not sure, either. I guess it had something to do with impressing the mother of his girlfriend. And he knew how much I loved it . . .' I trail off. 'That's the thing, Ma, what I keep coming back to. I'll never know why he did it. You know?'

Despite the time we spent together, there is still stuff about Ashish I don't know, questions I had slotted to ask on a later date, taking for granted that the 'later' would arrive. Now, those questions will forever remain unanswered. Why did he pretend to like rajma? When did he decide to surprise me in December? How did he tell his mother he wants to marry me? Who was his favourite of all his new friends at college?

Oh my god. His friends at college. Do they know?

Ma nods, kindly, emptily. 'You're going to get through this, baby.'

What is there to get through, though? What is exactly the through, what is the end to this? What does it look like? What can it possibly look like, if there is no Ashish on the other side?

'What if I don't want to get through this, Ma? What if this is right where I want to be? Forever?'

I expect something sagely, something that throws a rope for me to pull me out of this deep, deep well I've found myself in. But even my mother can't mother me out of this. She can only hold a torch and let me climb my own way up.

So instead, she says, 'Then you get to do that too, Sana. You get to decide.'

It's entirely unhelpful. It's also exactly what I need.

* * *

I haven't seen Bani in three weeks.

For the lack of a better word, a shudder-inducing prospect for a literature student, it has been hard—dealing with the fact that she survived something Ashish succumbed to. The last time I saw her was right after Ashish's cremation. I walked into her hospital room at Fortis, the same white building I'd crossed everyday coming home from school, stared at the monitors around her, took in the fact that she was conscious and looking right at me and sighed. Not the good kind of, 'Thank god, you're here' sigh. More like 'Oh, *you're* still here' kind of sigh. The realization disgusted me and I wondered if Bani could see through my relief.

Here's the line the doctors used when I was around. 'It's a miracle nothing worse happened!'

What do you mean nothing worse happened? I wanted to yell! *My boyfriend died. He sat a feet away from her and he died. Worse did happen. The worst happened.*

But they don't care. Why would they? He was not their patient.

He never was a patient at all.

While Bani was okay, the accident still caused major trauma. She had acquired a mild concussion and whiplash injury in her neck which would only go away with physiotherapy and broken ribs that would, unquestionably, take months to heal. The doctor's verdict? Not so bad, considering what happened to the other guy. I swallowed all of this, pushing down the bile in my throat that arose at the doctor's words. When the doctor left just as casually as she waltzed in, neither Bani nor I spoke about Ashish. Neither of us cried. Instead, we talked about how she was doing, how bad the pain was and the weather. When I left, I told myself I'd call her a day later to check up on her. I didn't. She didn't text either. Before I realized it, it had already been weeks of no contact.

I roll out of bed to grab breakfast, a little more on my feet lately than I had been the few weeks before. Bani, Bani, Bani, the voice in my head keeps prodding the inner corner of my skull. Not today, I keep telling it. Maybe tomorrow.

'Ma, why do you still do all of that manually?' I say as I grab a parantha out of the steel casserole placed on the dining table, as Ma sits at the opposite end, rummaging through a pile of bills and letters like it's 1998.

As I scoop up some dahi, I feel my mother's glare sit on me. She looks oddly contemplative for someone who is just doing monthly bills. 'Sana, baby, sit down for a second.'

This can't be good. A 'sit down for a second' rarely ever is. That's what she led with when I got my period for the second time at thirteen and she explained that it was going to happen every month. 'WHAT?! I thought it happens just once and then never again,' I squealed before rushing to my room and locking myself into the washroom as I bled through my underwear in protest. It also happened to be the way *I* led the conversations when the tables turned and I told her about Ashish.

'Please tell me you're not already having sex.'

'Gross, Ma.'

'Promise me you'll tell me when you start having sex. I'll get you the condoms. And if something happens, you come to me.'

Her being so chill with Ashish wasn't something I'd expected. Her practically encouraging me to have sex was a little much.

'I got a call from your college,' my mother says. I gulp. 'You've been absent for a while now, and . . . they don't allow bereavement leave for your . . . situation.' I already know what's coming next. 'They said if you want to move on to second year, you need to come back and maintain perfect attendance.'

'And if I don't?'

She pauses before she adds, 'You'll have to redo the first year.'

I am not ready for this. This is like being told there's a tsunami hitting in thirty seconds while I'm swimming in the ocean. I flail my arms and try to grab hold of something, but I keep coming up short. A sudden constriction of air in my lungs makes me feel like I'm really drowning. How can I be, though, when I'm sitting right here on my dining table?

'Ma, I'm not going back,' I declare.

She takes off her spectacles and pinches her eyes. 'Sana, you can't sit at home forever.'

It's like being asked to just start walking when I have broken a bone in my ankle. 'How?!' I want to yell. 'Can't you see? Can't you see how broken I am?' But that's the thing. Physically, I look unbroken. The fact that I'm serving myself breakfast proves I'm better at least by some degree.

'There is no way I'm going back,' I say, suddenly not hungry any more.

'Sana, baby, you have to get out of the house. You have to be doing something. Otherwise, this grief . . . it will consume you.'

'Ma, you don't get it. I can't physically go back.'

I can feel it—me tugging at the last ropes of her patience. Finally, her frustration peers through. 'So what? What are you going to do? Sit here forever?'

Is it the fact that I have put on 10 kg since Ashish died? Is it that my room stinks because I don't bathe often enough? Or is it that I run to her, mid-sleep, panic-attack stricken, and beg her to pull me out of this nightmare? What part of this has made her hate me?

'Wow,' I say, looking down at my plate, all the hunger in my body leaving my system. 'So that was your plan? To let me cry for a bit and then say "chop-chop, time to act normal now"?'

'I'm not asking you to act normal, Sana,' she says, frustratedly. 'I'm just saying . . . I'm just saying that you have to do something. This is not going to feel okay by just sitting at home all day.'

'And you would know because? How many times has this happened to you?'

My mother's face stiffens with anger. 'Behave, Sana.'

'And what if I don't? What will you do? Ground me?' I let out a little chuckle and my mother sharpens her eyes at me.

What has all her stupid strictness been for?

'If you would've just let me go, I would've had one last good memory with Ashish,' I spew in her face. 'You took that away from me.'

The fact that I am here, living this life, in part, is the consequence of her decisions. Far from saving me from the big, bad, terrible things of the world, her actions handed them to me right on a platter.

'Maybe he wouldn't have even died,' I say, finally.

'If you really think I would've wanted any of this to happen to you, Sana, you don't know your mother. Not one bit,' she adds, sullenly. 'You're going back to college tomorrow. This is not a discussion.'

How long till the decisions in my life actually become a discussion? That I get to take the call and live with the consequences of my actions?

I run to my room, grab a sling bag from the back hooks of my door and stuff my keys in it. I wear the first pair of shoes I can locate in my shoe rack and slam the front door shut loud enough to let her know that just because she gave me life, does not mean she gets to dictate how I live it. She wants me to get out of the house? Here's me, getting out.

By the time I'm downstairs, though, the adrenaline is quickly tapering off as my brain starts doing the math: Where do you want to go? Where *can* you go? To what world can you run to, to escape all of this, when everything is upside down and Ashish is dead instead of sitting in his dorm, studying. Oh my god, his dorm, my mind throws up, like shrapnel. What's going to happen to everything there? Will his parents fly down and retrieve it? The things Bani and I helped him pack—what will become of them?

Bani.

When everything else fades, she is all I have left. Even though I have wondered why *she* was the one left behind for me, in my weakest moments.

I book an Uber auto and on the ride to Bani's place, I try to think of the things to say. Why I didn't visit, why I didn't call. There is nothing I can say that she won't see through. When Bani's mother flings open the door after I have buzzed the doorbell ten times within a few seconds, her initial, annoyed expression quickly softens. 'Sana,' she says calmly.

'I'm sorry, Aunty, but can I please go see Bani?'

Her mother holds the door wide open for me, as though saying, 'You never have to ask,' and I run to Bani's bedroom—the way I have after every fight with Ma, misunderstandings with Ashish, or days when Bani called me crying and asked me to just show up.

I knock on her door before rushing in, how I would've done before. 'It's open,' I hear Bani's voice call out, lacking its usual gusto.

She looks up from the bed, straight at me, and smiles. It's not a happy smile. It's more like: I'm glad you're here. I can't pretend it hasn't happened any more, either.

And so I climb into her bed and though Bani oohs and ouches, she makes space for me to move in closer.

We still don't talk. We just sit, together for the first time, with the fact that it happened. And as it sinks in, we hold each other. In the background, through her window, we watch the sky turn indigo, as the weight of the loss that painted our lives a deep, dark cobalt blue envelopes us.

Chapter Twelve

Eventually, it isn't Ma who convinces me to bite the bullet and go to college. It is Bani.

'I feel like I'll die if I go back, Bani,' I whisper softly after recounting what had happened before I ran to her place.

She holds my hand and squeezes it, just the way Ashish would. If he were here. *If*.

'Why?'

'I am not ready to face the world. To have this conversation. For it to become more real than it already is.'

'Is it any less real *abhi*?' she asks. 'And do you think it'll ever become easy enough to face?'

I shake my head no.

'If you go to college a year later, start over, make new friends, will it ever be easy to recount if they ask you if you have a boyfriend?'

'You didn't go back too, Bani,' I say, referencing her father's death, something we don't usually talk about. 'You stayed home for a whole year, too,' I say, defensive.

'Yeah. I stayed home a whole year, sat in front of his framed photo in his bedroom and cried. All day. Everyday. For a whole-ass year.'

Looking at Bani, I feel my heart breaking. '*And* got bullied because of it. *And* made lifelong enemies out of it.'

'You got me out of it.'

'I know, Sana, and that's a big, fat silver lining,' she says. 'But I can't sit here and tell you that staying home did me any good. In fact, it left me caged in the initial moments of his death the entire time,' Bani says, recalling. 'It was only when I returned, when we became friends and started hanging out together, did I feel like I'd finally begun grieving.'

I want to not take Bani's advice so badly. I want to toss it in the bin and convince myself, 'What does she know?'

But she knows better than I do. Better than Ma even.

When I don't respond, Bani grabs my hand. 'Besides, Sana, if I'm going to be honest, you have the option to go. I'm stuck in this bed for I don't even know how long. I'm practically back where I was, so many years ago. If I had the option to escape, I would take it so fast,' she says. 'All I can do here is sit and think about Ashish. About Papa.'

I let the moment fade as I feel Bani's steady hand on mine.

'Very "grass is greener on the other side" of you,' I quip, now that it has finally dawned on me what I must do.

'Very English honours student of you,' she pokes me, joking.

And that's all we speak about Ashish. Because neither of us can stand to speak of him any more.

* * *

My biggest realization on my first day back to college after everything? I can't listen to music any more. And not listening to music instantly makes any commute last twice as long. My playlists are a blend of songs Ashish introduced me to, songs I listened to thinking about him, songs he hated and would ban me from playing on shuffle (mostly One Direction and Prateek Kuhad). I have nothing to do but people-watch my way through and dissect the stories behind the early morning eyes. You, are you in love? And you, over there, fixing your bangs in the front camera, are you headed to a date? Or you, sitting next to me, staring aimlessly at nothing, have you lost someone too?

Standing at the front gate, it takes me fifteen minutes to find the timetable for this semester. I tug at my shirt as I make my way to the lecture hall for the first period. It's only when I start walking that I realize all our second semester classes are in a completely different nook of the campus.

I'm in my own world, so hyper aware of every move I make that when I hear a 'Where have you *been*?!' launched at me from across the lecture hall, it sends shock waves through my system.

I look up and there she is: Aanchal, standing with both her hands on her waist. Next to her, there's a banana peel and an empty bottle of protein shake. *Shit*, I mutter under my breath as I feel Aanchal glaring at me with disbelief. I'm going to have to do this a lot earlier than I expected.

'Is that really you or am I seeing a ghost?'

'Hi, Aanchal,' is all I can muster.

She smacks my shoulder in disbelief. 'You can't disappear for a month and then just say hey like it's normal. Where were you? I thought you were dead? What happened?' she spitballs. 'I texted Ashish and he didn't respond either!' The volume of her questions overwhelms me, but it's the last part that's the real sucker punch.

'Actually, Ashish . . .' I begin to exhale, when she interrupts me.

'Wait. Please, please, please don't tell me you guys broke up. Not after that rom-com surprise he pulled.'

Oh. I had forgotten about that. Every happy moment with Ashish will almost always be dulled by the razor-edge realization of how it all ended, I guess.

'So?' Aanchal asks, interrupting my thoughts. 'What happened? Is there any chance you guys might get back together?' She looks so desperate for a positive response that it breaks me a little, the fact that I can't give it to her.

How simple a world that would be to live in; one where Ashish and I just broke up, where the idea of our future ended with a question mark instead of a full stop etched in permanent marker.

Before Aanchal can get another word in, I follow it up with the inevitable. 'No, we didn't break up.' I add, 'He actually passed away. Car accident. New Year's Eve.'

It feels like Aanchal is processing everything I have said at the speed of one word per minute. I let her take her time to catch up with what has been my life for the last month.

There is no dramatic hug, no 'I'm so sorry, Sana.' There is none of that conventional bullshit. Minutes later, the first thing Aanchal says is, 'How are you doing today?'

The addition of a simple word and the entire meaning of a question flips. Today, I can handle. Today, I have an answer for. 'I'm doing better than yesterday.'

Aanchal moves closer to hug me. We stay like that for a while, only breaking apart as Professor Sarin walks in and the lecture hall goes quiet. From the other side of the hall, I spot Preksha and Samira, sitting not too far away us, and wave at them.

'I don't know how to keep saying it again and again,' I say to Aanchal.

Aanchal places her hand over mine. 'I've got this.'

Suddenly, Professor Sarin's throaty voice fills the room. 'Saksham?'

'Present, professor.'

'Sakshi?'

'Present ma'am!'

'Sana?' She hurries over my name.

'Here, professor,' I whimper from the back of the hall. All of the faces seated at the front turn around to look at me.

'Nice of you to join us, Sana,' she quips, her eyes meeting mine in one swift motion before turning back to her register. 'Stay back after the lecture is over, please.'

'Sanchit?' She goes on, not waiting for a response.

* * *

When the bell rings, I finally walk up to Professor Sarin. Aanchal promises to wait for me outside. While she is clearing out her table, I am playing with my fingers and waiting, looking down at the floor.

'I heard,' she blurts out, suddenly.

'How?' I ask, stunned.

'Ashish's family lives in my colony, I'm friends with his mother,' she says. A piece of the jigsaw puzzle suddenly fits. Ashish had mentioned that a close family friend of his taught at my college when I had learned that my marks met the cut-off requirement, but I was so ecstatic that I hadn't paid attention to the name.

'And you probably don't remember but I was there at the cremation ground, too,' she says, lifting her spectacles off and resting them gently on her palm.

'I'm sorry, I don't remember seeing you.'

Professor Sarin sighs as she takes me in. 'I'm *extremely* sorry for your loss, Sana.'

No one has said these words to me until just now.

'About your absence from class,' she says as the moment passes and I try to hide a disappointed frown on my face.

I interrupt her: 'Yes, Professor, I know I've been gone for a month. I'm hoping to make up for it in the coming months if . . .'

'That's . . . not where I was going with this, Sana. I had a chat with all your professors from this semester. We've decided to waive off your attendance requirements,' she says.

'You'll still be expected to turn assignments in, but we can work on an extension basis so you can catch up with what you've missed out on.'

'But . . . just yesterday the admin called my mom saying I'll be held back if . . .?'

'I know. I heard of that phone call after it was made, which is when I got the professors together and told them about your . . . special case, and we decided to negotiate with the admin.'

I feel my eyelids being weighed down by the size of the tears I am holding back. I hadn't expected this kindness, so I don't know how to react to it. 'I don't know what to say. Thank you, Professor.'

'You don't have to thank me, Sana,' she says, before returning to her register; a sign that I'm dismissed.

Stepping out of the lecture hall, I notice Aanchal standing there, leaning against a pillar as she waits for me. Entangling her arm with mine, she commands my gait. 'Come now, let's get something to eat.'

We walk across the hallway and take the steps towards the canteen. The same path I have walked countless times before suddenly feels unfamiliar, as though I'm invading a space I no longer belong in. I stifle that feeling, when, from across the canteen gate, my eyes catch Pranav's. It takes less than a second for him to dart through and take me into a hug.

He pulls away from me and I can see his eyes wet. 'You should've texted us.' It hits me that Aanchal must've texted him in the time I was talking to Professor Sarin.

'I know,' I say, averting my gaze. 'I'm sorry.'

'Don't you dare say sorry.'

I just stand there as Pranav holds me, his hand stroking the back of my head. It seems to go on for hours. I wish it would last longer. 'I've got you. Okay?'

When I don't respond, he holds me by my shoulders. 'Sana, are you listening to me?' he asks, nudging my jaw to make me look at him, his eyes. 'I'm right here. I've got you.'

I nod, as if any of this matters.

Chapter Thirteen

Word around college moves fast. But word around colleges that have Tanya Shroff moves at the speed of light. Or sound. I'm not sure. I'm an English student.

At the one week point, I learn that everyone, to the exception of my friends, already knew, because Tanya had been going around, wearing white, flaunting her concealer-less puffy eyes, telling anyone who dared to ask that the 'greatest love of her life' and someone she had a crush on for ten years, passed away in a tragic car accident right after they spent some time together at a New Year's Eve party. Aanchal and Pranav had heard it through the grapevine too, but they hadn't assumed it would be Ashish at all. Tanya's descriptions hardly matched the person they knew him to be through me.

'She was going around telling people she had a moment with him at the party,' Aanchal tells me, although the hesitation on her face shows she's not sure if I'm up for discussing petty gossip about the situation, just yet. 'I should've known better, I should've known what she was referring to,' she says, extending her hand towards mine.

'She has always been like this, I'm not surprised.'

'Were they even friends?'

'Who? Ashish and Tanya?' I ask and Aanchal nods.

I tip my head back, letting the back-room wall hold my head. 'Once upon a long, long time ago, she called dibs on him. That's the extent of whatever relationship they had with each other.'

'And then what happened?'

'Then he fell for me,' I say, smiling. 'And that pissed her off, because she was used to getting all the guys.'

Aanchal joins me in for a laugh and then proceeds to hold my hand. 'Sure you're going to be okay?'

'Of course, don't worry about me.'

For the next whole week and a little bit of the one after that, Aanchal will be away from college. The yearly sports tournaments across Delhi University are lining up and she'll mostly be on the road, travelling from one college to another, representing our team.

'Okay, I'm going to head now. Coach will kill me if I'm late,' she says as the lecture hall begins to fill up. She had just come to say hi. 'Preksha and Samira will be here, okay?'

'Of course. Kick ass. Win every game.'

Aanchal smiles sadly at me. I didn't know there was a way to do that. 'I'll try.'

As Aanchal leaves, my hope is still alive that Preksha and Samira will show up and take the seat that I have saved for them.

When they walk inside the hall, I catch Samira's eyes. Samira and Preksha wave back and walk up to me, hesitation riddled in their stance, taking the seat right in front of me.

'Hi, Sana,' Preksha says, almost too high-pitched to be normal. She always smells like strawberries, but today, as she hugs me, I realize the smell is a tad pungent when she is close up. 'How are you doing, baby?'

Samira runs her hand down my back, rubbing it like she's helping a kid let out a cough. 'Doing okay?'

I force a smile—because they are trying. But I don't know how to do this either. This is my first time as someone who has lost someone, too. 'I'm fine! I missed you guys,' I say as they get seated. 'What's been up?'

'Lots yaar, we'll catch you up after the lecture, okay?' Samira says before turning around to face the front of the lecture hall. 'Oh, Sana, by the way, you still have that copy of *The Bell Jar* borrowed from the library na?'

I had forgotten about it. I borrowed it right as the exams were ending and was due to return it the first week of college.

'Can you *pleeeeease* bring it back? I really want to read it and you've had it for ages! You've read it na?' she asks.

'Uh, yeah, of course. I'll give it to you tomorrow.'

'Thanks babe,' Samira says, turning back to face the front of the lecture hall.

For the rest of the lecture, I sit alone, in silence, wondering if this is how it had always been. If this is how it's always going to be.

* * *

I'm almost certain I'm wearing Harry Potter's invisibility cloak all around college. Everywhere I go, people I would normally say hi to avert their gaze as though I didn't just wave at them. Professors don't even look me in the eye. Preksha and Samira, too, rarely ever text on the group I have with them and Aanchal. Mostly, the seat next to mine, as well as the pair of seats in front of me, remain empty.

None of this is a problem, though. In this new life that has become my normal, I don't mind going from one lecture to the next and leaving for home the second I'm done. But today, I have a three-hour break between lectures that feels impossible to fill up. I *could* bury myself in assignments. There are also about a hundred pages of readings I am behind on and more that keep piling on daily as I fail to catch up. Or I could go home, curl up in bed and go to sleep. The latter proposition is so tempting, I feel myself falling for it, until I see that Pranav has texted.

Pranav: *coffee? Bloom's?*

I feel like a dog that's been thrown a bone. I can't afford to miss any more lectures, even though Professor

Sarin guaranteed me an attendance waiver. Nothing is codified and they could turn their backs on me if they want.

Sana: *yes please*

'Hi buddy,' Pranav says, pulling me into another one of his generous hugs. 'Good to go?' he asks and I nod.

Pranav leads the way, humming quietly, and we begin our walk to Bloom's, running adjacent to our college boundary wall. We've been down the same path before, but this time it feels like a completely new route. As we reach Bloom's, he holds the door for me and I walk inside, beelining for my favourite seat that's luckily empty—the one right next to the window, overlooking a garden of daffodils. It's the same one we sat on the first time we were here. But before I can pull the chair out for myself, Pranav beats me to it. He's not pulling the chair out for me though, he has sat down in it, himself.

'Hey, that's my favourite seat,' I say, protesting.

'It's my favourite too,' he replies, grabbing the menu from another table to our side.

'If I had known it was a race, I would've run faster,' I say, grumpy, as I set my bag down on the floor and sit opposite Pranav.

'You can always sit down next to me like we did the first time,' he says, smiling.

I shake my head no. 'No, that's okay.'

Without asking me, Pranav orders me my regular—an iced latte with vanilla syrup, 'But not too much syrup, okay?' he adds on my behalf and gets himself his usual, coffee gasoline. I mean, coffee black. Or is it cortado?

'*Ek* sandwich *bhi lagado*, bhaiya,' Pranav says to Taran bhaiya, the server who doubles as the manager at Bloom's.

'Classic? Paneer and cheese?' He asks Pranav.

Pranav nods enthusiastically before returning his attention to me, noticing that I have been smiling at him this entire time.

I see him tighten up a little, suddenly conscious.

'What are you smiling about?' he asks.

'Nothing, nothing,' I say, looking outside the window.

'Tell me,' Pranav asks gently.

'Thank you.'

'For what?'

'I don't know . . .' I say. 'For treating me normally? I guess? But not too normally? If you know what I mean?'

'I don't, exactly,' Pranav says, looking down at the menu, concealing a smile, 'but you're welcome.'

From the corner of my eye, I see Taran bringing us our drinks on a tray.

'So,' Pranav says.

'So . . .'

'How did it happen?' he asks, before I have had the chance to stir the unmixed coffee and milk in my cup.

Okay, here we go: 'Car accident.'

'When?'

'New Year's Eve.'

'Was the other guy . . . ?'

'Drunk? Yep.'

'Was Ashish?'

I've not thought of this before, I realize. 'I don't know, it never came up. The drunk guy banged into him, so I guess they didn't care to check,' I say, stirring my coffee cup nonchalantly, as though this is a totally normal coffee conversation.

Pranav nods. For a brief moment, he looks away. He reverts his gaze on me to ask: 'Was he alone?'

I shake my head no. I don't remember if I've told Aanchal this, either. 'My best friend, Bani. She was with him too.'

Pranav's face shrinks and I see he's expecting more bad information.

'She's fine. I mean, injured. But alive,' I say with an acrid taste in my mouth that I wish weren't there.

When Pranav doesn't say anything but just stares at me, I fill the gap in our conversation myself. 'I think I could be a lot worse.'

'What do you mean?'

'I don't know,' I say, looking away. 'I mean, Ashish wasn't only my boyfriend but also my best friend,' I say, as I fear the tears knocking. 'Bani and Ashish are . . . were my entire world. And suddenly, overnight, my world snapped into half. *Literally*. You know?'

'Yeah, I can understand,' Pranav says, his eyes so gentle and kind.

'So, yeah, I don't know. I keep thinking, all things considered, that I could be a lot worse. I was, for a while. Every morning I would wake up and think,

"Oh, I have to call him," realize he's dead, and then it would be like the first day all over again. That was bleak. But now it's more like . . . it feels like this 50 kg ankle weight. I can walk, yeah, but even going from my bedroom to the fridge feels like exercise.'

Pranav smiles faintly at me.

'Still walking though,' I say, forcing a smile.

'Do you want to hear the story about my dog?'

I feel myself light up. 'Yes, of course. I can't believe I've gone so long without hearing it.'

'I think maybe it's a good thing I didn't tell you before,' Pranav says, taking another sip of his coffee.

'Wait, this is not a third date though. Will you still tell me?'

'I can make an exception,' Pranav says, winking, but I see something shift in his eyes. This is not how a boy looks when he's pulling a move on you. 'I live on the second storey of this building that directly faces the main road. So . . . no footpath, nothing. Just straight up cars, all day long. One evening, when I was thirteen, I couldn't find my dog, Shambhu, anywhere in the house. I had to take him for a walk. But I wasn't worried, he generally liked chilling in the parking lot,' Pranav says, before taking a deep breath in. 'Turns out, someone left the main gate open and he escaped. Didn't make it very far though. Some guy in a car, I think, hit him and left him there.'

I feel my heart drop at ever having joked about this.

'Anyway, to make things all that worse, he didn't die. Not immediately. But yeah . . . he had horrendous injuries and close to no quality of life left, so we had to put him down that evening. My parents were out of town so I went to the vet with my grandparents,' Pranav says, looking at his coffee. 'They tried to leave me at home, but there was no way I wasn't accompanying them. He died in my arms.'

'Aanchal said this story was a move, Pranav.'

'I mean, it's not *not* a move,' Pranav says, smiling. 'When he died, I got a tattoo of Shambhu,' he replies, stretching down his t-shirt to reveal his clavicle tattoo with an S written inside a paw. 'I had saved up some pocket money for this new watch. My parents were out of town. And I didn't know what to do with the pain. So I thought might as well distract myself with actual pain.'

'Did your parents not kill you for that?'

'They had bigger things to be worried about.'

I look at him. This is another layer. How many more till I get to the core of him?

'That's the story you tell as a move?' I ask.

'Correct.'

'Do you tell people the first half of it?'

He shakes his head no. 'Just the tattoo bit.'

'Tell me the full thing, Pranav.' I ask because I know there's more, because I see it on his face.

For the first time since I've known Pranav, I see him not have an answer at the tip of his tongue.

'You don't have to, if it's too personal,' I add.

'After Shambhu died, I was okay for a few days. I mean, shockingly okay. But then one day, it was so random, but mom got this fever, it wasn't even a big deal, and then suddenly, this . . . this strange paranoia set in. I don't know how to explain it other than that it felt like I had to go find him, I had to make sure he wasn't out on the street. And every single time, the realization would come to me, like a thunderbolt, that he is dead.'

'Eventually, I started waking up in the middle of the night and . . . I don't know, my chest would be so tight it would feel like someone had been sitting on it. I would have these strange, vivid dreams of my parents dying, getting hit by a car, falling down the stairs and cracking their heads open. At one point, I was walking to my parents' room every night to make sure they were still alive.'

'They probably figured I'd taken Shambhu's death a little too hard. But it never felt normal, you know? Not to me.'

'Anyway, when this didn't just naturally blow over, my parents were . . . a little spooked. Like, what is *wrong* with our kid? They took me to our family doctor and then, that doctor sent me to another and then, a few more,' he says, finally looking at me. 'They said it was obsessive compulsive disorder (OCD), with more of an obsessive bend to it, I guess. Apparently, I'd always had it but witnessing Shambhu's death was the trigger that made it obvious to me and everyone around me.'

'That's actually when I started reading,' he says. 'These mental images were so hard to turn off, and nothing helped. Not even the medicine, initially. Not watching TV, not listening to music. And then one day, electricity was out and I just grabbed this random book that was always on my mother's shelf and sat there and . . . the next time I got up, I had finished it. And those few hours were the most . . . I don't know, I guess "normal hours" I had experienced in months.'

'How is it now?'

'The OCD?'

'Yeah.'

'I don't know, so many years of having it, I don't remember life when I didn't have it. The medication helps. Reading helps. I'm okay 95 per cent of the time, but it does get bad sometimes.'

'Has it been bad recently?'

Pranav shifts his gaze away from me. He just nods.

'When?' I ask.

'Just . . . recently.'

'Tell me.'

He's still looking away when he answers: 'When you weren't replying.'

I feel my heart break. 'I'm sorry,' I say, and I watch Pranav shake his head. Like I shouldn't say that. 'What did you think . . . what did your brain tell you was going on?'

'Just thought you were dead. That's usually the first conclusion, and then I work backwards from there,' he says quietly. 'It doesn't really strike my brain that oh, she doesn't want to talk or she's busy. Just . . . dead. Or something really, really bad happened.'

'I can't believe Aanchal said this was a move.'

'It's not her fault. It's what her friends told her, that I made them fall for me by telling them a sad, dead-dog story.'

'Does she not know the full story either?'

He shakes his head no. 'You're actually the first person I've ever told.'

The realization sobers me up. Why? I want to ask.

'Do you have a picture of him?'

Instantly, Pranav whips his phone out to show me a photo of a much tinier, much more innocent looking version of him, with his hands wrapped around a mutt with brown eyelashes.

'You were a cute kid.'

'What do you mean? I'm not a cute adult?'

'Is that what I said?'

Pranav giggles. 'So you think I'm cute?'

I punch Pranav's arm. 'Do you miss him?' I ask. What a stupid question, I realize, as it makes its way out.

'All the time. He was the best dog in the world,' he says, looking down at his empty cup, before he looks up again to ask me, 'Do you miss *him*?'

'It feels a little too early for that. I feel like I'm still mostly just coming to terms with the fact that . . . I don't know . . . he's never coming back. Ever.'

'Tell me about him,' he says quietly.

I tip my head back and laugh. 'Where do I even start?'

'At the beginning,' Pranav replies, like there is nothing he would rather do than hear a love story that isn't one any more. 'You know I love love stories.'

'This one has quite the tragic ending.'

'Doesn't make it any less epic, Sana.'

And so, per Pranav's instructions, I start at the beginning.

Chapter Fourteen

Time flies when you're having fun. Time jet-skis through the sky faster than a Challenger when you're wishing for it to stand still. Time, also, actively tries to make things better, which works against the grain when the thing that it's trying to make better is the loss of a person. Because it getting better means forgetting; and I never, ever want to forget Ashish. Missing someone, and grief in general, I'm realizing, is tricky. You hate it but it's also right where you want to stay. The tiniest flicker of things feeling 'normal' and the guilt kicks in. *How dare you put on kajal today? Look at you, wondering if your top matches your skirt, when he died three months ago? Tch tch tch, it wasn't a funny enough joke to laugh that hard in the first place, especially considering your . . . situation.*

Take, for instance, the fact that the March trip to Nainital with the girls and Pranav is already due for next week and how I'm just a little butt-hurt that

Aanchal hasn't even asked me if I'm coming. I last overheard Aanchal talking to Samira and Preksha about their plans, if they were still on, and waited for her to ask me, too. But she didn't.

As I sit next to her in class, I can't help but wrestle through my feelings. I don't even want to go, so why does it bother me—not being asked? And why does Aanchal seem so crabby right now? Her mind seems to be on everything but the lecture, her fingers constantly fidgeting through ten apps on her phone.

When Aanchal launches out of her seat to walk out of the lecture, possibly towards the washroom, my curiosity, fuelled by my insecurity, gets the best of me. I grab her phone, that she left unlocked on the desk, and try and see what's going on. I suddenly fear if I'll live Sukriti's fate, a girl in my school who went through her boyfriend's chats in a moment of weakness and found that he had been sending the same horny texts, word for word, to three more people.

Pushing that thought away, I open her WhatsApp and find the text right on top is one from Pranav.

Pranav: *just you and I will go?*

Pranav: *it'll be fun i promise*

Is this about the trip? Wasn't it just yesterday that I heard Preksha and Samira confirming they're on board? I scroll up a little for more context.

Aanchal: *pissed off*

Pranav: *what happened? call?*

Aanchal: *in lecture. Preksha and Samira both cancelled just now*

Aanchal: *they legit said haan pakka 100% yesterday*

Pranav: *wtf, it's in a week?!*

Aanchal: *i know. They didn't even have the decency to tell me in person after canning like that, just texted a 'btw we can't make it'*

Pranav: *urgh. what to do now?*

Aanchal: *idk. i'm really annoyed, pranav, mom has been on the phone with the manager arranging everything for the last week*

Aanchal: *i don't even wanna talk about this with sana because she will feel guilty for backing out too when this is OBVIOUSLY not about her! I don't want her to think I'm forcing her to come or something, but I just want to bitch to her about the two of them*

Pranav: *no no I get exactly what you're saying*

Aanchal: *do you think I should ask her? If she wants to come, still?*

Pranav: *I think you should let her bring it up. I don't know, knowing Sana, she probably won't say no if you asked*

Aanchal: *no, you're right*

Aanchal: *URGHHHHHH*

Aanchal: *I want to cry, Pranav. I planned all this especially for her and now I have to cancel*

Pranav: *just you and I will go?*

Pranav: *it'll be fun I promise*

What does this mean? Aanchal planned the trip just . . . for *me*? That doesn't make any sense. Or wait . . . does it? I remember now, how the plan for the trip even came to be, how I was complaining to the girls about feeling like an adult-baby living at home because of how strict Ma can be. Had she planned this just for me?

As a getaway from my sheltered life? Is this why she is so disappointed that everyone, including me, is bailing?

'Hey, what did I miss?' Aanchal says, returning a few moments later.

'Oh nothing, just Sarin going on about mobiles in lectures again,' I say, looking down at the blank page of my notebook sitting in front of me, as though I'm waiting for the right words to appear, magically. I want to kick myself for looking through her chat. If I hadn't, I wouldn't know what's going on. But now, knowing that Aanchal is feeling so gutted about it all, that both Preksha and Samira have cancelled last minute, I can't help but feel the guilt I know they aren't feeling.

And so, I know what I have to do. Even if I absolutely don't want to do it.

'Hey, by the way, we're on for our trip na?'

She looks back at me, shocked. 'Umm, I thought you wouldn't want to go, San.'

'Maybe it'll be a nice change,' I say, faking it so well, I'm almost fooling myself. Would it be a nice change, though? Could it be exactly what I need?

'You really wanna go?' she asks, excitedly.

I only nod and Aanchal squeals, wrapping her arms all around me until Professor Sarin's glare simmers her back down.

Aanchal *changed the group name to 'HILLS ARE CALLING'*
Aanchal: *GUYS WE'RE GOING TO NAINITAL!!!!!!*
Pranav: *No way! Sana, you in?*
Sana: *yes! should be fun*
Aanchal: *the hills are CALLING*
Pranav: *okay. relax.*

I want to push the pedal on the brakes. What have I just done? Do I really want to go? And if I do, is it for Aanchal or is it the FOMO? And do I even deserve to go? Has it been long enough to do something like this and not feel like I'm being an absolute stone-hearted bitch?

A few seconds later, I see that Pranav has messaged me privately, too.

Pranav: *you're sure you want to come Sana?*

Sana: *yeah, it'll be nice I think. unless you don't want me to*

Pranav: *don't be an idiot*

Pranav: *just don't do this for any reason other than really wanting to come, okay?*

Sana: *don't worry, I really want to come, I promise. what will I do at college without you two anyway*

When I get home from college, I realize I skipped over the part where I can't just spontaneously agree to things like these, that I almost always need permission from my mother who has a tendency to say no without even hearing the full story.

'How was your day, baby?' Ma greets me as I enter home, unlocking it with my key.

'Good,' I say flatly. 'Back home early?'

She shrugs. 'Slow news day.'

Out with it, I order myself. 'Is it okay if I go on a trip with Aanchal and Pranav?'

Ma turns to look at me. She appears as confused as I feel about this decision.

'Uh, yeah, of course,' she says, taking off her spectacles. Of course?! My mother has that phrase in her vocabulary? 'Where is this coming from, though?'

'We'd been planning it for a while. And then . . . well, you know,' I smile faintly. 'Aanchal is really sad because everyone is cancelling so I thought . . . besides, I figured the change might help?'

'Are you sure this is what you want to do?'

I shrug, like it doesn't matter. Like it's not a big deal at all.

And then Bani asks the same thing when I recount the whole sequence to her.

'Are you sure you want to go? Right now?'

'Yeah, what's the worst that could happen? Someone dies?' I joke.

I'm still waiting for when I start finding it funny.

* * *

There is type A, which is mostly what I am, and then there is type whatever the hell Aanchal is—Bridezilla, travel edition. As I walk towards her, arriving at the Kashmere Gate metro station ten minutes later than when she had instructed me to, she points to the watch on her wrist, her foot tapping like a schoolteacher's.

'You're late,' she says so plainly that I think, for a second, that she'll disallow me from accompanying her because of the fact.

'Sorry ma'am,' I say, pulling my suitcase towards her and hoping a hug dampens her anger.

Behind Aanchal, I notice Pranav in the background, walking inside a McDonald's, waving at me. 'Hey bud. Want something?'

I shake my head no and he disappears into the yellowy-brightness, walking out seconds later with a burger in one hand and fries in another, while Aanchal stands waiting, arms crossed in front of her chest. 'Are you done feasting? Do you want us to miss the bus?'

'We're not in *Mission Impossible*,' he says, grabbing his bag from Aanchal's shoulder, not before gulping a huge bite of his McSpicy chicken burger. 'Chill out.'

'Would it kill you to hurry? The bus is reaching in ten minutes.'

'And we're *literally* ten metres away from where it's reaching.'

Right as the three of us finally make it to the pick-up point, a dingy, poorly lit bus, with the words 'Bing Bing Buses' painted on it in ivory white, halts in front of us. It looks less like a piece of transport, more a portable pub.

'That doesn't seem . . . very safe,' I say.

'Or sanitary,' Pranav remarks, looking in Aanchal's direction. 'I can't believe you wouldn't let us drive there.'

'I don't trust your driving,' Aanchal scoffs, stepping on to the bus.

'Oh, but you trust this strange guy?'

'Yes. He has more experience driving on hilly roads. Besides, he probably knows how to drive overnight without sleeping.'

The interiors are an instant sensory overload. Every last corner of the bus is shining with dizzying pink lights that flicker green on random intervals, while the seats are covered with a neon-yellow covers that make the seat numbers glow in the dark.

Before I've even sat down, I hear Aanchal and Pranav feuding again.

'Go sit over there,' he says, pointing to the empty seat next to me. I turn around to see what's up and realize Aanchal has taken the lone seat of the three tickets we booked, the one that was obviously meant for Pranav.

'What's your problem? I want to sit here.'

'Aanchal, it's an overnight bus and you could have a creepy dude sitting next to you,'

'You think you can throw a punch harder than I can?' Aanchal asks, raising her eyes. I don't *not* agree with her. She is the stronger of the two by a mile.

Before Pranav can respond, though, there is an interruption.

'Excuse me, could you please move? That's my seat,' a girl announces, tapping on Pranav's shoulder. He turns around, visibly defeated, to make space for her to sit.

'Now will you leave me alone?' Aanchal says, putting her earphones on as Pranav saunters back to where I'm sitting.

'You're comfy?' He asks. It's only when he's sat next to me, though, that I realize how snug our arrangement is.

I nod. 'I never pegged you as a protective elder brother.'

'I'm not.'

'What was that, then?'

'I would've done that for you, too.'

'Oh, so we've gone from relentless flirting to brother–sister now? What's next? Should I tie you a *rakhi*?' I ask, narrowing my eyes.

'Sana,' Pranav says as he rests his head on the seat in front of us in a way that he can look me straight in the eyes, 'please don't *ever* say that again.'

I flush red all over, which I hide by turning my head to the view outside my window, which is still very much Delhi roads and plenty of trucks.

'How long until we make it to Nainital?' I ask Pranav when I'm convinced my skin is back to yellow.

'Could take anywhere between seven to nine hours.'

'So we should be there by . . . six?'

Pranav nods. 'Approximately, yeah.'

'Gives us enough time to sleep then,' I say, stretching out as much of my limbs as I can. The guy sitting in front of me has pushed his chair all the way back to the point that his seat is practically in my lap; forget sleeping, even sitting is uncomfortable. Pranav looks down at my feet, at how I'm booby-trapped inside here, until suddenly, he's standing up.

'Where are you going?' I ask him.

'Hey man, do you mind pulling your seat back a little?' Pranav says, tapping on the guy's shoulder, who is busy watching YouTube videos without headphones.

I am instantly embarrassed, but when I feel the vastness of the space open up in front of me, I'm grateful for Pranav's intervention.

'Thanks,' I say meekly. 'You didn't have to do that, though.'

'Why not?'

'I don't know . . .'

'Would you have rather been uncomfortable the entire time?'

Curling into my seat and sinking in a little further, I notice Pranav uncomfortably upright. 'You're not sleeping?'

'I . . . am not entirely sure about the safety of this situation,' he replies. 'Maybe in a while.'

'Okay if I sleep?' I ask.

'Of course. That's why I'm here.'

Just as quickly as I fall asleep, am I ripped out of my slumber by the sensation of plummeting to my death into a valley. I open my eyes to realize it wasn't just a sensation. The driver has gone full throttle on the brake for no reason whatsoever. I turn to my left and notice Pranav is not sitting next to me. His place has been taken by both of our bags lined on top of each other, mimicking a head rest for me.

'*Aise thorri hota hai*?' I hear Aanchal's voice, all the way from the front of the bus. '*Yeh booking karne ke time batana hota hai*!' Pranav is standing right next to her, calming her down.

'Guys, what's wrong?' I call out to them.

Turns out, the bus is not *really* stopping at Nainital. It's headed in the right direction but its final halt is about twenty kilometres *before* it and we are just now being told of the change in plans. This wouldn't be the problem that it is if we weren't reaching the drop off point in half an hour, which is, at four in the morning.

'Did you not read?' Pranav asks Aanchal, irritated.

'Of course I read it, yaar, there was nothing!' she yells, loud enough for people to turn back in their seat and watch the drama unfold. 'How are we going to find someone to take us to Nainital at four in the morning? I'm going to go and have a word with this stupid bus manager.'

'*Chup chaap* sit down,' Pranav tells her. 'I'll figure this out.'

'Arre, but,' Aanchal begins saying.

'Shush.'

Half an hour later, Aanchal and I follow Pranav's lead and get off the bus at the final stopping point.

'You were right, by the way,' Pranav says to Aanchal as she steps off, right behind him.

'About what?'

'There was nothing about this drop off thing on the bus booking,' Pranav says like it pains him to admit. 'I double-checked it. They just changed their plans because there's a lot of unexpected tourist overflow and a bunch of restrictions that these guys didn't expect.'

Aanchal almost lunges towards the conductor, but Pranav pulls her back, holding the straps of her bag.

'STOP IT! I want to yell at that conductor,' Aanchal screams, trying, and desperately failing, to get out of Pranav's grip.

'Journal about it,' Pranav announces, before reversing Aanchal in the direction of the cab waiting for us, the one that Pranav had arranged while Aanchal and I sat panicking.

* * *

Even though it is 4 a.m., it takes us nearly two hours to reach Aanchal's parent's cottage. The ride *would* be picturesque, if it wasn't barely dawn. Right now, though, everything looks grey-ish blue tinted, like a sad, boring, war film.

Finally, a steep incline leads us to the front gate, which has spokes with sharp edges. The gate shines like white marble, even though I'm certain it's not made of marble.

As I step out of the car, we walk into the front lawns of a little cottage right out of a movie—tucked in the middle of so much greenery that you almost miss how rustic and well-intentioned every part of its architecture is. The sun is coming up right from behind it as it's just getting to be light when we reach, and this illumination from the back makes it all seem a little less real and a little more like we left Delhi and entered wonderland. The cottage seems to have four levels, each marked with faded, white wooden windows that make the whole building appear even more majestic. Instantly, my brain goes: this is a perfect romantic getaway spot.

I'm lost in admiration when I notice Pranav carrying my bag on one shoulder and his own on the other.

'Oh, I'm so sorry. Give it to me?'

'No no, it's totally cool,' he says.

I look to Aanchal. 'This is exquisite. Is it really your parents'?'

'It was my mom's parents' and they passed it on to mom. Parents handle it collectively now,' she says, motioning us to the front door, leading towards the reception. 'It's honestly not that fancy.'

We enter the hall, my mouth still agape, to a yellow-light speckled reception area, where a busboy greets us with something that looks like watermelon juice. I take a sip and realize that rich people have better watermelons too.

While Aanchal completes the formalities of our check-in, I walk around to take the interiors in. On the inside, the carpet matches the drapes—it's a boho amalgamation of woody furniture, pastel linen and light wood panels. No two couches are the same colour, the cushions are of different sizes and shapes, and the carpet is a strange, but intentional blend of more art forms than I care to count. Everything is a confusing mess, but the kind that has a touch of thoughtfulness attached to it.

'Have you ever been here before?' I ask Pranav.

'Once, when I was very young, I think. It's always crazy sold out,' he says, pointing me towards the couch, before sprawling all over it. 'When Aanchal made the plan, I was 100 per cent sure it was going to get cancelled, because every time we've planned to come here as a family, we've had to cancel because of a storm of international bookings.'

'Your mother is the younger sister, no?' I ask, taking the spot next to him. 'So, she owns it too?'

He nods. 'On paper, yes,' Pranav says. 'But Aanchal's parents like running the place day to day. My mum handles the boring, financial side of things.'

'Are they close?'

'Annoyingly close. They tried so hard to make sure Aanchal and I bonded too, because they were practically together twenty-four-seven.'

'Did that work?'

'Honestly? Not at all,' he laughs. 'We hated each other until like the ninth grade. Probably her wacky teenage girl hormones.'

'Hey,' I snub Pranav, punching him in the arm.

'I'm kidding, I'm kidding.'

Before I can ask follow up questions, Aanchal scurries over.

'Dude, last time I was here, they had actual keys for the rooms,' she says, excitedly holding up the key cards.

'I'm assuming I have the solo room?' Pranav says, grabbing one of the cards out of her hands.

'Unless you want to share the room with me, big brother,' Aanchal retorts, cheekily.

'Yuck,' Pranav says, fake-gagging. 'If you guys don't mind, I'm going to catch up on some sleep. Unlike you princesses who slept the entire way through.'

Chapter Fifteen

While Aanchal has allowed Pranav two hours of naptime before we start our day, I'm using the same allotment to wash the bus-grime off of me. Checking in with myself, I notice that although I felt okay coming all the way here, my heart suddenly feels heavy. As I lather up the shampoo in my hair, my roots already oily even though I'd just washed them yesterday, I piece together where this feeling comes from.

It's simple.

It's this room, it's the stupid swans arranged on the bed as though it's a honeymoon suite. It's the bathtub large enough for two. It's the view of the valley. It's everything Ashish and I dreamed about and never got to do. It's that daily, every morning, rinse and repeat dose of Ashish I never got, enough for me to get sick and tired of him. *Would* I get sick of him? Or would I want more, over and over?

Blaming the shampoo in my eyes, I turn off the shower and pat myself dry, when a loud banging knocks me out of my thoughts. It feels like someone is pounding on our door.

'Aanchal, will you get that?' I yell.

I am busy blow-drying my hair, wearing a bath-gown before I put a fresh pair of clothes on, when I realize I can still hear, even feel, the thumping.

'Aanchal!' I yell, 'What's going on?'

There is a white sheen of unblended sunscreen on my face, but I walk out of the washroom to take stock of the matter. Peeping out of the keyhole on our bedroom door, I notice that there isn't anyone outside, at all. I open the door to see what's going on, turning my head right and left, when I finally locate the source of the noise. Aanchal.

'What the hell, Aanchal?' I yell at her from across the hallway, while making my way to her.

'I'm just trying to wake Pranav up,' Aanchal says, looking up from her glare on Pranav's door towards me, to add, 'You look like a ghost.'

When Aanchal reaches for Pranav's door again, I move to grab her arm, afraid she's making enough of a scene for more people to come out of their rooms. Pranav tips the door open mid-knock and causes Aanchal to trip inward, inside his bedroom.

'Have you lost your mind?' he asks.

My eyes immediately pan from Aanchal's arm to Pranav, standing there shirtless in only his boxers, his hair ruffled and eyes puffed. He's just waking up. It's not like I expect Pranav to be any less good looking without clothing, but the realization of *just* how good looking he really is dawns on me at this moment. I see why the girls fall for him; dead dog story and all.

Suddenly, I am very aware of my body. Especially the fact that under this flimsy bath gown, I am completely naked.

'I've been calling you for an hour and your phone has been switched off,' Aanchal yells in Pranav's face. 'I told you two hours, maximum. We're already late.'

'Leave me alone, you weirdo,' Pranav says, shutting the door, but Aanchal grabs hold of it.

'Get ready, right now,' she announces. 'We leave in ten minutes.'

* * *

'It's been an hour!' Aanchal yells, with a disregard for decorum you can only have when you own the hotel. Aanchal and I have been waiting for forty minutes since she went ballistic on Pranav and he's just now casually trodding into the lobby as though Aanchal does not terrify him.

'I thought we came here to relax,' Pranav says, sitting down next to me. 'Hey, Sana,' he pats my thigh, 'Nice outfit,' he says, as he scans me top to bottom in my little floral dress that barely runs to my knees, one that Bani passed down to me when she bought it online and realized it didn't fit.

'Thanks,' I mutter, clutching my cardigan tighter, still embarrassed from when I last saw him.

'I prefer what you had on before though,' he says, winking.

I look around, waiting for some portal in which I could jump and disappear. Was my flimsy bath gown *too* flimsy? Was it . . . see-through?

'Whatever,' Aanchal announces, before sparking up her enthusiasm. 'Okay, so today we're going to do the trek to Tiffin top. It'll be a little tiring but mostly fun, and then we're just going to come back and chill in the cottage for the rest of the day!'

'What time will the chilling begin, officer? 1800 hours?' Pranav asks and I stifle a laugh. Aanchal might not scare Pranav, but I'm afraid of getting on any of her nerves right now.

The trek is a considerable distance away from our hotel and Aanchal's family has been kind enough to arrange a car for us. After Aanchal's great betrayal— not letting Pranav drive here—Pranav has designated himself as the driver. As we walk towards the car, he elbows me away from Aanchal.

'Don't you know how to make her act less crazy?'

'She's your sister! *You* should know.'

'I've been trying for years.'

'TODAY!' Aanchal yells from across the porch, standing next to a silver Honda City. As we quicken our pace to walk towards her, she waits for Pranav to unlock the door to ask me if she can take the back seat. 'The front makes me carsick.'

I open the door to the passenger seat as confirmation and fix my belt as Pranav prepares to reverse. 'Wait. Don't people get car sick in the back?'

'I was born different,' Aanchal says dramatically before using the seat to lie down.

I look over to my right to notice Pranav almost out of the gate and point to his seat belt, not on.

'I was going to do it after reversing,' he replies.

'You should do it the second you get in the car.'

While I expect him to explain himself, he simply nods, grabs his seat belt, and fixes it on.

'We're going to get breakfast first, because apparently this one can't do a trek that kids do if he doesn't have some food in his tummy,' Aanchal announces from the back.

'Honestly, I could do with some food too,' I add.

As Aanchal groans in the back, Pranav holds out his fist to mine in a fist bump.

'She's still my best friend.'

'For now,' Pranav replies.

The tiffin trek is a quick walk from the Mall Road, where our pit stop for breakfast turns into a two-hour gossip session about people we know from college. Tanya takes up a lot of talking time and I'm disappointed, but not surprised, that her ridiculous antics have followed me around this long.

'What problem does she have with you anyway?' Pranav asks once I've given him the low-down on our dodgy history, while he fidgets with the remaining bits of his English breakfast that Aanchal was so sure he wouldn't finish.

Because I don't answer, Aanchal speaks for me. 'Apparently she was pissed that Ashish picked Sana over her.'

I add, 'She was used to getting all the boys,' for context.

Pranav looks at me stunned. 'Wait. *She* was the pretty, popular one in your school?'

'Obviously. Why?'

He shakes his head in disbelief. 'Wow.'

'Wow what?' I ask.

'I don't know,' Pranav says casually. 'I would've thought that that would've been you.'

* * *

When we reach the starting point of the trek, Aanchal is steadfast against getting us a guide, despite many of them passionately soliciting us.

'Please. I practically grew up here,' she says to one of them, '*I* could be the guide!'

Since it is the off season, the trek is largely empty and as soon as we ascend just a little, the landscape changes from the commercial, high-energy feel of the Mall Road to a tree-capped, green-speckled wonderland. While the lush greenery is inviting and breathtaking, this is hardly a steep climb and my everyday shoes do just the job—even though Aanchal had insisted that Pranav and I buy a special hiking pair before the trip.

'It's not that serious,' Pranav had sneered in her direction. 'We're not in LA going for a hike every morning.'

'It doesn't matter where you are, Pranav. It's the mindset,' Aanchal had said, chuckling. 'That's the thing about athletes. It's always serious for us.'

But even though it is not steep, it still is a lot of activity for someone (me) who has spent the majority of her days after college under her blanket in bed.

Nearly ten minutes in, as Aanchal is soaring like this is her daily morning walk, I am struggling to breathe one full round in. Pranav is walking behind me, a little winded too. I pause as he approaches me.

'Can we take a sec?' I ask, heaving.

He nods.

Unintentionally, we pause at a picturesque sight. It has just rained a few days prior, according to the locals I overheard, and the green on the trees looks extra pigmented, like someone coated them just for us. The spot we're in currently feels like being cocooned in nature's lap. Years ago, I remember Ma telling me how, when she was a kid, she would run to the park where she played with her friends, take her chappals off and just lie down on the grass whenever her parents frustrated her. Being close to nature, she said, was the only way she knew how to fight stress. 'We didn't have Calm or Headspace,' she said, jerking her head, when I'd asked her to pay for my subscription to an overpriced meditation app that I only used for a month.

Standing here, so many feet above the ground, watching the candy floss clouds in the sky feel so close yet so far, I think I finally understand. It's not that this fixes anything. Nothing ever can. I just feel small here. The good kind.

'Ready to go?' Pranav asks.

As I take the first step, I feel the rocky land under my feet and before I can step off what I have stepped on, my left foot coils and my body starts falling sideward. Flailing my arms, I try to grab hold of something before preparing myself for the landing, the inevitable smashing open of my head. But something intervenes, breaking gravity's plans. Strong, calloused hands tug at my waist, holding all my weight upright while I've already surrendered to the fall.

I look up and see Pranav's face, his brow crinkled, his forehead fuzzy.

'That was close,' he says as he helps me stand back on my feet, his hands on me still. 'Are you okay? Are you hurt?' There is a sense of urgency in his voice that I don't know what to say to adequately soothe.

'I'm okay,' I reply, letting him hold me, letting him feel that I'm okay. 'You saved me . . .' I say, before suddenly hesitating. 'I mean, you probably saved me from some major head trauma.'

'Sure you're okay?'

I nod. 'Are *you* okay?' I ask.

Pranav fidgets with the rocks around my feet, shoving them all out of my way. He looks back up to say, 'Yeah. I'm okay.'

It takes Pranav and I ten minutes to catch up to Aanchal's silhouette. The entire time, he walks a little behind me. The three of us finally unite when the trek is about to reach its culmination point.

'Guys! This view. It's so good. It's even better than what I remember,' Aanchal says, making the first turn towards the summit, the 'tiffin' point of the trek where people sit and eat the meals they have packed for the journey. 'This was so worth it.'

I glare at her, and then at the view, unimpressed. It's average, at best, a little corner overlooking a valley. It's just about the standard experience you'd get from any hill station.

'I don't know, kind of a *meh* end to a good hike,' Pranav says.

Aanchal gasps at Pranav's disagreement. 'So you're saying this was all for nothing?'

He throws his head back a little, his hands in his pockets, like he's really thinking about it, before leaning forward to look right at me. He shakes his head. 'No, I liked the climb,' he says, staring so deep into my eyes, I wonder if there's something more important behind me that he is trying to look at, if I should look away.

I turn around and there's nothing.

* * *

'Remember your promise,' Pranav announces as the three of us are almost at the parking lot. 'No micromanaging, no itinerary. Only chilling tonight.'

Aanchal sighs dramatically, before holding up her thumb in Pranav's face.

As we move into the passenger and driver's seat respectively, I can feel Pranav's eyes on me. When I'm certain he's looking, determined by a quick glance from the corner of my eye, I turn sideways and catch him. 'What?'

'Do you know how to drive?'

That is not the question I was expecting.

The quick answer is yes, the long answer is . . . depends on who you ask.

Ashish was the one who taught me how to drive in the few months before he left for college.

'Okay, so when you let go of the clutch, you have to do it extremely, extremely gently, like you're setting a baby down for a nap,' Ashish explained, as I put my foot on the pedal, putting the car in the first gear.

'Do you think I put babies down for naps daily?' I asked him, frustrated.

I did not want to do this. While Ashish was concerned that with him gone, there would be no one to drive me around, I had taken issue with this entire suggestion. Firstly, how un-feminist of him! Bani knew how to drive! And secondly, I had no interest in driving. It felt like a waste of time that could be better spent doing anything else. And besides, it was my Delhi Metro era!

But Ashish had somehow won that argument and here we were, on the cusp of another.

Steadfast on being as patient as ever, Ashish ignored my brattiness. 'Just be gentle, baby. That's all.'

'Good, now a little push to the accelerator.'

'I know this much, Ashish, I'm not a child.'

On Ashish's suggestion, I took push to mean shove and pressed hard on the accelerator. Quickly, his car shot a few feet forward and then fizzled out of ignition.

'What?! What did I do wrong?' I screamed, exasperated. 'I told you I didn't want to learn!'

'You're being really difficult, Sana. I'm trying to teach you something and you're not listening to me.'

'No, you're not trying to teach me. You're expecting that I already know how to drive and when you tell me, I just follow your instructions. That's not how teaching works,' I yelled, storming out of his car.

Later, we decided that it was not the best idea to introduce a teacher–student relationship in our dynamic. Bani finished the lesson and the follow-up practice sessions, while Ashish sat in the back and tried very hard to keep quiet.

It feels like all of that has led up to this moment, as Pranav asks me: 'So?'

'Huh?'

'Do you know how to drive?' he asks again.

'Oh, yeah, uh, I do,' I reply. 'Yes, I do'

'Do you want to drive?'

'Oh, no, no, no. You drive. I'm not that great.'

'The roads are completely empty. Want to try?'

I can almost feel Ashish challenging me in my mind. *He's going to find out you can't drive.*

I can drive.

A mocking laughter. *'That's not how I remember it.'*
'That's because you're a terrible teacher.'

In my head, Ashish is smirking as I think: What the hell? Why not? What could go wrong? When I feel the weighted responsibility of the driver's seat hitting me, I realize a lot. I turn to my left to tell Pranav I don't want to do this and see that the first thing he's doing is putting his seat belt on.

'Are you doing that because you're scared that I'm driving? You know I can totally not? This was your idea.'

'What? Oh, no. I just . . . you were right. About the whole seat belt thing.'

'Oh,' I say, a little startled.

On Pranav's count, I turn the ignition on and before I can decide to freak myself out about it, I am already on the main road, driving, manoeuvring traffic and doing all of this like I do it every day. Meanwhile, Pranav just sits there, silently observing me. No clenched jaw, no terrified look on his face like he has just handed me a death wish. The only instructions he offers are direction-related.

I turn right onto the street that eventually leads towards the cottage and as the incline approaches, I turn the ignition off, pull up the handbrake, and undo my seat belt.

'I don't think I can take it uphill, do you want to switch?'

From the back, Aanchal zips out of the car. Our windows are down and through them, she screams,

'Guys, you continue your driving lesson, I really need to pee,' making a run for the gate.

'It's really simple, I promise. Just put the car in first gear and make sure you press the accelerator super hard, with all your force.'

'That doesn't sound right,' I interject. 'I thought you had to go gentle with the pedal in the first gear.'

'Normally, yes. But you're facing an incline,' he says, pointing to the path that lies ahead. 'You need to give the engine that boost to sustain the climb. As soon as you're back on flat land, you go back to being gentle.'

'Okay, here I go.'

Pranav interrupts before I can turn the engine back on. 'Seat belt,' he says, cockily.

I make a face. 'But we're here,' I protest.

He shrugs, raising his hands. 'I don't make the rules.'

Unlike with Ashish, I follow Pranav's instructions word for word. To my surprise, it goes exactly as he describes it. The accelerator takes the force and the Honda City feels like it's tethered to a tractor pulling it from the other side. Only when we finally make it uphill can I confidently confirm that there was no tractor. It was all me.

'How did I do?' I ask, feeling like a kid woefully underprepared for a math exam that turned out to be incredibly easy.

'You did perfect,' Pranav says, before hopping out of the car.

* * *

After my much-needed nap, I walk to Pranav's room at 5.58 p.m. sharp, the designated hanging out spot for the night, and I notice that Aanchal is already pouring us all beers. Behind our three filled mugs are fifteen more cans lining the table.

'FINALLY! I've had like, ten beers already,' Aanchal retorts as I walk in after Pranav opens the door.

Internally, I'm still thinking about what Pranav said to me the second he opened the door.

'You've just woken up, haven't you?'

'How do you know?'

'Your eyes.'

'Hmm?'

'They look different.'

'Wow. You mean they're puffy and ugly.'

'Is that what I said?'

'No, but that's what you meant!'

He turned around. All his attention on my face, then at my lips. His eyes like piercing lasers digging into mine. 'If I told you what I meant, you wouldn't believe me.'

Aanchal steals my attention as she announces, 'Guys, the plan is to get super, super drunk and confess all our dirty secrets to each other. If we don't wake up with a raging hangover tomorrow, we didn't do it right.'

Alcohol and I share a strange relationship. I love how it makes me feel but I hate how it tastes; which is why I prefer a shot of vodka or tequila so I can just do with the buzz, instead of having to sip on gasoline the entire time. Beer is not my scene.

So, as the three of us are chilling and talking about more random college drama we can conjure up from our WhatsApp chats and Instagram stalking, my beer bottle is sitting only half-empty in my hand.

'Sana, you're barely drinking,' Aanchal complains, noticing my pace. 'I'm opening another can for you. Drink that one quickly.'

'Arre I just don't like beer.'

'You should've just said that! What do you want? We can have anything!'

I keep forgetting that this is Aanchal's hotel. 'Um, tequila? Can we do that?'

'We can do whatever you want, babe,' Aanchal replies, grabbing the phone.

Three shots chased by a little bit of coke later, I realize that maybe it isn't a good idea to down hard liquor on a relatively empty stomach. But it does feel like the best idea ever, at the same time.

Over the next hour, Aanchal and I drink our weight in shots. The first one makes me feel better than I have in months, the second shot is that, but with a little bit of icing on top, and by the third or fourth one, I have already lost count of how many we have downed. Every few minutes, Pranav tries to barge in to take the bottle away from us, but Aanchal and I are feral enough to claw it right out of his hands.

It is somewhere around the sixth shot point that he intervenes, like the big brother he is, and takes away the bottle.

'He's hidden the bottle yaar, Aanchal,' I say, sulking.

'I'll go look in the washroom,' Aanchal announces like she has just had the best idea ever.

As she skips on over, Pranav comes and stands next to me.

'Doing okay there, bud?' he asks, taking the shot glass out of my hand. The remaining bits of tequila splash out of it left and right as the alcohol in my body is buoys me off balance like I'm a flimsy boat in the Indian ocean. In the background, Aanchal's playlist is filling up the room with indie music—it's either The Local Train or When Chai Met Toast, I can never tell the difference between the two—and I'm swaying to the beats.

'Super,' I say, holding up a thumb. 'Why are you not drinkinggggg?'

Pranav giggles. 'I'm drinking. Just not as much as you,' he replies, holding my waist and steadying me. 'Which, by the way, won't be a totally terribly idea to pause now.'

'Can you pass me a beer pleasssseeeee?' I ask Pranav, ignoring everything he has just said.

'You've had a lot already, Sana.'

'Don't be a bore na,' I reply, grabbing myself a pint from the table. I flip open the tab and chug half of it in record time. 'FUCKKK, Pranav, this beer is so good. Have you tried it?' I ask, holding the bottle right to his face.

'You mean the same beer I've been having all night? Yeah, I've tried it. It's really nice.'

'You're making fun of me,' I reply, making an exaggeratedly sad, puppy face. 'You're making fun of me because I'm *sooooo* drunk and I've had so little, and you're *soooo* sober when you've had so much.'

When Pranav doesn't reply, I say, 'You think you're very cool right?'

'I actually haven't had much at all.'

'Why not?'

'I have you two to look after,' Pranav says, matter-of-factly.

'PRANAVV DON'T BE A BORE YAAR!' I scream at the top of my lungs.

He shakes his head at me, smiling. 'You're such a stupid fool,' he says to me, tapping me on my forehead.

Any filter I have is long gone.

'Why were you so tensed when I almost fell on the trek?'

Pranav looks startled under the weight of my question. 'What?'

'When I almost fell today, why were you so . . . *worried*?'

'I wasn't.'

I move closer to him. 'You were. Tell me why?'

'I don't know why either,' Pranav says, looking away. 'I was just worried you'd hurt yourself, that you'd twisted an ankle or something.'

'So what?'

'Or that you'd get a fracture, that I won't be able to get you off the trek in time to get some help.' I have never seen Pranav like this. The pretence is gone and the wall that protects him from the rest of the world seems to be temporarily put away. Finally, he looks up from the corner he's been glancing into. 'It just worries me.'

'What worries you?'

'The idea of people I lov . . . people I care about,' he says.

'Mm-hmm?'

'People I care about getting hurt.'

'Is this . . .?' I ask, but not wanting to say it. Is this a symptom of a condition? Is this who you are? Are those two things one and the same?

He answers: 'Yep.'

'But you knew I wasn't hurt,' I say, holding his gaze. 'I was okay.'

'It takes a second to kick in,' he responds.

I have more to add, more things to ask, when Aanchal comes bursting out of the washroom.

'FOUND IT!' she yells, holding up the bottle of tequila in her hands. 'Although,' she says, covering her mouth, 'I think I'm going to be sick.'

'Shit,' Pranav mutters under his breath, like he's mad at this interruption too.

Aanchal rushes back to the washroom, the bottle still in her hand, and I hear the first rounds of her throwing up everything we've had in the last few hours.

'I should probably go check on her,' Pranav says, without looking at me.

By the time Aanchal is all puked out and crashed into Pranav's bed, I am half-sober too.

'Let her sleep in here tonight,' Pranav says, tucking Aanchal into his blanket. 'You'll be okay by yourself?'

I nod. 'Yeah, of course. I'll go get some sleep too.'

'Call me if you need me,' Pranav says as I turn around to leave his room.

'Sana?' he calls out when I don't respond. 'I'm serious,' he reiterates. 'Call me if you need me. Anything at all.'

'Goodnight, Pranav.'

Chapter Sixteen

The morning after the drinking scene, I wake up to a mild hangover. Tossing and turning in bed, I try to force myself to sleep, but to no avail. My body is fully awake and my brain is throbbing with pain. It's barely daybreak outside as I reach to grab my phone from the bed stand to start my day, when . . .

Wait. It can't be.

No. I can't possibly have forgotten.

Getting up from the bed, I feel my body on the brink of convulsions. The fact that on the midnight of Ashish's birthday, I was drunk out of my mind, swaying to music . . . I feel a burning urge to throw up. I force myself to calm down, to take a breath, when a message from Bani shoots my heart rate up, once again. It's a picture from his eighteenth birthday, a glimmer in his eyes, vanilla cake smashed on his face, Bani and I at his sides.

Walking over to the balcony, I sit on the edge of a stool and stare at the photo. In it, I'm smiling so hard and no one but Ashish and I would ever know why. Right as the photo was being clicked, with his house full of relatives from every corner of the country, he was holding my hand under the table. It was a private world, one that existed without anyone knowing about it.

This is why I haven't gone back to the pictures. Every last one stirs up memories. But what's worse is that photos are the only places where he'll ever *really* exist again. And my waning memory keeps going soft on the edges, forgetting details I once swore I couldn't forget if I tried. Now, I feel parts of him fading every day as I race to catch him; like sand in my hands, the harder I hold, the quicker he keeps slipping out. What was the shape of his eyebrows? Did he have a mole on his palm? Did he squeeze my hand two times or three?

I look down at my phone, tears stinging my eyes, pain banging in my chest, and wonder what today would be like if Ashish were alive. The answer is simple: we would be long-distance and I would be writing him a cheesy message about how much I love and miss him. None of what I feel has changed, even though there is a longer distance between us than either of us ever anticipated there being.

Opening WhatsApp, I search for Ashish's name—I never needed to search, once upon a time—and begin typing.

Sana: *Happy birthday, baby. Do I start by saying I miss you or is that too obvious? I'll say it anyway. I miss you, Ashish.*

I'm so mad at you. How do I celebrate this day without having you around? How do I ever do a 20th March without waking up and wanting to yell Happy Birthday to you at the top of my lungs? How do I go another day without kissing you? While you're answering all of these questions, answer this one too: What am I expected to do now that you're gone?

You know that thing I once told you, when you were feeling homesick and I was missing you a little too much? That no matter how near or far you were, I could hear your voice inside my head? That still happens. I hear you all the time, Ashish. I can hear you right now. I can feel you caressing my cheek, telling me to stop crying, wiping away my tears, handing me your hanky. If you're gone, if you're really dead, how come I feel you all over me? I know you never believed in ghosts, so if this is the ghost of you, I know you're probably feeling egoistic about it. But just give me any sign and I'll take it and I won't tell anyone. I promise.

My heart hurts every single second of every single day. Even when I'm okay I'm hurting. I don't know how to go on but everyone keeps telling me I have to. I keep waiting for you to come show me the way, like you always used to. Something tells me that's never going to happen, is it?

Anyway. Happy birthday, baby. I love you so much. I will love you into whatever forever awaits me and then some more.

As I press send, I feel worse than I have in weeks. The sunshine falls straight into my eyes but I feel less and less awake. There is no way I am doing anything other than staying under the blanket. Before I take to my slumber, I drop Aanchal and Pranav a text.

Sana: *Not feeling well guys. Rain check on today's plans. Will join back tomorrow.*

Resting my heavy head on my pillow, I call Ashish to my dreams, hoping this time, he shows up. He has to—it's his birthday, after all.

* * *

Hours later, I wake up from another dreamless state to the sound of knocking. I walk like a zombie to the door, my head pounding from the alcohol, the oversleeping, the trauma. Pranav's face, holding a massive tray, greets me. He's wearing beige khakis with a half-sleeved, brown button down and seems dressed up enough to have just returned from dinner.

'You need to eat,' Pranav says, walking inside the room. He doesn't wait for my permission.

'What time is it?'

'Almost nine. You've been asleep for fifteen hours.'

'How do you know I woke up at all?'

'I saw you from my balcony,' Pranav explains, looking down at the food he's setting on the bed for me.

'What?' I say. 'You can see our balcony from your room?!'

Pranav nods. And just like that, he asks: 'Ashish?'

'It's his birthday,' I say, moving a plate from the tray on to my lap, the blanket between the tray and my skin. I open the cloche to paranthas that look potato stuffed, a mango pickle and some curd on the side.

'And I forgot. That it was his birthday.'

Pranav looks at me, waiting for me to add more. 'How could I forget, Pranav?'

He doesn't answer. Instead, he asks, 'How old would he have turned?'

'Twenty.'

'He was a year older than you?'

'He started school a little late,' I say, talking with my mouth full. I am hungrier than I realized. 'His parents put him in kindergarten, but he was homesick to the point of throwing up every day, so the school pretty much just returned him.' The recollection of this story still makes me chuckle.

For Pranav though, it makes him think. 'Lucky for you.'

I stop eating. 'How?'

'Who knows? Maybe if he would've stayed in school that year, you would've never been classmates, probably wouldn't have met?'

Never meeting Ashish.

Would I trade it all away if it would take this pain away too?

I don't know the answer. I don't think I ever will.

'Yeah, lucky me.'

Pranav suddenly looks uncomfortable. 'I'm sorry, I obviously did not mean . . . I just don't know what to say.' I see him stand up and move towards the door.

'Wait.'

Pranav turns around and just looks at me. 'Stay,' I whisper. 'Can you stay? For a while?'

'Of course.' This time, he sits down next to me, as I sprawl out over the bed and lie down. 'How can I help, Sana?' he asks.

'You can't,' I say, honestly. I am lying down next to him as he is half upright.

Pranav moves the hair out of my face. 'I know. God, do I know that.'

I catch his eyes as he plays with my hair a touch too long, an attempt to fondle rather than to fix.

'I'm okay, Pranav,' I try to assure him.

'You're not.'

'I'm not, but you . . . you being here helps. More than most things do,' I say, grabbing his hand. 'You can't fix this for me.'

He throws his head back on the headboard, then up at the ceiling. 'Let me make it easier, at least.'

'You already do,' I say simply.

He thinks I don't hear him when he mutters to himself: 'I can do more.'

'Okay if I go to sleep?' I ask.

He nods.

'Can you stay here? Till I'm asleep?'

'I'll stay all night, if you want,' he says quietly.

When I'm almost asleep, I feel his hand stroke my head, the back of his fingers gliding against my face, almost reaching my lips until they suddenly disappear.

I keep my eyes pressed shut to pretend I am too asleep to notice it all.

* * *

'Today has to be epic, guys,' Aanchal says on the car ride to our next destination, as Pranav swerves in and

out of unkempt streets, trying to get us out of the
woods. Today is, in Aanchal's words, the Best Day
Ever of the trip. You know, that day in your week-long
vacation where you pack in the most fun activities, the
best restaurant visits, the one you save your comfiest,
but most stylish outfit and shoes for? That.

I don't know what I had been expecting when this is
how Aanchal sold this day to us, but it wasn't *camping*.

'So the event,' she says, holding up her fingers
in a double quote, 'starts this evening and lasts until
breakfast tomorrow morning.'

'This is such a pretentious white kid thing to do,
Aanchal,' Pranav says, distractedly. The ride is bumpy
and I have already hit my head twice on the window.
'You okay?' he asks, rubbing the corner of my head
with one hand on the steering wheel.

'All good,' I smile back at him.

Aanchal, though, does not care. 'Shut up. It'll be so
much fun, you guys won't stop talking about it for the
rest of your life.'

'I don't know why you're so excited to sleep with
ants and flies and whatnot,' Pranav says as he takes a
sharp left. 'Where do I park?' Pranav asks, turning into
the corner where the navigation ends.

'Right here,' Aanchal says, gesturing to a bare
patch of land.

'Here means what?' Pranav asks me. 'This is . . .
literally just . . . nothing.'

After the number Aanchal's cottage did on me when
I first saw it, I was expecting some fancy expedition with

flag poles and signboards everywhere. Maybe even some portable washrooms. This is just a tad underwhelming.

There are seven people, total, camping on a large swathe of patchy green right amid a forest. After we're done collecting all our basic camping gear and equipment, the organizers lead us all towards a shaded area under the trees and Aanchal's face instantly lights up, the wheels of nostalgia whirring in her eyes.

'Let's set up our tents?' Aanchal squeals, bubbling with energy. 'Pranav, can you help Sana set up ours? I'm going to help that girl over there. She's all alone,' she says, winking at him and skipping off, before he can respond.

'That was . . . weird,' I say, looking at Pranav.

'By now, nothing Aanchal does should surprise you,' he says, unfurling the tarpaulin and passing over the instruction pamphlet to me.

At the fifteen-minute point, every expectation I had of us making a good team has been proven unfounded.

'You're anchoring it incorrectly, Pranav,' I yell, as the tent falls lopsided and collapses in front of us.

'Oh, and how many times have you done this, before?'

'I'm the one who is reading the instructions!'

'And I'm the one who is doing all the heavy lifting. If you know how to do it so well, by all means, have at it,' he says, annoyingly flinging the poles in my direction.

Somehow, with a little more back and forth and a lot of Googling, we manage to get this thing to stand upright.

'This is a little . . . tiny for three people, isn't it?' I say as the two of us walk inside to check if it all looks good.

'Guys! Come! Campfire,' Aanchal screams, storming inside our tent.

'Of course there's a campfire,' Pranav scoffs. 'What are we doing next? Making 'smores?'

'That's *exactly* what we're doing.'

While Aanchal walks towards the bonfire with us, she quickly evades my attempt to chalk out space for the three of us to sit together. Instead, she takes the spot next to the same girl, Sherry, whose tent she helped set up.

'You're not going to sit with us?' I ask Aanchal, as she's already halfway across through the bonfire. Ever since we've arrived at the campsite, Aanchal has been a moth to the flame of Sherry. I thought this was supposed to be our big vacation night, but it's turning out to be quite different from what I had expected.

She turns around and scratches her head. 'Umm, I just . . . Sherry and I were in the middle of this one topic, let me finish that right up and we'll all chill?'

The sun has just set and the evening sky is fading from a light to a deep blue when some of our co-campers come up with a (not) brilliant idea.

'Guys, Sunil has a great horror story, if everyone's down,' one of the boys sitting right next to Pranav proposes.

Even though this is my least preferred genre of activities, I do not protest because everyone else, including Pranav, seems to be pumped for it. That is before they realize that Sunil's story is about this very campsite we're at and the main character is a camper, just like us, who came here a few years ago and never left.

'Despite a full week of searching, they didn't find the body. To this day, no one has any idea what happened to him,' Sunil says, his voice dramatically low. 'Ever since, everyone who camps here claims to hear a rustling sound on the ground at three in the night . . . like someone is choking.'

Pranav is laughing in Sunil's face. 'Good one, dude, very original,' he says, nonchalantly, before Sunil points him in my direction, visibly petrified with my knees close to my chest.

'Are you really scared?' Pranav asks, lowering his head down to meet my eyes that have sunk into my arms.

'Was this needed?' I whisper in his direction. 'Now I'm not going to be able to sleep all night,' I say.

'Please don't tell me you believe in ghosts,' Pranav snickers in my direction. 'Come on, Sana.'

'I believe,' I say, trying to calm myself down now that everyone's eyes are on me, 'that unless someone can confidently prove ghosts aren't real, I will choose not to anger them by dismissing their existence.'

'But that's not how the world works.'

'Why not?'

'Proving something doesn't exist . . . that's impossible. On another planet, there are probably living beings that have noses where we have feet. I can't prove that's not true. But living in this world, I can conclude, to a reasonable degree, that that's not possible.'

'But that's not enough for me. I need to know to believe.'

'Okay, let me put it this way. What about God?'

'What about God what?'

'Do you think he exists?'

'First of all, they. You don't know God isn't a woman,' I sneer at him. 'And I don't know. I like to believe so, yes.'

'Do you think there's evidence God exists?'

'No, I don't think so.'

'If you need proof something doesn't exist, why don't you need proof something does exist?'

'Hmm.' I'm stumped. 'I haven't thought about it that way.'

'See, there's a lot I can add to your life,' he says, following it up with a classic smirk.

'What do you get from this? From all your flirting?'

'Who says I was flirting with you?'

'What else is this then?' I point to his raised eyebrow. 'I'm sure that's a move.'

'By now, you've thought my dead dog and my eyebrow are a move, Sana,' he says, annoyed. 'What's it going to be next? The way I walk?'

'Now that I think about it, you do walk in a very "Come hither" kind of way.'

'Who talks like that, yaar,' he says, shaking his head and forcing a smile.

'Why don't you tell me one of your classic moves?'

Looking up at me, he seems to hesitate for a second.

'Okay, a classic Pranav move, hmm. I guess, eye contact.'

'That's not a move!'

'Trust me, it is. With a 100 per cent blushing rate, if I may add.'

'I doubt it.'

'You're doubting my *actual* move?' Pranav says, staring deep into my eyes, making me look away. I hate it when he does that.

Wait: he does it very often, doesn't he?

'Sana,' Pranav says, forcing me to look up.

'What?' I ask.

'You're blushing.'

'I'm not.' I *so* am.

'You know a move is a good one if it works on the most difficult of people.'

'I'm difficult?!'

'Difficult to flirt with, yes.'

'So you *do* try to flirt with me.'

'I used to,' Pranav says. 'I don't any more.'

Ashish was right, I realize. I won't be able to tell him though.

'Ouch,' I pretend to be hurt. 'Why? Found someone worth stopping for?'

'Yeah, something like that,' he says, smiling to himself.

* * *

Despite our riveting conversation, Pranav and I have both been yawning for the last hour, even after consuming copious amounts of 'smores on top of the Maggi, waiting for Aanchal to join us, as she said she would, hours ago. And while I slept enough for two days combined last night, the idea of being horizontal again is enticing.

'Aanchal, we're heading off to sleep. Are you coming?' I ask, standing right behind her. Aanchal lifts up her head that is dropped on Sherry's shoulder, as Sherry's arm wraps around her waist, and I wonder what's going on. Since when are they so close, I think to myself, and why hasn't Aanchal mentioned this girl even once before?

'Our sleeping bags are ready,' I add, sensing Aanchal's hesitation to leaving her comfortable position. The entire time at the campfire, Aanchal and Sherry have been too close and cuddly for comfort, and the realization fills me with a strange jealousy.

Am I less fun now? Does Aanchal not enjoy being around me as much as she enjoys her other friends' company? Does she wish I hadn't brought up the trip at all?

On her tippy-toes, Aanchal follows me to the tent, patting her new friend on the knees, as I lie down next to my sleeping bag.

'Um, guys, is it okay if I sleep in Sherry's tent?' she asks Pranav and me, right as my insecurity is beginning to calm down, now that she's finally joining us.

'Hello? Stranger danger? You barely know her,' I point out, irritated, unable to understand what's up with her or if I have done something to mess things up. 'What's going on here? Who is this girl?'

Aanchal looks at Pranav, a sheepish smile on her face. 'Actually, I've camped with her before. We've both been coming here since we were kids.'

'Oh. Why didn't you tell me that before?'

'Pranav, can you tell her everything?' Aanchal asks.

'Hello? I'm right here! You can just tell me right now? Who is she? Is she a spy? Is she working undercover?'

Aanchal ignores me. So does Pranav. Instead, he glares right back at her. 'Everything?'

'Everything,' she says, nodding confidently.

'You're sure?' he asks, concerned.

'Absolutely.'

'What the *hell* is going on?' I ask, interrupting. 'I'm standing right here!'

'Sana,' Aanchal says grabbing both of my hands, 'I promise Pranav will explain everything, okay? Can I please sleep in her tent tonight? *Please?*' she asks and her eyes shimmer like a puppy's.

'Of course, as long as you think it's safe, go ahead.'

Aanchal doesn't miss a beat.

As Aanchal leaves, it suddenly appears to me that the space between Pranav and my sleeping bags has shrunk. I lie down, still, stretching my legs out uncomfortably, making sure I'm not laying them on top of Pranav's. Even though we just shared the same bed last night, that was a queen's size in a hotel room. This is a tent not large enough to hold one adult properly.

I feel Pranav's hesitation in how he is laying down: stiff, the opposite of relaxed. 'You're sure you're okay with this? I don't . . . you know, I really don't need to sleep. I can just chill by the campsite, outside.'

'Don't be silly,' I say, moving a little inwards so I can make space for Pranav's giant legs. 'Unless you snore. In which case, please see yourself out.'

'You do know that *you* snore?'

I gasp. 'What are you saying?! I do not! Have you seen this nose? It breathes perfectly through the night.'

'Sana, I have watched you sleep two times in the last three days now and you have snored like a pig both times.'

'How rude.' I scowl, looking up through the transparent ceiling of our tent.

'A cute pig.'

'I'm still sure I don't snore,' I say, ignoring the compliment.

'Oh, you do. And you jitter when you're asleep, like someone is tickling you. Every five minutes, or so.'

'Wait, what?'

'Yeah, it's really funny to watch . . . I'm assuming it's because you're dreaming.'

I sigh, because that couldn't be further from reality. 'I haven't had a dream in ages.'

Pranav gets up for a second to turn off the portable light that is brightening up our tent. As soon as the dark washes in, the stupid horror story echoes in my mind.

'What if that story is true?

'Sana . . .'

'No, even if you don't believe in ghosts. What if it's true?'

'That's not what I was going to say,' Pranav replies.

'Oh, then what?'

'Just that,' he says, 'if it's true, I promise I'll push you in the ghost's direction and make a run for it.'

'Asshole,' I reply, smacking him in the chest.

'But that won't happen because they're not real.'

'Okay, and if they are? Then?'

'Then I'll protect you.'

'Who will protect you?'

'I'm hoping you'll protect me too,' he smiles.

This entire trip, it feels like Pranav has been speaking to me in code. Like right now.

'Let's just hope, for both of our sakes, that they aren't real,' I say, a huge yawn escaping my mouth.

'You feeling sleepy yet?'

'Not really. You?'

'Same,' Pranav says, before turning his glare to the roof of our tent. 'It's nice to see stars up here. And strange.'

'Yeah, always a little bit of a shocker to see what other cities have that Delhi does not.'

'SANA! That one's . . . wait, look in that direction,' he says, holding my jaw and angling my face towards where he is looking.

'WHAT?! What am I seeing?'

'It's a shooting star, you idiot,' he says, holding my head. 'Do you see it?'

'Wait, is that . . .' I say, concentrating. 'Oh my God, Pranav, I see it.'

He holds my hand and with my index finger, he traces the rise and fall of the star till it disappears into the deep blue of the sky. For a few seconds, we sit and marvel at the timing of it all.

'What is the most romantic thing you've ever done?' He asks.

There is so much material I can dig from, but the inside of my mind feels like that drawer in your cabinet that is so messy that you can't retrieve a thing out of it.

'I can't think of anything specific,' I say, despondent. 'What about you?'

'This, I guess,' he says simply and my entire face flushes red. Suddenly, I'm grateful that the lights are turned off and he can't see. 'The stars, you, the nip in the air. I don't think anything else cuts it,' he adds, looking sideways at me.

'What's going on with Aanchal, by the way?' I say, changing the topic, after pausing for long enough to make things a little awkward.

Pranav rests his head down on his left arm, snuggling over his bicep. 'It's a long story.'

'Isn't that exactly what you do on a camping trip? Tell long stories?'

Chapter Seventeen

'You're not being serious?'

Pranav laughs. 'I am.'

'Aanchal is *gay*?!'

'Yes.'

'And that girl . . .'

'Is her sort of situationship, yes.'

'I can't believe this!'

In a quick recap of their dramatic, super Bollywood-coded story, Pranav tells me how Aanchal and Sherry have known each other and have been hooking up, for years. It all started with Aanchal's family sending her to this camping expedition when she was fourteen, where she found Sherry and quickly fell in love. Even though Sherry lived in Nainital, it was not a problem because Aanchal was visiting once every other month. While they weren't ever exclusive, it had carried on this way for years and years, until suddenly, they were both grown up and Sherry had decided to go to college in the UK. And so this was a farewell trip: a big, dramatic goodbye. Suddenly, I feel the fog clearing on why Aanchal had been so giddy to make it all happen, that I wasn't the 'her' she was talking about in her texts with Pranav. It was Sherry.

'I did not see that coming. At all.'

'Really? I feel like it's pretty obvious. Think about it. Have you ever seen her looking at a guy? Calling him hot?'

I pause to reflect.

'Who is her favourite actor?'

I answer: 'She doesn't have one. Unless you count Anne Hathaway.'

'And Anne Hathaway is . . .?'

'Okay, okay, I'm not five years old,' I say, frustrated—both at the fact that some missing pieces of Aanchal finally add up and that it took me so long to put them together. 'Wait, Pranav, shouldn't she . . . *she* should be the one telling me this herself . . .'

'Don't worry.' Pranav shakes his head. 'Her telling me to tell you is her way of coming out to you. She would've done it herself if she wasn't so horny,' he says, laughing. But seeing my face, the worry on it, Pranav puts his hand on mine. 'Arre, Sana, I know her. We talked about this. She wanted me to tell you.'

'Why wouldn't she want to tell me herself?'

'I don't know, maybe it's the fact that you guys are new friends and she's worried you'll judge her?'

'I would never . . .' I say, trying to think of strong enough words. 'I *love* her.'

'I know. But she's had friends she's tried to come out to and they've . . . started acting weird. So I can imagine it's a little tough, having to come out to every new person you meet, over and over again,' he says, pausing a little before adding the next bit, 'That's also why I'm glad all the girls cancelled. I don't think she's there yet, with the both of them.'

'Hmm?' I hum, lost in thought.

'If I'm being honest, I'm glad they cancelled too,' he adds, his voice fading into silence towards the end of that sentence.

'Why?' I ask.

'I don't know,' he responds. 'If they were around, I probably wouldn't have gotten to spend so much time with you. Definitely wouldn't be sharing a tent with you.'

'We have spent plenty of time together, before,' I add, unnecessarily leading the conversation on. I feel a calmer, more rational version of me knocking at my head: *What the hell do you think you're doing?*

'Is it so bad that I want more of it?'

I flinch. 'Well, you have it now.'

And because we're locked in eye contact, I notice the millisecond shift between him looking at my eyes and then my lips. I catch him, he knows, and he moves away, embarrassed. Everything, including the air around us in this tent, feels heavy.

'You drive really well, by the way, I don't think I told you that day.'

This declaration breaks the tension. 'What are you saying?! I'm a horrible driver.'

'Who told you that? You're honestly really good. Alert, good reflexes, smooth.'

'That's funny.'

'Why?'

'Ashish used to say I was terrible. Even though he's the one who taught me how to drive!'

Pranav doesn't respond to what I say. Instead, he asks: 'How are you doing?'

'I'm okay,' I say, quickly realizing that for the first time, I really mean it. I'm . . . okay.

'Really?'

'Yeah, really. I don't think it's going to kill me, you know, which I really thought it would, the first few weeks.'

'I don't think anything could kill you, Sana, I've never met someone stronger than you,' he says, his hand finding mine in the darkness.

I shy under the weight of the compliment. I shiver under the touch of his hand.

'That's not true,' I reply. 'I'm quite weak and fragile, honestly.'

Pranav's hand grips mine, until our fingers are intertwined. 'Sana, I'm not a good liar, so when I say I respect the hell out of you, it's the truth. You're stronger than I could ever be.'

'That's not true, what about Shambhu?' I say. 'And everything else.'

'We both know that's not the same.'

I shake my head because that doesn't matter. 'Still, you get it.'

'I do,' he says.

'Sometimes, I feel like you're the only one that gets it,' I say.

I can feel Pranav's thumb circling my palm. It feels like he's trying to write something, but my heart is beating too fast in my chest to decipher it.

'Is that a bad thing?'

'Not a bad thing. Just strange.'

'Why is it strange?' I feel Pranav's other hand find my waist in the dark, holding it so gently, I can almost miss it's even there.

'We don't know each other that well,' I say, plainly.

'I think I know you better than you realize.'

'Oh?' I glance at him. 'What makes you say that?'

'You want to test me?'

'No, I want you to prove yourself.'

'Okay, first, I can tell you're distracted because you're trying to read what I'm scribbling on your palm.'

I can't think of anything to say to out-match him.

'Second, I know, even though I can't see, that one eye of yours is on me and the other eye is staring at my hand that's trying to hold you. That eye is half of the reason why I can't tighten my grip.'

I'm worried Pranav can hear my breath, how loud and desperate and stupid it sounds.

'Do you want more?' he asks, teasing.

'Yeah, I'm not convinced.'

'You're still trying to figure out what I'm scribbling, as we speak.'

I can feel my frustration building up.

'Am I wrong?'

'Why don't you just tell me instead?'

'Because,' he says, pausing, 'if I tell you, you won't be able to say no.'

'That's very presumptuous of you,' I say. 'What is it?'

I can feel Pranav's hand sweat on my waist. He was fearless enough to drag it inside my shirt. 'That I want to kiss you.'

'And you think I won't be able to say no?'

Something changes in Pranav's eyes. An innocence peaks through all that cockiness I'm so used to ignoring. 'No, I just wish you wouldn't.'

'Why?'

'Why do you have to make everything so hard?' he says, and I burst out laughing. 'THAT'S NOT WHAT I MEANT!'

'Sure, sure,' I say, giggling, and I feel Pranav's hand leave my waist.

'Fuck off.'

'Ask me again,' I hear myself tell him.

'And? If I do?'

'I don't know. But just ask.'

'You know that deal works really badly for me, Sana?' he says, before moving towards me, this time grabbing my waist with proper intention. In a way that I can't miss it.

'Let me kiss you, Sana,' he says, almost pleading. Like I've kept this thing from him. Like it's his to take. 'Will you? Let me?'

'What if I don't?'

'Then I'm going to turn around and asphyxiate myself in my sleeping bag out of embarrassment, if you don't mind.'

'That'll be a tad dramatic, no?'

'Sana.'

'I'm scared.'

'So am I.'

'What do you have to be scared of?'

'So much. So fucking much.'

It happens slowly and then all at once, like a flight taking off. In one swift move, Pranav pulls me towards him, my chest against his, his breath heavy on my neck. I steady myself by grabbing his shoulder and he one-ups me by taking my jaw in his hand.

My entire body heats up in the process. I'm afraid I'll combust if I get more of his touch. It doesn't matter that his lips haven't touched mine yet. It's already done. I am already there.

'Sana.'

'Hmm?' I ask, my eyes now shut, in preparation.

'You know you're supposed to wish on a shooting star, no?'

I open my eyes and find him looking at me, so intently. I nod.

'This. I wished for this.'

Pranav's hand steadies my jaw as his lips part mine, making space for him. All at once, it feels like he is touching every last nerve ending on my body. I move into him as though there is more space to cover, any distance at all to close, until my body might as well be glued to his. Pranav's hand alternates from my jaw to my hair, pulling me in as his tongue meets mine. I can feel him dare, I can feel the shape of his hand cupping me, almost there but terrified of touching me in a way that can't be undone.

'Do it.' I don't explain myself. I hope, so desperately, in this moment, that Pranav will get it.

Slipping his hand inside my shirt, he unhooks my bra.

The tingles travel up and down my body, resting tight between my legs, where I so terribly hope his hands will go. Does he move first? Do I? How do we play this?

As his tongue explores mine, his hands squeeze my butt in a bid to pull me even closer to him. I have so many questions I want to ask. Why? Why did you wish for this? Why are you kissing me right now? Why aren't your hands between my legs already?

Taking a break from my lips, as though coming up for fresh air before he dives right back in, Pranav throws up an answer, like he has just read my mind.

'I've wanted to do this since the day I saw you.'

* * *

Even though Pranav and I wake up in the morning in each other's arms, even though my head is on his chest, my saliva dripping all over his t-shirt, his hand under my shirt, neither of us talk about it. Not then, not when we get in the car, not when we check out of the hotel, not at all. I don't know why he doesn't mention the events of last night, but I know why I don't: because when I woke up in Pranav's arms in the morning, for a hint of a second, I thought it was Ashish. And when I realized it wasn't, I couldn't stand to see Pranav's face or think of what we'd done the night before.

I especially could not stand the fact that I couldn't wait until we did it again.

By the time I am home, I wonder if it even happened. Did I dream this up? The kiss that felt like coming back to life? His hands over me, that might as well have been electric current running through, restarting my lifeless body? Or the sweet, sweet touch of Pranav's lips on my forehead, that felt like a balm to everything my life has been lately? It feels like jet lag, this feeling—back there, I was living a future-tense version of my life, until suddenly, I'm in my bedroom with countless questions running through my mind, including how I could possibly let this happen. The biggest question of all though: how did it not happen sooner?

I'm going over it all in my head—his hand, its explorations, his soft, soft lips and how good he tasted. It's so fresh, so new, that I can still feel it all over if I try hard enough. When my phone buzzes on my chest, it's a much-needed distraction.

Bani: *sanaaaaa how was trip!!!!*

Sana: *great timing . . . i need you*

Bani: *you wanna come over in a bit?*

Sana: *cool, be at your place in 10*

When I finally see Bani, I try to skirt around the story, to get to the point without having to make it—until she asks me to cut the bullshit. I comply.

'YOU KISSED HIM?!' she yells, right as I wrap up the whole thing. I pray her mother can't hear us.

'He kissed ME!'

'Are you saying you didn't kiss him back?'

'No, of course I did.'

'Did you not want to?'

I can feel my heart go from breaking to mending to breaking, every time I think about it. 'That's the problem, Bani. I really wanted to. And then I did it.'

'But why is that a problem?'

'Bani, it's been, like . . . *four* months.'

She reaches her hand out towards mine. Holding it, she says, 'So what, Sana?'

I can already feel my throat constricting.

'Would it have felt any better had it been, I don't know, six months?' she asks. 'No one gets to decide when and how you move on, Sana. Just you, just your heart.'

'That's all easier said than done.'

'What are you so afraid of?'

'I don't know . . . I guess, just by kissing Pranav, I have taken away some of my right to . . . grieve Ashish. And I don't think I'm ready to let go of that,' I say. 'I still miss him. Constantly.'

'You're going to be grieving Ashish for the rest of your life, Sana.'

'That . . . doesn't quite help,' I reply, lightly chuckling.

'It sucks, but you know that is true. And it's a good thing. In that way, he's always going to be a part of you. But just because you will always be thinking of your past, does not mean you can't have an eye out for your future, too, right?'

'That's not how it works, Bani. The guilt is ginormous. It feels like I cheated on him.'

'Everyone carries their own guilt. Look at me. I'm never going to wake up a single day and not think that I should've died too.'

Her confession sends ripples through my body. Suddenly, Pranav is the last thing on my mind.

'Bani, don't you dare say that ever again, okay?' Hearing the thought I have ruminated upon in my deepest, darkest moments being said out loud feels like my diary being read in the school assembly. I feel like Bani read the feeling all over me and internalized it.

'Sana, you don't know . . .'

How it happened. That's what she means. We haven't talked about it, not even once, because I have convinced myself that I don't want to know. Learning how the last few seconds of Ashish's life played out will only mean that I spend the rest of my life thinking about how, if I changed anything about the moments leading up to it, things could've ended differently.

But seeing Bani's face right now, I know I need to know. For me to really put this to rest. For her to not feel like she cheated fate, every day. For the both of us to have a shot at moving on.

'Tell me,' I say, scooting in closer, grabbing her hand and placing it on mine. 'Tell me how it happened.' I owe Bani this.

She is already tearing up and we aren't even at the start of the story. I nudge her again. 'Tell me, Bani.'

It's like she had been waiting for permission all along.

'It was nothing, Sana. I keep going back in my head and replaying that moment, but it was really, really . . . so, I don't know what's the word for it . . . unremarkable. I was extremely drunk, maybe a little more than I should've been . . .'

'Why?'

'Tanya was being a bitch at the party.'

'Anything different from her usual self?'

'No, but because you weren't there, she didn't have to tone it down at all.'

'What did she say?' I ask, my chest seething with fury.

Wiping her nose, Bani tells me, 'We were playing this stupid truth or kiss game. I forced Ashish into it, he did not want to play because he saw Tanya was playing too, but I was already drunk and the party was damn boring and I thought . . . I thought it might be fun.'

'And it was, it was fun for a second, and then the bottle landed on Ashish, and Tanya asked him to point to the prettiest girl in the room. It was Tanya being attention-seeking, thinking Ashish will point to her, and Ashish knew that, so he pointed at me,' Bani says.

'Sana, you won't believe the way she laughed just at the idea of Ashish finding me pretty. And then . . . everyone joined in.'

'Then what?' I ask, pushing down the murderous rage I feel for Tanya. If I saw her right now, I wouldn't trust myself to not get violent.

'Same thing, her old bullshit. In front of everyone, she asked Ashish if the rumours were true, if he was actually dating me and just pretended to date you so he didn't have to feel judged by people.'

'What is wrong with her? She said that out *loud*?'

'Yeah. And then she started going on about how you would feel if you found out Ashish had pointed to me . . .'

I interrupt. 'I would feel like he was goddamn right. Like I would've pointed to you no matter if Miss India herself was in the room.'

'Anyway, something about that threw me over the edge, Sana. I already was feeling lonely because all of these people around me were making out, plus I had this bitch, who has messed with me my entire life, practically call me ugly in front of the entire batch. So I just . . . I ran to the bar and did the stupidest thing, which was take as many shots of vodka as possible.'

I rub Bani's hand with my palm as she goes on.

'I got drunk really quick, obviously. I was getting . . . bad, saying stuff around Tanya, calling her out, calling her a slut . . . just wrong things. I was pissed off and this resentment came out from years and years of her bullying the crap out of me because of what? Papa's death?'

'Anyway, Ashish said he was going to take me home. He asked if I felt like throwing up first and obviously, I said no. There was no way I was going to let anyone at that party see me in that condition after what Tanya did.'

'But by the time we were halfway through, it was all starting to come out and I made him park the car on that road . . .'

This is it, I tell myself.

'I was throwing up and Ashish was rubbing my back. I don't think he had his eyes on the road at all,' Bani says, breaking down. 'Why would he, Sana? We were parked.' Bani's voice cracks towards the end, like a radio station losing signal in a tunnel.

I feel myself gulp down all the saliva in my throat, my mouth suddenly so dry I couldn't speak a word if I tried.

'It happened when I was finally done. When I was getting back up. The headlights, I saw them. I saw that car coming. And I couldn't say a thing. I couldn't say a word.'

Bani wipes off a tear that trickles down her cheek. I just sit there watching it.

'I really thought it was over the second I saw the car coming towards us. And in my mind I just went, this is it. This is when I die. Before I could get myself to speak and ask Ashish to look ahead, it had already happened.'

Bani telling me all of this feels like a boulder that has finally rolled off the cliff after teetering on the edge for forever.

'What do you remember next?' I ask.

'Nothing,' Bani says. 'That's all I remember. After that, it's just black and then the hospital room.'

We sit in a silence for a bit, before Bani asks, 'Do you hate me?'

It catches me by surprise, despite it once being a threatening, heart-breaking thought in my head. Because how could I possibly hate her? I do the math in my head—the number of things that I would have to change to make it mean that Ashish left the party alive. The easiest solution I come up with is this: if I never met Bani, I wouldn't have met Ashish. Tanya would not have had to call dibs. I would not have ignored her dibs. She wouldn't have ended up hating Bani, or me. They might even have been friends. Maybe Tanya and Ashish would've dated. Maybe he would still be alive.

The only person to hate in this entire equation is me. I'm the problem. Not Bani.

'Bani, there is not a world in which I could possibly hate you.'

'If I had said something, Sana . . .' Bani says.

'Then what, Bani? What would've happened?' I ask. I feel like I'm speaking more to myself than I am to her. 'You would've yelled, he would've tried to turn the ignition on, put the car into first gear . . . and even before all of this, what had to happen would've happened already.'

'You don't know that.'

'Yes, I do. I wish I didn't know that, I wish I could believe that you saying something would've changed things,' I say, thinking out loud. 'But it wouldn't have.

I know we can both sit here and think about all the things we could've done differently, as if any of it would make a difference, but it won't.'

'Bani, look at me?' I say, holding her face. 'You froze. A car was coming at you in full speed and you were drunk, and you thought you were going to die and you froze. Your body did that, you didn't. You don't need to blame yourself for this because you didn't do this. You didn't kill him,' I say. 'He would've died regardless.'

I find that the realization hits me, too. All at once. He would've died anyway. No matter the circumstances, regardless of whether I went to the party or not—at the end of the night, things would've probably worked out in a way that led to Ashish no longer being here.

It was time. He had to go.

'How do I stop feeling like I cheated him out of getting a shot at being alive?' she asks, trembling.

'The same way I try to feel like I didn't cheat on him by kissing Pranav.'

Chapter Eighteen

I have to tell Pranav how I feel. If there's anything I've learned in the last few months, it's that life is short (cliché, yes)—but it's terrifying how many things I keep putting off for the future when no such thing is guaranteed to me. To any of us. And while I have no idea what I will do with these feelings I have for Pranav—hell, I don't even know what these feelings are—I know they need to exist outside my body. Maybe I'll find what they are as I'm saying them out loud.

It is the only thing on my mind on the way back home from Bani's and in the metro ride from home to college the next morning. But when I see Aanchal in the lecture hall, sitting on the last seat as usual, her face sunk into her palms, I'm temporarily distracted.

'Hey,' I say as I walk towards her, resting my bag down on the floor. 'What's wrong?'

Aanchal looks up at me. 'Nothing.'

I place my arm around her shoulder. 'It's Sherry, isn't it?'

We haven't talked about Sherry, or everything else, ever since we've been back—at least not explicitly. But there has been a tacit understanding that I know. That I love her. That I love whoever she loves.

She nods. 'She broke up with me, Sana.'

'Why? What happened?'

'She's leaving the country,' Aanchal says, wiping her nose.

'But that's not for a few months.'

'She said she doesn't want the relationship to feel like a time bomb. And that it would be better if we end it now rather than later, on a good note,' Aanchal says, scoffing.

'But . . . you guys could always do long distance?'

Aanchal shakes her head no. 'We never wanted that . . . to feel trapped by our love for each other. That's why we never made it exclusive either.'

'But this isn't any better, no?'

I can see the finality written all over Aanchal's face, I can sense it in her tone. It rips me apart, the fact that I learn the beginning, middle and ending of Aanchal's love story—pretty much all at once.

'Is there no way to change her mind?'

Aanchal wipes the tears off her face, as though deciding that it would be the last time she would cry about this. 'No, it's done.'

When the bell rings, Aanchal tells me she's going to be gone for the rest of the day.

'Badminton doesn't wait for heartbreak,' she says, winking and picking up her bag and pulling it around her shoulder.

* * *

When Aanchal leaves, I feel my resolve strengthen. Doesn't this feel like a time bomb too? Pranav and I sitting on these feelings, waiting until they consume and destroy us?

I text Pranav to meet me outside the canteen. He replies instantly.

On my way there, I feel delirious. In one step, I feel like I'm making a huge mistake. In another, it feels as though I will burst if I don't say it out loud. With every step, it starts making sense: both those conclusions can coexist.

I'm so lost in my mind, debating it all with complex pros and cons lists, that when Tanya passes me by, calls out my name, and I don't respond, her grabbing me by the shoulder to grab my attention makes me yell.

As my scream settles down, Tanya contorts her face into a faux-sympathetic expression.

'Sorry for scaring you yaar, but I've been calling your name out *tabse*,' she sing-songs as she normally does, the way that makes me cringe. And then everything Bani told me comes back to me and my blood starts to boil.

I look at her flatly. 'Oh, sorry. I was . . . on my way to somewhere.'

'*Ohooo*, to Pranav, haan?'

His name catches my attention, despite being all that my brain has been repeating over and over, anyway. The inflection Tanya attaches to it triggers a response.

'Yes, why?'

Tanya shakes her head. 'No-no, no reason,' she says, before adding, 'I heard you guys went on a trip together. You and Aanchal and . . . Pranav?'

'Yeah, we did,' I say curtly.

'Nice-nice, yaar. You two are a damn cute couple, Sannu,' Tanya says.

'What?'

'Arre, you and Pranav, dating only na?'

'Um, no we're not?'

'Oh? Accha? I *toh* heard from some sources that you guys are getting very close, you know?' she says, making kissing noises by puckering up her lips in my face. It makes me want to throw up, looking at her, hearing her talk.

'We're not together.'

'Oh, anyway, I just think it's nice you were able to move on so fast.'

'What did you just say?'

'Arre! Don't take it the wrong way, na! Just that if it was me, it would take me *sooo* long, dude. Like, even *I* was crushed when Ashish died.'

I try to think of something to say that will end this conversation and deliver the singular message that I don't want to have another one with her, ever again.

'You know what Tanya? Go fuck yourself,' I say, storming off.

It's not that innovative, but it's the best I can come up with.

When I spot Pranav waiting for me outside the canteen, I am fuming.

'Hey,' Pranav says, smiling, because he does not know his words have travelled far enough down the grapevine to reach me. Who else knows? Who else is talking about Sana, the girl whose boyfriend died four months ago, who is now shoving her tongue down a new guy's throat?

'Hi,' I say, my arms crossed around my waist.

'I missed you,' Pranav says, reaching for my hand to hold. I flinch and push him away.

'What are you doing?' I ask, my eyes narrow.

'Is everything okay?'

'No, Pranav, everything is obviously not okay.'

'Sana, what is going on?'

'How could you tell people we kissed?'

'What are you talking about?'

'Pranav, please don't try to lie your way out of this. Tanya is going around telling people there is something between us a week after we kissed. Do you expect me to believe that's a coincidence?'

I see the smile that was plastered on Pranav's face from the very second he saw me, change into a solemn sadness. 'You think that the first thing I would do after kissing you, something I've been dying to do since the day I saw you, is go tell people so Tanya can gossip about it?'

'Tell me how she knows then, Pranav. Explain that.'

Pranav holds his forehead in his hand. 'You really think I told people, don't you?'

'What else am I supposed to believe?!'

'That this person,' he says, his words dripping with frustration, 'has a history of doing this? That she has *literally* done this to you, to Bani before? That we hang out constantly and it's obvious we're close, which could lead anyone to make up stupid rumours?' he says, looking straight at me. 'Why is your first conclusion that I said something?'

It's either the fact that he is making sense or that I can see he's close to tears that knocks the wind out of me. Meanwhile, I just stand there, saying nothing.

'What?' Pranav asks, breaking my thoughts.

I look at him, my head blank. The anger I felt just moments before has dissipated. Suddenly, I feel nothing at all.

'Nothing,' I whisper.

Of course, he didn't tell Tanya. Of course, Tanya made it up. But it's not about Tanya any more. It never was.

'Sana,' Pranav turns his gaze down. He doesn't look at me. 'I didn't even tell Aanchal. I decided I won't tell her at all unless it comes from you first. Just in case you decided you wanted it to mean nothing . . . And you thought I told a stranger, or evil spawn Tanya herself, after I know the kind of things she has said about you, about Bani.'

'Pranav, what else was I supposed to think?'

'I just know that you were supposed to not think the worst of me just because you're scared and you think it's better to turn me into the bad guy than to face your own feelings.'

'What's that supposed to mean?'

Pranav scratches his head. People keep passing us by, but he doesn't seem to care. Neither do I. 'Let it go, Sana.'

'No, tell me what you mean by that.'

Pranav grits his teeth before continuing. 'I just know that you feel something here and it's petrifying for you, for obvious reasons. Reasons that I understand better than you think I do,' he says, looking at me. 'You feel something and because it scares you, you took your first chance of lighting it on fire.'

But is that not the opposite of what I was doing? I was on my way to tell him how I felt, when all of this happened. I wasn't running away. I was running *to* him.

'You can't tolerate the fact that I'm here, I'm right here, and so in love with you. You don't want to see it because then you'll have to do something about it. Either admit that you feel it too or tell me it's just in my head.'

I stare at Pranav, and he grabs my hand. 'I can't stop this. From the moment I saw you, I couldn't see anyone else. It's just you. This is it. You are the one.'

'Pranav, I can't,' I say, because I cannot. I force my hands out of his touch, before I say, 'I cannot do this.'

'Why? Because you don't want to or because you think you can't? Because you feel it's wrong?'

'You have no idea what it feels like.'

Pranav raises his head, looking to the sky, frustrated. 'No one is ever going to want to try and understand more than I do,' he says, looking back down at me.

'Don't you think it scares me?' he asks. 'All my life, for years, I thought I couldn't risk adding another person in my life that I love so much that losing them could kill me. I couldn't . . . I couldn't torment myself with the thoughts of more people I love dying in a thousand, excruciating ways.'

His voice is tired, hurt, expectant. 'And then you walk into my life. And I see you and I think, "Please, God, please, don't let anything happen to her. She's so good." That's what I thought when you introduced yourself on the first day, that's what your love for *Jab We Met* made me feel.'

'And then . . . another person I touch, another person I . . . love, crumbles. Every single time I see you cry or hurt, it feels like a hammer to my chest. All I want is to make sure you don't feel that way, Sana. The moment I found out about Ashish from Aanchal . . . I don't know. I couldn't *physically* stand it. What am I supposed to do with this? With all of this, everything that I feel for you?'

Standing here in front of him, hearing him say the things I would've said to him had Tanya not interrupted my thinking, I feel like there's a coin being tossed in the sky in painful slow motion. Land on heads, I think. Heads means I love you. Please just land on heads.

But it doesn't. It's tails.

Because this situation is too reminiscent of the last one. Me, entering a pre-existing group, befriending one person, falling in love with another, causing everything to implode. It's funny that Pranav is worried that everything he touches crumbles when everything I touch has turned to ashes. But not this.

Not Pranav. Not him.

Just like that, I know what I have to do, even if it's not what I want.

What I have to do is this: not do this ever again. Spare Pranav and I the hurt of this breaking in a million ways it can. Spare him the torture of ever having to go through what I'm going through. Because if it almost killed me, it'll most certainly maul him.

'I'm sorry, Pranav,' I say. 'I can't do this.'

I am already walking away, not waiting for him to respond.

'Don't do this, Sana,' I hear Pranav calling me out. 'I love you. Please. At least tell me that you feel something here, too.'

I wish I could. I wish I could tell you that your eyes hypnotize me, so much so that I wish you would save them just for me. That I find myself thinking about you even when you're right in front of me, that when you tell me things you're thinking about, I hope I'm the first one you think of telling them to. I wish I could tell you that I want this, that I can do this, that I can be strong enough for the two of us. I could tell you all of this and most of it would be true. But that's no longer enough.

'I'm sorry, Pranav,' I say, walking away.

I walk till I'm outside the college gate. I walk till I can't feel my feet any more.

Chapter Nineteen

It's happening again. I feel myself opening my eyes to the interiors of the same hole that I slipped into when Ashish passed. At least this time, I have exams to blame. The texts roll in, Bani's follow-ups, Aanchal's questions about how much I have prepared, the usual buzz on my phone screen from the thousand texts per minute exchanged on our class WhatsApp group. But Pranav's silence rings the loudest.

He won't even try to claw his way in. But it's for the best. With the thickness of the walls around me, I'm sparing his fingernails permanent damage.

In the group chat, Pranav and I pretend nothing has happened. It's a tacit agreement that we seem to have made without ever discussing it. And despite everything feeling normal, nothing *is* normal. Any minute, my brain thinks. Any minute and he'll come around.

'What's going on, Sana?' I hear my mother's voice at my door, flung wide open at midnight. I have two books in front of me on my study desk, but my eyes are glued to the floor. My mind is in another galaxy.

'Huh?' I ask, looking up to find her staring at me from the edge of my door.

Ma walks towards me and sits on the bed, turning my chair around with her so I can face her. 'You're not doing okay. What is going on?'

'I'm okay.'

She shakes her head. 'No, you're not. You were . . . in the middle,' she says, 'but right now, you're not.'

I just want to say it, all the things that keep me up at night, including the fact that I'm in love with someone new at the same time as being in love with my boyfriend who is dead.

'Tell me,' she says, her hand on my thigh.

'I don't know, Ma. Everything feels so, so wrong,' I say, finally exhaling a breath I have been holding for far too long. 'I sometimes feel like it would be easier if I didn't exist at all.'

Instantly, I feel my mother's weight plunge towards me. She holds me inside her arms and I can feel her heartbeat loud against my chest.

'Don't ever say that, Sana,' my mother says, caressing my hair. 'Please don't. Promise me,' she says, holding my chin up.

I look up from the hug. I look at her face and see pain coursing through it. My mother, the strongest woman I have ever known, suddenly looks like a child.

'Everything feels hard, Ma. I don't know if this will ever be okay,' I say, exasperated.

'Sana, you're made of . . . literal iron. There is nothing you cannot get through.'

I shake my head. 'That's not true. I'm not you,' I say, exhaling a laugh. 'I'm not strong the way you are, Ma.'

'What makes you think I was born this way, baby?'

Shrugging, I say, 'It just feels like you were.'

Shaking her head, Ma says: 'Before your dad came into the picture, there was someone else. Ali. We knew each other from school, but never really spoke. Only when we landed up in the same college, did we start talking at this *thela* we would both go to, to get lunch.'

'Both of us loved the egg chow mein roll there,' she says, her eyes glimmering with nostalgia. 'It started with getting one roll together and him paying for mine because I was out of money. Before I knew it, we were having lunch together every day,' she adds, smiling. 'My entire life, leading up to that point, I never once thought about love. I was constantly told it was going to be decided for me. And so I thought, fine, let's focus on what I can control, which was my education. My career,' she says, recalling. 'And then love hit me in the face when I was looking the opposite way.'

I know this story does not have a happy ending. Because I'm here.

'Then what happened?'

'Then . . . nothing. Before it could go further, I was in my third year and my parents were already looking for a groom,' she says as her eyes filled with regret.

'Ali and I would've never worked out. But I was newly in love and I really thought I could fight it, somehow.'

'And?'

'And I lost. As soon as college was over, I was married to your father,' she says definitively, like she has had her time to make peace with this conclusion. 'They certainly did not predict he would leave me for a younger girl in a few years, that instead of having the *dhabba* of an inter-religion marriage on their face, they would have one of a divorced daughter instead.'

'What happened to Ali?'

She looks at her hands crossed on her lap. 'When your father left, I was still young enough to do the love thing again. Plus, my parents really could not say anything any more. So I tracked him down through some old friends.'

'And?'

'And, well, he is . . . very happy, has a wife, three kids, and is living his best life in London, I think,' she says and it feels like her heart is breaking into a million pieces.

'Both of us moved on, but his version was better than mine.' Then she looks at me. 'But I got you out of it all, and for that, I am willing to sacrifice anything and everything. Over and over again,' she adds. 'That heartbreak with Ali, marrying someone who wasn't right for me, and then a heartbreak again of knowing he has moved on . . . I thought I couldn't possibly survive that, Sana. But every time I looked at your face, I knew I had to. I knew I would survive it over and over again if it meant I got you out of it.'

'I know I have been strict, to the point where I sheltered you too much. I know other kids your age have had it easy. But I thought, the one thing I could give you freedom for is this . . . to fall in love. The way I couldn't.' She nestles my hair behind my ear as she says, 'That's why I always, always loved Ashish. And I would have supported you, loved you, if it were any other guy *or* girl, just as long as they were good to you. I never wanted you to have my experience with love.'

'Ma, you don't have to explain,' I say, sincerely. 'I will never, ever blame you for protecting me.'

'But I couldn't protect you from this,' she says, breaking down. A few minutes ago, she was holding me. Now it feels like we are holding each other. 'I couldn't save you from this.'

Everything, from not wanting me to be at Ashish's place for too long, watching him lying lifeless on the floor, trying to take me away from the cremation, to forcing me to get out of the house a month after his death—suddenly, all of my mother's actions, decisions, make sense to me. She was cursing herself for the freedom she gave me to love, which left me caged in the darkest prison I have ever known. She was atoning for her mistakes.

She was just trying her best, after already trying her hardest to protect me, all those years.

I hold her hand. I caress her head this time. 'You already did, Ma. You've been protecting me all along,' I say before resting my head on her shoulder.

Finally, every tear I have held back in the last few weeks comes trickling out. Ma cries with me, too.

* * *

'ID?'

'*Didi*, why would I come to a college at eight in the morning if I did not study here?'

'ID card *dikhaiye.*'

It is the second last exam, but this debate is timeless and about as pointless as the exam I'm about to go write. I bring my backpack from my shoulder to my chest, hunting for my ID card which is usually in my front pocket. But the zip is open and the pocket is empty, other than some loose ten-rupee notes. Where did it go? They won't let me inside without it and I don't have enough time to go back and get it.

'Here, you dropped this,' a voice accompanies a tap on my shoulder, right as I'm about to panic.

Turning around, I put a face to it. Pranav.

Only when I hear his voice after a month do I realize how much I have missed him, how easily my heart turns to him. I try to hide the excitement in my cheeks caused by his sudden appearance, his proximity and the fact that we'll finally have a conversation better than the one we last had.

'Um, thanks,' I say, taking it from his hands and putting it around my neck.

Before I can say anything else, Pranav is already walking away.

'Best of luck, Sana,' Pranav says, shooting a smile at me that feels like a bullet wound to an already punctured heart. He walks away from me without waiting for a response, before disappearing into the crowd of students holding their heads down to their books and readings. I try to follow him until I can't any more.

Fitting, I think. Pranav in my life: once in focus, then suddenly, not at all.

Walking inside the exam hall, Aanchal's gleeful smile at having spotted me helps dull the anticlimactic exchange with Pranav.

'Finally! It feels like I haven't seen you in ages,' she says pulling me into a hug. I am so happy to finally see her usual, happy self, after the breakup. 'This exam business sucks dude.'

'It's kind of why we're here,' I quip. 'You smell great, by the way.'

'Endorphins baby,' she says, kissing her bicep. 'Also, what are you wearing for my party?'

For her birthday, Aanchal is flying out to Bali with her family and so, the only available date for the party, based on all her various friend groups' schedules, happened to fall on the last day of our exams. And because Pranav and I were the ones who planned it all with her, my being there was as obvious as Aanchal's being there.

'Oh, I'm just going to borrow something from Bani,' I say, looking at Aanchal. 'Who all will I know, by the way?'

'So, obviously, Preksha and Samira aren't coming.'

'Biiiiiig surprise.' I can't remember the last time I saw them, forget talked to them.

'But it doesn't matter na, you'll have Pranav,' she says matter-of-factly, with an eyebrow raised. 'Unless you have something to tell me?'

I shake my head furiously. 'Yeah, no, of course . . . you're right,' I say, pushing away the thought that I *had* him, that I have nothing to tell Aanchal because there's nothing there any more. 'I'll have Pranav.'

* * *

'Something better, Bani, please,' I plead, sitting across from her on her bedroom floor.

'Okay, how about a classic cold and fever? No one's going to want to catch that, especially not Aanchal before her trip.'

'She doesn't get sick only yaar, that's not a reason enough to scare her,' I say. 'Crazy immune system. She will call my bluff in one second.'

Bani scratches her head, hunting for another idea that will help me get out of Aanchal's birthday party. As much as it pains me to do this, I am not in any shape to handle being in the same space with Pranav for hours—not when it will be spent ignoring each other.

'What if you say you're on your way and then your cab breaks down and then a bunch of traffic policeman drama happens, and now you're just going home because you're exhausted?'

'Too complicated. I can't lie about so many variables.'

'Sana, you can't ask me to tell you a good lie and then say you can't tell a bunch of other lies to support it. Get a grip.'

'Please, Bani.'

The last exam of my first year is already over and while I should be celebrating, I am instead finding reasons to ditch a party I helped plan.

'I'm seeing you at seven,' Aanchal had said as I told her I want to go home to get fresh before the party. We had just walked out of the exam hall and the glowing smile on Aanchal's face told me how much she was looking forward to tonight. Especially after everything that went down with Sherry.

'Of course,' I smiled in her direction. 'Wouldn't miss it for the world.'

Instantly, I ran to Bani's place. She would know how to help me get out of this, I had thought. But as I'm here, sitting across from her as she throws up ideas I could've thought in my sleep, I'm second-guessing my blind faith in her.

'BANI,' I yell, stealing her attention back from her phone. 'Help. Please.'

Something in Bani's face switches. What she says next is not a suggestion. 'Would it really be terrible to just go, Sana?'

'It absolutely would be, Bani.'

She stands up and joins me on the floor. 'Sana, come on, what is this about?' she asks, a faint whisper in my ear. 'What happened?'

'Nothing happened,' I say, looking down at my feet.

'Obviously, something did. And obviously, this is about Pranav,' she replies. 'Just tell me.'

I look over at her and wonder if there's any point delaying the discussion. I can't come up with a reason to. And so I catch Bani up to speed, reliving the moments in my mind until the climax snaps me out of a dreamlike haze and back to this moment.

'That bitch. I will *kill* her,' Bani says fuming.

'I don't even care about her, honestly.'

And it's true. While Tanya was just the catalyst that got everything to combust, in the end, it was self-sabotage.

'Okay, will you do me one favour? Tell me what it feels like when you're around Pranav.'

'Bani yaar . . .'

'Just try?'

I close my eyes and try to imagine it, recreate it. 'I don't know . . . how to explain it, but when I'm with him, I feel like . . . it's just a constant feeling of floating. Like I'm up in the sky, unbothered, having the time of my life. And as soon as he goes away, I'm back on the ground and my life is a mess and everything sucks. But . . .'

'But?'

'But those moments when I am with him, when I feel weightless, they make me keep wanting to be next to him. I feel like being next to him all the time and then I want to not be next to him because I feel like shit about it all, and then because I feel like shit, I want him more.'

'Why are you so dead against the idea that you might be in love with him too?'

'No. I can't . . . that's never going to happen. I don't love him. I can't.'

'You *can't* or you don't?'

I break my gaze from the floor and look at her: 'Bani . . .'

'Sana, do you really not love him or do you think you're not *allowed* to love him? At least not . . . *yet*?'

'I love *Ashish*.'

'Will there ever be a day you don't?'

'No, but that doesn't matter.'

'Okay, think of it this way. Imagine I make a friend in college, a guy friend who I spend hours talking to, who I'm obsessed with because he gets me in all the ways I want to be understood, maybe even a little more than you understand me,' she says, squeezing my hand. 'Would you say I can't be friends with him? That I would be betraying my absolute insane amounts of love for Ashish, because I made a new friend?'

I shake my head no.

'So if *I'm* allowed to love someone else, if *I'm* allowed to find someone to fill the hole he left in my life as a best friend, as a brother, why can't you?'

My eyes sting with tears. 'I feel like I'll forget him, Bani.'

'You never, ever will. That's my point, Sana. Ashish is always going to be there, right here,' she says, pointing to my heart. 'But what about here?' she says, pointing to the empty space around me. 'Is it the worst idea? Making enough space to love two people at once?'

Looking down at my palm, picking at scabs of my dry skin, I say, 'It doesn't matter any more. I have already messed all of it up. I don't think he even wants to talk to me.'

That's all it takes to put Bani in action mode. She tugs at my shoulder. 'Get up,' Bani announces, before walking towards her wardrobe determinedly. Pulling a dress out of a hanger, a little black one from Marks and Spencer that I have always had my eyes on, she shoves it in my face. 'Put this on,' she says.

'What the fuck?' I say, confused, picking the dress up from the floor where it falls in front of me.

'We're going to the party.'

I stare at her. 'We?!'

'Yes. We.'

'*We*,' I say pointing to her and me, but mostly her, 'are not invited. And *I* am not going.'

'Aanchal sounds like a chill girl who won't mind. Get up and get dressed.'

'Bani, please, I don't want to go.'

She settles, sitting down next to me. 'Tell me honestly that you don't want to see Pranav, that you don't want to talk to him,' she says, before adding, 'that you don't want to kiss him, and I won't force you.'

I can't tell her that. Not honestly. And so, I just grab the dress out of her hand and do as she says.

'Do you have eyeliner?' I ask.

Bani turns around to give me the widest smile possible.

Chapter Twenty

Even though *I* already know Aanchal is Richie Rich after staying at her 'little cottage' in Nainital, I still find it comical when the realization dawns on Bani as her eyes pan vertically to catch the full scope of her Vasant Vihar mansion as we exit the auto. The five cars parked outside and the two peeking through from the basement don't help her mouth's extreme curvature.

'Where *are* we?' she asks, suddenly conscious. 'We're . . . not dressed for this. I think this is the first auto to enter these streets, like, ever.'

I'm wearing the little black dress Bani gave me and she's in her usual pick for parties—an off-shoulder white moment with a low-cut sweetheart neckline that accentuates her clavicle and makes, in her words, her 'larger' waist disappear. I always disagree. There isn't a bit about Bani that should disappear for her to become more beautiful.

'Chill, she's too normal. Abnormally normal for how loaded her parents are,' I say, pulling her inside.

Bani shakes her head, walking next to me. 'I would love for this to be my normal too . . .'

Ignoring Bani, I hold open Aanchal's front gate, left ajar for the guests. We've known each other a little less than a year, but I'm already in half of all the photos that sit framed in her bedroom, which is probably why Aanchal's house manager, Kamlesh didi, lets Bani and I through.

If it looked grand on the outside, nothing prepares us for what Aanchal's home looks like on the inside. Her living room is half opulent couches and half a gigantic crystal chandelier that towers over us as we walk in. There is enough light coming out of it to illuminate this entire house.

I find Aanchal right there, sorting through a tray of food leaving to go upstairs, which I can tell where the party is by the speaker's bass.

'You're here,' Aanchal says, tiptoeing across the room and pulling me into a hug. She smells like expensive perfume and newly discovered joy. When she breaks away from our hug, she takes a second to be sure, before adding, 'And you brought Bani!'

'Sorry for showing up unannounced,' Bani says, stretching out her hand, 'but also not really, because, you know, security is not all that tight here,' she says, pointing to Kamlesh didi at the gate, using her phone.

Aanchal narrows her eyes. 'Oh, you know, I just told her to let all the pretty girls pass through,' she says, smirking at Bani. 'Besides, I was honestly going to ask Sana to bring you,' Aanchal says. 'I'm not sure how I forgot.'

As they're speaking, my eyes are fixed on the staircase. Is he here? Where is he?

'Where's Pranav?' I ask, interrupting their banter.

I see Aanchal look at me suspiciously. 'What's going on between you two?'

'Nothing.'

'By nothing she means everything,' Bani interrupts. 'They kissed.'

'WHAT!' Aanchal yells. 'WHEN?! I *knew* something was going on with how weirdly you two were texting on the group. How could you not tell me?!'

'Not now. Where is he, Aanchal?' I ask, my voice dripping with desperation.

It's like time is running out. Like how Geet feels when she's almost getting married to Anshuman, but her heart is throbbing for Aditya, who is walking away. It's like the train is leaving the platform with Pranav on it. I need him to get out. I need someone to pull the chain.

'He's on the balcony,' Aanchal says, pointing to the open door on the first floor, visible from the ground floor living room where we are standing.

I nod. 'Okay, I'm gonna . . .'

'Go,' Bani says, shoving me towards the staircase.

I climb up the steps, my heart beating out of control—because of fear, because of the joy of what lies ahead of a conversation I am dreading.

Let's just say, I wasn't dreading the right thing.

This shouldn't be surprising. That it took him thirty days to move on shouldn't make my throat feel itchy and dry. This is . . . this is who he is. Still, standing here, next to Aanchal's first floor balcony, I *let* my heart shatter into a million little pieces all over again. Both his hands on her waist, her staring into his eyes, the lack of any distance between them, the pleading look on Pranav's face.

'This is it, you're the one.' Hadn't he said those words to me just days ago? Did he mean 'the one . . . for the time being?'

At the end of the staircase, I see Aanchal and Bani still standing there as I make my way to them as quietly as possible.

Bani notices the red in my eyes and asks, instantly. 'What happened?'

'Let's go, please.'

Aanchal holds my hand. 'Hey, what's wrong, Sana? I thought you were going to . . .'

'I did too, Aanchal. But you were right about your brother,' I reply, my voice dripping with bitterness. For him, for Aanchal who didn't warn me enough. 'He has another girl in there and he seems pretty happy and I don't want to . . . I can't afford to do this to myself,' I say as I feel myself choking up. 'Bani, can we please go?'

'Oh hell no,' she says, grabbing my hand and pulling me towards the staircase. I'm holding my weight back, protesting against Bani doing what she seems to want to be doing, but before I can reasonably hold myself back, she bumps into Pranav on the stairs. Aanchal is right behind us, watching it play out.

'Wait, Bani right?' Pranav says, looking at her.

I turn my face back, hoping to escape Bani's grip, but it's already too late.

'Sana,' I hear Pranav's voice call me out.

Bani does not respond to Pranav's question. Instead, she smacks his head. From the sound it makes, I can tell it was . . . hard.

'Ouch,' he says, rubbing his temple. 'What the hell?'

'Yeah, Pranav,' Bani says, crossing her arms around her chest. 'What the *hell* do you think you are doing?'

Pranav looks at her, shocked.

'I dragged her all the way here when she didn't want to come just because I thought you weren't an absolute dick, that you actually loved her, and you're here, frolicking with some random chick?' When Bani looks over to the balcony, it's suddenly empty.

Pointing her finger at him as he tries to get a word in, Bani announces, 'You listen to me. I will not let you treat my best friend like absolute crap, especially not after I have seen her being treated like the princess she is. Honestly, who do you think you are?'

She turns around and says, 'Let's go, Sana.'

Before we can leave, I can see Pranav grab hold of Bani's hand.

'Can I speak to you?' he asks, gently. His grip seems to be urgent rather than imposing.

She nods. 'Speak.'

'Privately,' Pranav replies, without looking at me. I wouldn't know, actually. I have fully hidden myself behind Bani's tiny frame.

Bani seems conflicted but says 'Okay' anyway.

'Go talk to him,' is all Bani says when she returns from the balcony where she and Pranav have been standing for the last ten minutes.

I can feel the vibrations on my face. 'A few seconds ago, you were going to drag me out of this party.'

'It's not what it looks like.'

'Wow, you sound like such a guy.'

'Listen to me, that girl . . . it wasn't anything.'

'Come on, Bani,' I say, scoffing. 'What are you going to say next? That he didn't mean it and being with her made him realize he only really wants me?'

'Sana, it was an ex who was incredibly drunk and came to him, slurring, asking him to kiss her. The only way he could stop her from forcefully kissing him was by holding her back.' She adds: 'I don't know. I have no reason to believe this, but he doesn't sound like a guy who likes to lie.'

'Why would he not want to kiss her?'

'Can you please not be so dense right now? He's in love with you,' she tells me firmly. 'It's written all over the poor guy's face.'

I wanted to believe, so desperately, that he had moved on, so I could tell myself this was a wrong decision, had been a wrong one this entire time.

How do I tell myself that now?

Bani tugs at my hand.

'If I do this, Bani, I can't take it back.'

Bani leaves this one up to me, because it is my decision after all. 'He's waiting for you on the balcony,' she adds, before climbing down the steps to join Aanchal.

* * *

'Need a refill?' I ask, sneaking up behind him. This time, thank God, he's alone.

Instantly, he turns around. A rush of excitement and then he is poker-faced again.

'I'm good,' he says, turning around, placing his empty glass on the thick railing of Aanchal's balcony.

I know this is going to be hard. He put his heart on his sleeve and I left it sitting there. Love is selfish, after all. It always wants something back.

All he really wanted, though, was to hear me tell him that I loved him, too.

I walk closer to him and tug at his t-shirt. 'Pranav, yaar, look at me?'

He turns around, but his eyes look empty. I take the seat next to him and try to grab hold of his arms, but feel too scared to touch him just yet. Instead, I say, 'Can we talk?'

'Actually, can I go first?'

I hesitate, but shrug, 'Sure.'

'I'm sorry. That was a stupid thing for me to do,' he says and I'm instantly surprised. 'I've been thinking about it all this while and I didn't know how to apologize. I piled all these feelings on to you, when they are not your problem. I don't . . . I don't know how I would've felt if I were in your position.'

Where is this going? Is he taking it all back? Is it ending before it even starts?

'I wasn't avoiding you, these last few days. I was just . . . I didn't want you to feel burdened by how I felt. That wasn't fair. I shouldn't have done that to you. I'm sorry.'

'Pranav, please. Stop.'

'Okay,' he says, dejected.

'I don't know how to do this,' I admit, truthfully.

'Do what, Sana?'

'Do this. Again,' I say, sighing, while moving closer to him. 'Fall in love again, do all of this again, when . . . when it's all so new, what happened.'

'When I was doing it the last time, I thought that I was done for life, as silly as that sounds,' I admit. 'And now I'm here, looking at you, looking at your eyes,' I feel Pranav's face soften, 'and I . . .' I'm struggling to find the words to make him understand, but I force my brain to dig something up.

'It feels like . . . it feels like I'm on a skydiving plane and the instructor is telling me to jump, and that I'll have the time of my life and that I'm safe. That nothing will go wrong. And I *know* all of this, I know I will love the fall, but there's this slight chance that the parachute doesn't open, that I crash into the ground again.'

Pranav grabs my hands.

'You don't need to do it again, Sana,' he says, sincerely. 'I'm sorry. Saying the things I said, predicting your feelings for me, all of that was really inconsiderate. You don't have to rush it. For me, for anyone.'

'You're not listening to me,' I say, grabbing his jaw. I feel him fidget under my touch, like this is the last thing he expected. I also feel the sparks take flight all around us.

'I'm saying, I don't know how to do this again,' I tell him, looking straight into his eyes. 'But here I am, doing it.'

'Doing what?'

'You know what.'

'Say it anyway.'

'Falling in love with you,' I confess. 'I can't stop doing it.'

'What if you didn't stop?' He says this as he grabs my waist and closes the distance between us. It's not his touch but the way he peers into my soul when he says this that makes my knees wobble, my chest constrict.

I look away. 'There's no way I can go on and not feel like I'm . . .'

'Like you're what, Sana?' he asks, tipping my chin up to look at him.

'Like I'm cheating on him.'

'What if I tell you I don't need you to love me more than him?'

'What?'

He grabs both of my hands. 'I think, and correct me if I'm wrong, but I think you're scared of . . . not *loving* me more than him, but the possibility of it happening someday. Because we have more time ahead of us and he . . . doesn't. And you,' he tries to find the perfect words, 'you want to love Ashish the most, forever.'

My throat dries up as I listen to Pranav lay out all these complex emotions in simple words. Because as much as I want to love Ashish the most, forever, here I am, holding hands with a boy I am falling in love with.

'What if you don't have to love me more?' he asks, sincerely. 'All I want from you, Sana, is for you to tell me that you feel how I feel, that you can't stop thinking about me, that you wait for the exact second I text you, that you run over the reply a thousand times in your mind because you want to make me laugh,' he says, pausing before he finishes: 'That when you kissed me, when you fell asleep in my arms, you felt like . . . this is it, this is what you and I have been waiting for.'

'Pranav,' I say, helpless. 'I hate that I can't stop thinking about you. Because you're not the one I'm supposed to be thinking about. You're not the one I'm supposed to be missing when you don't text me back. But I am. And it kills me, but I am.'

'You don't have to miss me, you know that.'

'What if . . .'

'What if what?'

'I don't ever want you to go through this, Pranav. And I don't know if I can . . . give you that without fearing, every single day, that you'll end up like me. That what I went through, you'll go through, and it'll kill you.'

'I'd rather die at your hands than be alive without you,' he replies, in an instant. 'Gosh. That's dramatic. But you have to know it's true, Sana. I don't mind sharing. I don't mind if half of your heart is somewhere else. All I want is a piece of you.' Pranav looks at me with the whole world in his eyes, like I have the power to make or break him in one swift blow. 'Can you?'

'Can I what?'

'Give me a piece of you?'

'Feels like you're taking it with or without permission.'

'Can you say it? Even if we decide this won't work or you just . . . can't do it?' he says, his eyes on me. 'Can you do that for me?'

Maybe it's the thunder in the sky. Or maybe it's just what it feels like in my body—the idea of giving myself to someone again, letting lightning crash all around me as I marvel at the sight of it, hoping it doesn't strike and kill me.

'I think,' I say, pausing a little, 'I think I'm in love with you.'

Pranav pulls me even closer, if it's possible. He props my face up to his, until our eyes are having their own conversation. 'What's it going to take for you to know for sure?'

My eyes dart between his eyes and his lips. Before I can say it, that I do love you, that I can't stop loving you, Pranav's lips meet mine. It's a meeting, a hello, a hug, a why-did-you-leave-me-hanging, and a I'm-so-glad-you're back. Pranav's lips meet mine and I think the following thoughts: Are my feet on the ground? Am I floating? Are we still here? What if we fall?

But when he grips his hand over my waist, so tight I can feel him in my bones, I know he'll hold me. If I fall, he'll cushion me.

I hold him back. I need to say it.

'I love you, Pranav.'

The fact that I say it, so simply, without prefixes, charges him up. The second time he grabs me, pulls me into him, is not like the first one. If the first was exploratory, this one's hungry. This one is like screaming, 'I thought I'd never get to do this again.' My hands are in Pranav's hair, brushing through it, as his tongue moves into my mouth. I can feel him panting as he's kissing me and eventually his breath slows down, like kissing me is breathing.

He pulls away, looks into my eyes, and says, 'I'm taking you to Aanchal's bedroom.'

I laugh, saying, 'That's a little gross, Pranav. She's my best friend and your sister,' as I follow him up the stairs.

The second he pushes the door shut, all these feelings that have been bubbling, struggling to stay below the surface, start overflowing as we sit down on Aanchal's bed and only take a few seconds to find each other's lips again.

'I can't believe you're here,' Pranav exhales, pulling back, his hands still on my jaw.

'I can't believe it either.'

'Do you want to know something?'

'Obviously.'

'That morning of the exam, when we ran into each other . . .'

'Hmm?'

'I unzipped your bag. And took your ID card out.'

'Why?'

'It had been twenty days, Sana. I saw your face and I just . . .'

'You what?'

'I wanted to touch you. So bad.'

'But you didn't touch me. Just my bag.'

Pranav nods. 'I wouldn't until you asked me to.'

I feel myself falling for him. I feel myself not wanting to make it stop.

'Can I?' he asks, interrupting my thoughts.

I throw my head back. 'Please.'

Right as his lips part mine, I hear the handle of the door being pushed open, until it swings wide in front of us. Bursting in walk Aanchal and Bani, their hands all over each other, embroiled in a kiss until I yell to its anticlimactic ending.

'WHAT THE FUCK?' I scream, looking at my two best friends, kissing each other. My best friends are kissing each other?! 'WHAT ARE YOU TWO DOING?'

'What are you two doing in *my* bedroom?' Aanchal asks, distracted.

'What are you two doing *together*?'

Bani looks at me cheekily. 'I really like her, Sana,' she says, squeezing Aanchal's butt in front of me. I want to throw up. 'Why wouldn't you introduce us earlier?'

'She probably wanted to keep you to herself,' Aanchal says, pulling Bani into a kiss.

This can't be happening. My best friends are kissing each other and have just walked into the room a minute after I have confessed love to my best friend's brother.

'Care to explain *this*?!' Aanchal says, pointing at us back.

'I'm in love with her,' Pranav says, casually, like he's reading out front page news from the paper. He locks the declaration in with a kiss on my cheek and both breaks and heals my heart at once. 'Care to explain . . . that? What about Sherry?'

Aanchal giggles. 'I moved on the second I saw Bani's face,' Aanchal says, pulling her in for another kiss. I see Bani blush at that confession.

Before I know it, I'm laughing. 'This is *so* weird.'

And for the first time in a long, long time, the only pain I feel is from my stomach cramping at the influx of giggles.

Chapter Twenty-One

'I think you would like him.'

Why is he not seeing this?

'I think I would absolutely not.'

He is dressed in white. Fitting, I guess, but I have rarely ever seen him in white before. Except . . . well, the one time. It brings out the brown in his eyes. I'm only now noticing how brown they are.

'You're not even trying to see it,' I say, frustrated.

'Would you like it if you were in my place? Would *you* see it?'

'You were the one who left!'

The horizon is white too, stretching into endless nothingness. Both of us are seated on a bench that seems to be floating in the sky or on water, I can't tell. All that really grounds me here is the sight of his hand on mine.

His face is a confusing blend of anger and understanding. 'You could've waited a little longer.'

Instantly, I feel my eyes well up with tears. 'That's not fair.'

'Why is that not fair?!'

'You don't get to leave and then decide how I move on,' I say, frustrated. 'Do you have any idea how hard it was? How hard it is every single day?'

'Come here,' he whispers, pulling me to him, making me dissolve in his embrace. I comply, but I feel nothing. 'Does he make you happy?' he asks.

'Yes.'

'You could've taken a second to think before you answered that, but okay.' He looks at me, his expression sincere, and says, 'I'm happy for you, Sana.'

'You're lying! You're not. You're jealous. Why else would you just now show up like this?'

I see him reaching for my hand again. I let him hold it. 'Because I miss you.'

'Then why'd you leave?'

'Wasn't in my control, na,' he says, kissing it lightly.

'Will you tell me something?'

'Anything.'

'Do you love him more than you love me?'

'And then you say you're not jealous,' I reply, moving away. This conversation is frustrating. Everything about this is frustrating. 'If I say yes, will you come back? Or haunt me? Or come back and haunt him?'

'That's not how it works,' he laughs. Like any of this is funny.

'I know, but can we just pretend for a bit?'

'We can,' Ashish says, squeezing my hand thrice, like he has always done. I can't remember how it feels any more.

I look at him, wondering if there is a timer buzzing around us that will ring and make Ashish disappear into pixels. 'I have a question.'

'Tell me?'

'Why haven't you showed up until now?'

'I had to wait until I was sure you were happy, Sana.'

'It would have made me happy had you just come.'

Ashish reaches out his hand to stroke my hair out of my face. 'I know. But I needed you to be really happy without me.'

I want to tell him that that's never going to happen, that there is a treasure chest of happiness I unlocked a few years ago, that is now forever out of reach. I will be happy, but I'll never be as happy as I feel, right here, next to him.

Just as I'm about to say it, I hear the screeching buzz of my alarm fill my ear, the slow escalation of the vibrations getting louder and louder.

'Please, no,' I beg.

This is the first time he has visited me.

I need more time.

There are things I want to say.

Questions I need answers to.

That's the thing though; I can't catch hold of time, just like I can't feel Ashish under the touch of my hand, no matter how much I tighten my grip.

The music blares through the room as I open my eyes. I roll over to check my phone and the date glares back at me: 1 January.

— THE END —

Acknowledgements

How does one begin an acknowledgements section for a book they never thought they'd get to—or be able to—write?

Here's how: one dives straight into gratitude.

Thank you to my parents, the wind beneath my wings, the best ones plucked from the universe and handed to me, for whatever reason—everything good about me is an outcome of your blood, sweat, tears and sacrifices. Thank you to my grandfather for always forcing me to read and write more. And to my grandparents, who are no longer with me but who have shaped me in a thousand beautiful ways to be who I am today. Thank you to Saharsh, my brother-in-law, for not only birthing this book idea, but helping me flesh it out through every iteration. And to Twinkle, my sister, my best friend, the North Star guiding me at all times, for calling it a crap draft when it was a crap draft. And for being patient as I turned it into a passable one.

Thank you to my first professional mentor, member of Parliament Gaurav Gogoi—if it weren't for you telling me I should focus on writing as a skill in our last feedback chat, I don't know if I would've ever taken this seriously. The hugest thanks to my professor at Ashoka University, Satyendra Singh, for being my first—and the best-ever—writing mentor. Everything you taught me continues to inform every word I write today.

This whole writing thing began as a joke between me and myself. I never thought people would find my pieces, cry to them, read them out to their partners on video calls or print them to keep as copies. Thank you, deeply, to all my internet readers. Every day, I pinch myself because I can't fathom how this book already has people waiting on it as impatiently as I am.

Thank you to my lovely editors: Gurveen, for taking a bet on a debut author with nothing much to her name but a 15,000 word draft with a bazillion typos; Anushree, for helping this book reach the finish line; and Saba, for making sure it reached there without any errors. And a huge thank you to Shreya Punj for helping me get noticed by the Penguin India team. Thank you to Anjali Mehta and Shadab Khan for the cover illustration and design of my dreams! A big thanks to everyone at Penguin who worked on my book in any way—every single one of your efforts has threaded together this dream project of mine.

I have been blessed with the best friends in the world and a million thanks for their love, support and constant 'You've got this!' won't suffice. Thank you to my friends-turned-sisters, Shruti and Somya, for loving me through every one of my phases and being kind enough to not call my 'writer phase' a phase. Some friendships are written in the stars and ours is one of them. Thank you to my best friend, Malavika, for reading the first draft of this book and being the best cheerleader one could ask for. Thank you to my college (and forever) best friend Harshita for inspiring two characters in this book and for giving me the kind of friendship I could keep writing about. Thank you to every last one of my friends (you know who you are)—who don't miss a beat to introduce me as their 'author-friend', for constantly bringing my book up in parties.

Most of all, thank you to my life partner (premature, maybe, but hey, I stand by it), Arjun. I'm so grateful that you read and marvel at everything I write (except this book, but you're forgiven), even when what I've written is at best average.

If I have missed your name, please know that this section was written in a state of emotional overwhelm and that I'll be expressing my gratitude to you in person, one way or another.

Finally, thank you, dear reader, for picking up this book. I hope you enjoy it. I hope it makes you cry (because Lord knows we all need a good cry).

I hope it meets you when you need it the most.

Scan QR code to access the
Penguin Random House India website